ADVANCE PRAISE

VIRGINIA'S RING

Virginia's Ring is a triumph and a tour de force. Lynn Seldon has written one of the best books about a military college ever written. With the publication of *Virginia's Ring*, he joins the distinguished ranks of our military academy graduates who have written about the life changing, fire tested tribe. It reminded me of James Webb's *A Sense of Honor* about the Naval Academy and Lucian Truscott's *Dress Gray* about West Point. But Mr. Seldon makes Virginia Military Institute a great test of the human spirit and one of the best places on earth to earn a college degree.
— Pat Conroy, author of *The Lords of Discipline*, *The Great Santini*, *The Death of Santini*, and many other bestsellers

All VMI alumni will smile and nod as they read this. It's a celebration of the many strong ties and emotions that define the VMI experience and a tribute to the sacrifice that is service to our country and our state. A tribute to the seasoning that occurs in all VMI men and women. A "must read" for alumni and friends of VMI of all ages.
— Teddy Gottwald, President of VMI Class of 1983 and President/CEO of New Market Corporation

Lynn Seldon's *Virginia's Ring* will resonate with every man and woman who has stood in the long gray line, eaten a square meal, and sweated at something euphemistically called a party. The man knows his school, VMI, and his love for all he experienced there comes through on every page. This is a story of shared sacrifice, communal values, and unbreakable friendships. It nails academy life, and in doing so summons the best in each of us.

— John Warley, The Citadel Class of 1967, author of *Bethesda's Child*, *The Moralist*, and *A Southern Girl*

Lynn Seldon really captured the patriotism and work ethic required by all VMI cadets, both male and female. My favorite thing about *Virginia's Ring* is that the female cadets are just as powerful as the males.

— Andrea "Andee" Walton, VMI Class of 2008

In this well written and accurately portrayed novel, Lynn Seldon shares his love and appreciation for his alma mater and VMI's unique educational experience. The main characters, cadets Nick Adams and Virginia Shields, tell their VMI stories in captivating, moving, and nostalgic reading. This is a must-read for all who wear the ring and for the entire VMI family.

— Greg Cavallaro, Class of 1984 and CEO of the VMI Keydet Club

After I began reading, I was hooked. I could not put the manuscript down. For me, it was much like Pat Conroy's *The Lords of Discipline*. Through his personal knowledge of VMI, Lynn has used his writing talents to weave the Institute's journey with co-education into a very exciting and believable novel.

— Mike Strickler, VMI Class of 1971 and former executive assistant to VMI's Superintendent

This is a book a Southern girl will read in bed, on the piazza, or on the beach.
— Nathalie Dupree, co-author of *Mastering the Art of Southern Cooking* and *Southern Biscuits* and author of *Nathalie Dupree's Southern Memories* and many other books

The Virginia Military Institute – it would be hard to imagine a school so influenced by the past as this one, where history and tradition shape personal relationships on a daily basis. Lynn Seldon takes us into this world as only one who has been there can. *Virginia's Ring* reveals the complex and at times conflicted legacy of fellowship and sacrifice inherited by the young men and young women of today. It is a moving story, spanning generations, propelled by characters we come to love.
— Dave Kennedy and Tom Farrell, writers and producers of "Field of Lost Shoes," a feature film about VMI cadets at the Battle of New Market

Lynn Seldon paints her [Virginia's] portrait with great care, sensitivity, and courage, and in doing so tells us not only her story, but his — he too wears the ring. Death haunts *Virginia's Ring*. It conquers all, but so do family, friendship, and love.
— Bernie Schein, author of *If Holden Caulfield Were in My Classroom* and *Famous All Over Town: A Novel*

My classmate Lynn Seldon scores big with *Virginia's Ring*. A delight for both alums and those intrigued with the Institute.
— Wade Branner, VMI Class of 1983 and veteran "Voice of the Keydets" broadcaster

C.1

Virginia's Ring

—◇—

DISCARD

STAUNTON PUBLIC LIBRARY

Lynn Seldon

Copyright © 2014 Lynn Seldon
Cover art copyright © 2014 by Wendell Minor
All rights reserved.

ISBN-10: 1495929469
ISBN-13: 9781495929465
Library of Congress Control Number: 2014903192
CreateSpace Independent Publishing Platform
North Charleston, South Carolina

**For Cele
My Spirit**

The VMI Spirit

Oh, Clear the way, VMI is out today,
We're here to win this game;
Our team will bring us fame,
In Alma Mater's name.
For though the odds be against us we'll not care.
You'll see us fight the same,
Always the same old Spirit,
And we'll triumph once again;
And though defeat seems certain, it's the same with VMI.
Our battle cry is Never Never Die.

Chorus:
For when our line starts to weaken, our backs fail to gain,
Our ends are so crippled, to win seems in vain;
The Corps roots the loudest, we'll yet win the day,
The team it will rally and fight — fight — fight! RAY!
We'll gain through the line and we'll circle the end,
Old Red White and Yellow will triumph again;
The Keydets will fight em and never say die,
That's the Spirit of VMI.

The Institute will be heard from today.

Gen. Thomas "Stonewall" Jackson

Acknowledgments

The seeds of this love letter to VMI were first planted in the shadows of The Citadel in Charleston, South Carolina, during lunch with Pat Conroy, Citadel Class of 1967. While sitting at a corner table at one of our favorite Charleston restaurants, Slightly North of Broad (SNOB), the famed author of *The Lords of Discipline* and many other bestsellers casually commented, "I think someone should write the VMI novel, and I think you should do it, Lynn."

Though it took me several years of carved out writing time, I've done just that. During the process, I've alternatively thanked and cursed Pat for the idea and support.

Writing fiction is every bit as hard as he says, and Pat has set the bar very high for the likes of fact-based journalists like me who thought making up stuff would come easy. It didn't.

Thanks, then, Pat, for putting me out on this long march down memory lane. Thanks also for setting the bar so high in all of your writing.

Pat's wife, the equally extraordinary novelist Cassandra King, has also set the bar high for me and others when it comes to writing about the South and Southern characters. I hope my Virginia-based novel does her proud as well.

Pat and Sandra welcomed me into their Lowcountry homes, and seeing the massive wood desk where Pat composed *The Great Santini* and other classics remains an inspiration to me every morning when I sit down, open a vein, and try to write about VMI and many more distant destinations. I will also never forget fortuitously placing the manuscript of this novel on Pat's desk atop a copy of Hemingway's *Death in the Afternoon*. Within days I received an encouraging call from Pat and a suggested title for the book: *Virginia's Ring*.

I consider it a great honor for Pat to have introduced me to his long-time cover artist, Wendell Minor. Wendell's art has graced the covers of most of Pat's books, as well as diverse authors like David McCollough, Fanny Flagg, Nathaniel Philbrick, Mary Higgins Clark, and Jodi Picoult. Thanks for a great cover and so much more, Wendell.

Pat also invited me to his mostly-weekly lunches in Beaufort at his favorite restaurant, Griffin Market, where Laura and Ricardo Bonino feature what Pat calls, "By a long shot, the best Italian food ever served in South Carolina." Over several lingering and quite tasty lunches, Pat introduced me to his long-time friend Bernie Schein (also a teacher and writer), Bernie's brother, Aaron, lawyer-writers John Warley and Scott Graber (both Citadel classmates of Pat's and novelists in their own right), and Jonathan Hannah, whose sharp wit keeps everyone on their conversational toes at lunch.

John Warley was kind enough to read my novel relatively late in the long process and made many suggestions that greatly improved the flow, tension, and conflict of the book. John's novels, including *Bethesda's Child* (2010), *The Moralist* (2011), and *A Southern Girl* (2014) are all highly recommended.

This is not *The Lords of Discipline Too* and was never intended to be. However, much like Pat's novel, it's most definitely a love letter to the concept of military schools in general and the Virginia Military Institute specifically.

It's also a love letter to all of the people who influenced my decision to attend VMI, stay at the Institute, and support the school and the extended VMI family in any way I could after graduation.

This love letter starts with my parents, who didn't try to talk me into — or out of — attending VMI. They listened to my anguished calls from VMI's bank of pay phones, my whining when I was back home in Winchester, and even a sobbing request that they come to VMI and take me home in the middle of my first semester of Third Class sophomore year.

They came as requested and even took me out to dinner at pretty Peaks of Otter in all its fall glory. But they left Lexington without me. Thank you, Mom and Dad, for knowing the best thing for me was to drop me back off at Barracks without a word about quitting.

My oldest brother, Greg, is VMI Class of 1975. I visited him several times during his cadetship, and I seem to recall he was often marching penalty tours due to some military infraction. That didn't discourage me from trying my hand at the Institute, and neither did Greg. Of course while I was a cadet, I often wished he had been more discouraging.

Middle brother Steve and sole sister Bev also both made visits to VMI an important way for me to keep my sanity while there. Those civilian sanity breaks included some good times over at Washington & Lee with soon-to-be brother-in-law and W&L 'mink' grad Dan Kniffen. I still remember that my parents,

Greg, Steve and his wonderful wife, Debbie, Bev, and Dan all somehow made it to my graduation. Thank you all for being there, always.

Cele, my wife of twenty-plus years, is truly my spirit. She's been there for every bloody word and mile of this book, including holding down the fort when I was up in Lexington hunkered down in Moody Hall or down in the South Carolina Lowcountry trying somehow to evoke the Conroy magic in my words during my many monastic writing sessions. This book is very much a love letter to her from me — and from one of my main characters, Nick Adams.

Of course many other people shaped my experience at VMI and beyond, including the eventual tone and texture of this book.

Influential VMI professors from those thankfully small classes include Ed Daley, Floyd Duncan (Class of 1964), Albert Chang, Alexander Morrison (Class of 1939), Bill Badgett (Class of 1953), T.Y. Greet, Dean Foster, and several more I'm sure I've forgotten over the years.

When I think of influential teachers, I'd also like to thank James Porterfield (VMI Class of 1965), who was a legendary teacher at John Handley High School in Winchester — which is one of the prettiest public schools in the country. Mr. Porterfield initially gave me a failing grade for a class my senior year, leading to some serious soul searching and studying to retake an exam and remove the provisional acceptance status VMI placed on me after learning of that F. Lesson learned, Mr. Porterfield, lesson learned.

Tennis coach, civil engineering professor extraordinaire, and true VMI man Donald "The Jammer" Jamison (Class of 1957) kept my VMI experience in perspective when I most needed it. I'm glad I still see him on Post and can thank him — again.

My brother's dyke, Vern Beitzel (Class of 1972), was a member of the administration during my cadetship and his on-Post home became a true haven for me at times. More recently, Vern was quite encouraging about this book and put me in touch with several female cadets and graduates who helped define Virginia, the female character in Part Two of this novel.

Former VMI English professor John Leland came to Lexington after I graduated. I contacted him after reading his excellent book, *A Guide to Hemingway's Paris* (I was pursuing a similar book about Hemingway's Key West at the time). Two of his other books, *Learning the Valley: Excursions into the Shenandoah Valley* and *Porcher's Creek: Lives Between the Tides*, are also highly-recommended. John was an insightful early reader of this novel.

I'd also like to thank Major Gen. James M. Morgan Jr., Class of 1935 and dean of the faculty during my cadetship. He was quite supportive of my unusual (at the time) pursuit of "study abroad" during my Second Class year. I seem to recall that his permission included a request that I send a monthly postcard from London, which I always wrote while wearing the VMI ring I'd earned the previous November.

Many members of my class, the Class of 1983 ("The Best Class in Barracks"), were there for me as a cadet, over the years since graduation, and recently when it came to researching and writing this novel (or tailgating before home games). These include class president Teddy Gottwald (who provided great insight to this novel), Wade Branner ("Voice of the Keydets"), Cal Murray (Wade's on-air partner for many football and basketball games), Charlie Luck, Richard Hewitt, Tray Adams, Jay Williams, Malachi Mills, Clayton Wagner, Franklin Hudgins, David Warriner, Jim Outland, John Dodge, Mark Sykes, Chip Shirley, Andy Jones,

Tracey Jones, Bob Mednikov, Tim Spencer, Al Toler, Kevin Keilty, Ed Kluckowski, Mike Laughon, Jay Lasek, Dan Martin, Paul McCusker, Mark Pappas, Graham Nuttycombe, Spence Westbrook, Tom Winkler, Owen Peery, John Preston, Duane Ray, fellow Handley and VMI grad Tom Radle, Max Rogers, Stephen Ross, Scott Belliveau (an early reader), Bruce Cohen, Owen Dunlap, Bruce Hazelgrove, Bobby Edwards, Warren Groseclose, Dave Clarke, Mark Jamison, Roger Fiedler, Steve Goddard, Scott Gines, Mark Heslep, Brent Dunahoe (First Class roommate and reader of several early drafts), Matt Waring (another First Class roomie), and, last, but never least, Skip Goodwillie (also a perceptive advance reader of the novel). Many of these men have proudly served our country. So, thanks to all Brother Rats and apologies to those I accidentally omitted.

Honorary class member Chaplain Charles Caudill was our chaplain during my cadetship and his son, Chris, was also in our class. The chaplain and I have a special bond over a bible that goes way beyond formal religion and is rekindled anytime we see each other back in Lexington.

Several spouses of classmates have also been encouraging and helpful in ways large and small over the years, including Paige Williams, Elizabeth Branner, Jodi Outland, Jeannie Murray, Staci Goodwillie, Cindy Warriner, Ann Parker Gottwald, Lisa Luck, Kathleen Mills, Lisa Dunahoe, Margaret Hazelgrove, Beth Sykes, Kate Wagner, Karen Adams, and Susan Waring, to name just a few. Thanks especially to Paige for her reading and insight from the female perspective, as well as comparisons to the writing of Pat Conroy and Cassandra King — high praise just when I needed it.

Several of my classmates and their wives had sons in the Class of 2012. We were fortunate enough to be included in their tailgates and other get-togethers, as well as seeing them receive their rings and diplomas. Thanks to my classmates for making us honorary parents and to their sons, Cam Murray, James Goodwillie, and Richard Luck — very special VMI men, just like their fathers.

The Class of 2012 also included that trio's roommate, Chris Baber from Richmond. He was one of those "fifth year" cadets I've always admired who had the fortitude to return to VMI for an extra semester to earn his diploma. Thanks also to his parents, Chris and Linda Baber, who I really enjoyed getting to know at VMI when they were there supporting their son. Parents like Chris and Linda often play a huge role in the success of their sons and daughters at VMI.

Chance McConnell roomed next to Cam, James, Richard, and Chris, and his parents are now part of the VMI family as well. Hailing from far away Hollywood, Lee and Angie McConnell fell in love with VMI and Lexington and actually moved to town during Chance's cadetship. Lee is well-known in the film industry for his special effects work, and if they ever make a film of this novel, I hope he'll be heavily involved.

The fictional main character of this novel, Nick Adams, is in the Class of 1984 because Conroy's seminal military school book, *The Lords of Discipline,* wasn't published until 1980, and I wanted Nick and other fictional characters to have legitimately been able to read the book before heading to VMI that August. Given this, I've also leaned on many Class of '84 members to join my march down memory lane.

First and foremost, Greg Cavallaro, Class of 1984, has been my biggest and most patient cheerleader and critic. Greg is the long-time CEO of the VMI Keydet Club and sees firsthand the life-changing benefits of attending VMI and participating in sports. It's our hope that this novel will expose potential scholar-athletes, both males and females, to the benefits of attending VMI. Thanks to Greg and his lovely wife, Marlene.

Other members from the Class of 1984 who chimed in with details about the Honor Court, drum outs, and more comical (at least now) memories and stories included Mark Morgan, Bill Janis, John Munno, Chris Caplice, Alex Thompson, Frank Kollmansberger, Barry Coceano, and Andy Protogyrou.

We talked to many female cadets and alumni, who provided much insight into their experiences at VMI. I'd especially like to thank Nichole Kramer, Class of 2003, Hannah Granger, Class of 2011, and Hope Hackemeyer, also Class of 2011.

Andrea "Andee" Walton, Class of 2008, was particularly insightful with Part Two of this novel and, as Wine Consultant at Quigley Fine Wines, made sure I paired the right wines with various fictional meals at the Southern Inn, Peaks of Otter, and elsewhere. Cheers, Andee.

Other alumni from various classes I want to thank include: my dyke, Clif Tinsley, '86, Dennis Hackemeyer, '80 (Hope Hackemeyer's father), Mark Weiss, '73, Ralph Costen,'70, Dan Sheahan, '76, Jim Mallon, '76, Bob Stransky, '72, Vic Arthur, '75, and many more.

Two members of VMI's extended and very loyal family who've also earned my thanks and gratitude include the Alumni Association's Carole Green (who helped with my many monk-like Moody Hall stays) and Traci Mierzwa, formerly of the VMI Foundation (and an early editor of this book).

When a Moody Hall room and bunk were unavailable or I needed a change of Lexington scenery, I made the historic Hampton Inn Col Alto my base — it's highly recommended. In addition, our class president Teddy Gottwald and his charming wife Ann Parker were on schedule to open a boutique downtown inn called The Georges about the time this book hits the streets of Lexington and you can bet I'll be among the first guests.

Mike Strickler, Class of 1971 and former executive assistant to the superintendent, proved especially supportive throughout this arduous process. Mike's office was adjacent to the superintendent's and I still get cold chills every time I enter Smith Hall, long known as "Puzzle Palace" to cadets.

I promised Mike's long-time boss, General J.H. Binford Peay III, VMI's fourteenth superintendent and Class of 1962, that — unlike Pat Conroy when *The Lords of Discipline* was first published — I'd always be welcomed back at my alma mater. I made that commitment in VMI's Marshall Hall following a speech by Pat where he referenced me and this book.

That day, after smilingly stating that he went to the best military school in the country and reaffirming a similar love of military colleges, Pat said, "There's a VMI graduate named Lynn Seldon that I'm trying to get to write a novel about VMI. I'm as excited about that publication as I can be." I hope the excitement and love that Pat has provided to me are evident on every page.

Foreword

This is a work of fiction. The main characters of this novel are completely creations of my imagination, though historic figures like Stonewall Jackson and George C. Marshall are very much a real part of the Virginia Military Institute's history, as are many other people and events during the time periods of this novel.

Of course, there is a very real VMI in the pretty college town of Lexington, Virginia. I'm a Winchester native and the Shenandoah Valley setting remains one of my favorite places in the world in reality and now in fiction.

The characters also visit many places that did exist during the periods of the novel (some are still there). However, I have occasionally taken the liberty of changing the timing and setting of certain events based on my VMI experiences and those of other male and female cadets to help the flow of the novel and to include many formative experiences.

For instance, the beloved Skip Castro Band didn't always perform when and where I have them play in the novel. They did, however, come back to Lexington for my twenty-fifth reunion in 2008, and it truly was a "Boogie at Midlife" night for many fans of their famed song "Boogie at Midnight" (which they played at about 10:30 p.m.). And, like in the novel, VMI really did beat the likes of Army and Virginia Tech back in the early 1980s. Really.

The fictional deaths readers experience in this book are very much a part of VMI and post-VMI life. It comes with the territory for cadets (who are sometimes called to active duty) and alumni, who have served this country during times of war and peace for almost two centuries.

Relatively late in the process of writing this novel, during a visit to the excellent VMI Museum in the basement of Jackson Memorial Hall, I learned for the first time that two VMI graduates died on September 11, 2001. Lieutenant Commander David Lucien Williams, Class of 1991, was killed at the Pentagon. Mr. Charles Mathers, Class of 1962, died at the World Trade Center. Since 9/11, more than a dozen VMI alumni have died while serving their country and fighting the global war on terrorism.

Death and VMI are inevitably intertwined in real life. So is service. I hope that my fictional words have faithfully rendered a service to the men and women of the VMI family. I'm very proud to be a part of a diverse group that still believes in the many definitions of service.

Sic semper tyrannis

Prologue: Nick

My name is Nick Adams and I wear the ring.
Well, that's not completely true. I often do remember to pull it out of my father's antique writing desk drawer when I'm going back to the lovely little town of Lexington. And until I got it resized, I had to wear it on my pinkie.

Every time I slip it on the chubby ring finger of my right hand, I feel an all-too-familiar cold chill blowing straight down from that hilltop Parade Ground at the Virginia Military Institute. However, the memories soon flow over me like the molten gold of my ring and they've mostly been too hot to touch the past thirty-plus years.

When I sent my ring back to Jostens in the late-1990s to get it resized, I also had them remove the Social Security number that was engraved into that expensive early-1980s gold. Many of us were naïve enough back then to have that singular number engraved in our rings, along with our last names. Back then we were certain our rings would be returned if we lost them, and we didn't think twice about including our Social Security number.

Today, as I write this more than a decade after 9/11, letting that number get into the wrong hands means you can lose your identity — and maybe much more. We were naïve about many things then.

I own and cherish the ring because I matriculated at VMI on a blistering hot August day in 1980 and graduated on a crystal clear spring day in May, more than 1,350 days later. I counted.

My decision to attend VMI was based on a teenager's inexperienced and immature desire to gain a father's love. That decision would haunt me and, at times, please me for those four long years in Lexington, another four years abroad with the U.S. Army, and many more trying days and nights that would follow.

My college choice would affect my life and the lives of many others in my class, other classes, and around the world. For a few it would even begin the march to their much-too-early deaths.

I didn't know then that people could actually die as a result of their college choice or that they could also send their sons and daughters there for the same life-and-death experiences. I know now.

This is my story and that of several others who wear the ring. These are my experiences and words as I remember them. There is life in these words. There is honor and there's dishonor. There's cheating death and there is also too much death, including that horrific day back in September, 2001. I experienced all of this and much more at VMI and in the thirty-plus years since I received my sheepskin diploma from the Institute.

It's also the story of a beautiful young woman named Virginia Shields, who graduated from VMI more than 20 years after me — and her father, Chip, who was my VMI roommate for four years and my best friend. Like me, Virginia tells her story and tales of others in her own true words, and it will be quickly apparent that she may eventually become a writer like me. She also wears the ring, and it still fits her like a glove more than a decade after I slipped it on her finger in VMI's Old Barracks courtyard. It's the same oversized VMI ring as the one her father also once wore so proudly.

Part One: Nick
1980–1984

It's a short drive but a long road between Richmond's Monument Avenue and VMI's Letcher Avenue in Lexington. From the first time I was dropped off in front of Barracks on matriculation day to the morning I left just after I graduated, I often dreaded heading up to VMI's monumental Barracks. But I also feared going back to the city of monuments for many years as well.

It was that first trip up that little Letcher Avenue hill to Barracks that would change my history — and the history of many other boys arriving that day — forever.

I'd heard all the stories about the difficulty and harshness of the Ratline. The shaved heads. The straining in Barracks. The yelling. Eating "square" meals while sitting at attention on the front three inches of your mess hall chair. The sweat parties. The lack of sleep, thanks to the late-night, middle-of-the-night, and early-morning mental and physical challenges. Drum outs for Honor Court violations. And so much more to endure for at least six months — only to then experience everything else VMI typically threw at you for another three-plus years.

I'd also heard the stories about VMI's storied dyke system, an interchangeable term for a Rat and his — and later her — First Class mentor who helped Rats navigate the tricky terrain of that first year. There were also many stories about the post-graduation bond of VMI men — and later women — who would do practically anything for others who wore the ring.

But those standalone stories couldn't and didn't prepare me or others for the accumulation of all of the trials thrown at me day after long day back in 1980 and into 1981. Those first days and nights were just the beginning of a laundry list of many bad times and a few quite good experiences I can only now recall and really appreciate.

They would last well past breaking out of the Ratline that first year, enduring Third Class sophomore year as a "Rat with a radio," a life-changing Second Class junior year as a "Rat with a ring," First Class senior year as a "Rat with a Rat," and graduating, only to have another four years of many good and bad experiences in the army. All of that due to a decision of that long-lost nineteen-year-old boy. Life — and death — really began for me that summer of 1980.

I didn't know all of this on that bright and hot day and very dark first night when the thunder and rain were almost as loud as the upperclassmen yelling at me. I just knew I needed to get through that single day and night — and then the next versions of both.

I'd already learned that life was an accumulation of days and decisions, and I'd already decided I was getting a VMI ring no matter what I had to endure during those trying times. But I'd soon learn that getting to wear that ring wasn't always a matter of simply deciding you could and would. Sometimes at VMI, like in life, others could control your destiny in ways you couldn't have imagined. And sometimes there was no control at all.

I won't go into too many details of my thankfully "normal" Rat year. It's different for everyone, but somehow the same — at least for those who stay. I can't speak for those who left. There were many of them.

Out of 427 who arrived on matriculation day, more than twenty would leave within the week, and dozens more would depart in the first few months. Only 300 or so of us would make it through the Ratline, and fewer than 200 would walk across the stage with me in 1984.

I stayed because I wanted to wear the ring back to Monument Avenue — for my dad, for me, and maybe even for Pat Conroy.

That summer of 1980, I'd sat on our little third story apartment's porch and read a book my father had given me before he died.

If you want to know what the first trying year was like back then at the likes of Lexington's VMI and The Citadel down in the bucolic town of Charleston, South Carolina, find a copy of the book I read that summer: *The Lords of Discipline*. Like mine, Pat Conroy's words are a love letter of sorts to military schools and the bonds between men — and now women — that develop there.

The book describes the Citadel Knob and VMI Rat years in microcosm and in words far better and truer than I have the capacity to create more than thirty years later. Conroy's fictional story came from someone, like me, who thought way too much for his own good.

Thinking too much is highly discouraged during Rat year, and it would sometimes make VMI and life more difficult for me and others. I still think too much, and it still comes at a high cost for those who know me or once knew me.

Upperclassmen at VMI and The Citadel who did read *The Lords of Discipline* over the years would employ some of Conroy's fictional tactics on Citadel Knobs and VMI Rats. I know because I read about the mental and physical adversity tactics and then got to experience them firsthand with far-from-fictional characters.

I thought Conroy and his truly singular book had prepared me for VMI, but I should have known that books can often be a pale comparison to real life when you're right in the middle of living it. I've found that to be true even with lyrical writers like Conroy, one of the many novelists I would grow to love like my father had once worshipped the likes of Steinbeck and Hemingway.

Yes, I came from Monument Avenue and from one of those big mansions near the fabled street's statue of Stonewall Jackson, an irony I couldn't resist noticing when saluting another statue of him on the VMI Parade Field just outside Jackson Arch.

However, it's not what most people initially thought when I would tell them my "upper class" address. I lived in a two-bedroom apartment with my father on the third floor of what had once been a stately eight-bedroom mansion for some Richmond tobacco tycoon who was now long dead from cancer.

My father was an English department professor at nearby Virginia Commonwealth University. He was a Hemingway scholar, and I was named after a frequent protagonist in many Ernest (and some would say less than earnest) Hemingway short stories. In fact, I was born the day Hemingway killed himself: July 2, 1961.

My mother was not a Hemingway fan, nor did she appreciate my father's attempts to emulate Hemingway's travels (he did this quite successfully) or writing style (he failed at this miserably). My mother also didn't appreciate my dad's attempts concerning pursuits of the same concepts for their only son. The jury's still out on me when it comes to travel and writing.

My mom left us when I was seven years old on the day my father gave me the first and only gun I'd ever own outright. It was a Ruger model 77, I think. I broke it down and threw it away long ago.

She kept our now-gunless West End house, and my father and I moved into the Monument Avenue apartment. She died within the year of breast cancer and it was my first brush with death. My father never remarried. I don't even remember him having a single date the next twelve years.

I grew up roaming the Fan, hitting tennis balls over in Byrd Park where Arthur Ashe learned to play, and sitting in on as many of my father's VCU classes as time allowed. In fact, he tried to schedule at least one of his classes after I got out of school for the day at Fox Elementary and later Albert Hill Middle School and Thomas Jefferson High School.

Try as I might through books and words, I was never anything like that Renaissance man and fellow Virginian Mr. Jefferson. Jefferson hunted, and so did my father.

Unlike my father, Jefferson, and Hemingway, I never liked guns. My dad was a crack shot, but I didn't even enjoy practicing with him using clay targets because I knew it was practice for killing something — or someone.

This would hold true for me with four rifles at VMI, several pistols in the army, and later, when my dear VMI roommate, Chip, whose parents had a Monument Avenue mansion all to themselves, once took me quail hunting at his family's river house. Well, I really only followed along as he and his father hunted. But I did, of course, eat the quail.

During many long nights lying awake in my cot at the Institute, I would sometimes wish my aversion to firearms had kept me from matriculating at VMI. But it wasn't enough of a deterrence for a boy wanting to be a man.

Many of my high school friends thought that because my father killed himself with his rifle the summer before I headed to Lexington it would keep me from going to a school where you were issued a rifle during your first week there. They were naïve about things like that. But then again, so was I.

At first I didn't think I'd ever understand exactly why my father killed himself. Before I would learn otherwise, I thought it might have been his failed writing career.

He'd taught several VCU students who had become successful novelists, and that had always seemed enough for him. At the time I also thought he simply may have wanted me to get on with my life without the large shadow cast by him or the likes of Hemingway and other larger-than-life writers that he'd shared with me on the printed page and out in the world.

The day before he shot himself in his VCU office, my dad actually signed a new four-year lease on our apartment and paid all of the rent in advance. I've renewed that lease every four years since, even though I've rarely slept there more than one hundred nights in any given year.

When I am back in Richmond, I still do many of the things I did when I was growing up. I hit balls against the wall in Byrd Park — and yes, I do see doing so as a metaphor for my life. I eat many of my meals at Joe's Inn, just as my father and I often did during summers when we were both out of school and not off traveling somewhere.

I still walk for hours along Monument Avenue and other streets in the Fan. At night, when I'm walking back to my apartment from Joe's, I peer through blurry old window panes at families eating their supper together and wonder at my life of wandering and meals in so many places around the globe — often alone.

I still recall eating in VMI's mess hall that first night, where I certainly wasn't left alone. At times I would have someone yelling in each ear and another red-faced Third Classman an inch away from my nose screaming at me to eat my spaghetti, square-meal style, faster.

It didn't help when my sauce-filled fork hit that Third's nose on the way to my mouth. He'd remind me of that mistake for months while I was completing countless push-ups for him. He was Class of 1983, and he loved to make me do eighty-three push-ups whenever his class was allowed to give the Rats a sweat party, which typically involved lots of push-ups, sit-ups, running in place, being yelled at, and sweating.

I remember thinking that night — and for many more meals at VMI — that I couldn't wait for a peaceful plate of food while sitting completely alone back home or at Joe's.

I generally got my mess hall peace once the Ratline ended, but eating a meal alone at VMI was rarely an option. Many solitary meals came later, and I sometimes even miss that red-faced Third Classman and his now-comical culinary company.

Even way back then and under those circumstances I found myself analyzing the food like my father and I had done during many meals in Richmond and on the road. I still recall that the pasta was overcooked and the sauce's greasy ground meat was way too fatty. It was that way all four years, and I probably ate that mess hall spaghetti more than a hundred times. I can still taste it.

I was often required to loudly recite spaghetti and other menu items dozens of times for upperclassman during my Rat year. It was one of many requirements of Rats, and if you didn't get the menu exactly right you could be sent to the Rat Disciplinary Committee for extra special treatment.

The RDC could sometimes play a big role in life at VMI, as well as in decisions to leave the Institute. The first time I was sent to the RDC was because — under pressure during a sweat party early one morning — I forgot that pancakes were on the menu an hour later. That resulting RDC workout late at night the following week up on the tiny fifth stoop annex was perhaps the hardest workout I had as a Rat. And that's saying something.

Even then I enjoyed food and liked thinking about it — even bad food like those pancakes. Growing up in Richmond with a father who liked to cook and frequently dine at local Fan restaurants, I'd acquired a taste for good, hearty, and simple food that would prove to be yet another problem during my years at VMI. Except for a few MRE (meals ready to eat) rations in the field, that problem would change for the better when the army sent me to Europe and I discovered Michelin chefs and stars.

In a tasty twist of fate, my time at VMI learning what sometimes bad food could taste like and then my U.S Army time in Europe eating my way through the Michelin restaurant guides actually led to what I've done ever since the day I got out of the army: write about food. Back in 1980, little did my English 101 professor know she was teaching a future restaurant critic on that scalding hot August morning in Scott Shipp Hall in my very first VMI academic class.

By the time I was in that English class, I'd made it through the first week of VMI relatively unscathed. My arms and shoulders ached from push-ups, my ears were ringing from the yelling, and my brain was bursting with all of the information I was trying to memorize from the Rat Bible, a pocket-sized book filled with minutia about VMI history and life that we were required to quickly learn and recite. After our initial "Hell Week," the upperclassmen had returned, and this had added yet another nuance to the Rat experience — multiplying the number of people yelling at us about Rat Bible facts, our uniforms, and more almost tenfold.

With that first stressful week behind us, it was good to get my head around something beyond the names of the ten cadets who died at New Market and what was for lunch that day. English class and several other English Department classes during my four years at VMI would save most of my sanity. Classrooms and Scott Shipp Hall became my havens and recovery rooms from all of the physical and mental stress during that first year and even the next three.

Quite simply, I found solace in the words of Shakespeare and, later, Julia Child and M.F.K. Fisher. There was also sometimes solace in my own writing even back then, as I tried to make sense of the transformation I was experiencing in Lexington and occasionally back home in Richmond.

—⟋⟍—

Thoughts of Richmond still lead to two people: my father and my roommate of four years, Winston Charles Shields IV. Called Chip at birth by his father Win and then everyone else the rest of his all-too-short life, my dark haired Richmond-born-and-bred roommate grew up on Monument Avenue and lived in one of those historic old mansions just like me.

But among many differences that actually drew us closer, Chip's parents owned the entire 10,000-square-foot three-story brick home where he'd grown up two blocks from me without us ever meeting. While my father had paid for our apartment's rent four years in advance, Chip's folks could certainly afford their mortgage as well, since they, and eventually their descendents, were heirs to thousands of shares in one of the largest tobacco companies in the world.

From the first day we met in Room 441 up on the fourth stoop just around the corner from where Old Barracks connects with New Barracks, Chip and I began a friendship that would last through the many trials and a few joys at VMI, back in Richmond, and around the world.

We'd somehow find camaraderie in the pain of many things that would happen to one or both of us, but we'd also find great joy in happy events that would pass in the next decade as well. I wish we'd had many more decades together on this crazy planet.

I don't remember if we shook hands when we met that August afternoon in Room 441. In the years to follow, we'd lock hands and look each other in the eyes after any separation of more than a day or two.

Some may label this tradition some sort of brotherhood macho ritual related to our time at the Institute, but for Chip and me, it would become more of a physical affirmation that we were bonded beyond words.

I do remember noticing Chip's eyes the day we first met. They were the slate gray color of our cadet blouses and they contrasted his black hair — when it grew out again — perfectly. His daughter Virginia has the same eyes and hair.

While Chip's Monument Avenue upbringing could have and did ruin many people in similar situations, his hands were not stained by either the green of dollar bills or the brown of tobacco leaves. Unless someone told you — because he certainly wouldn't — you'd never have known about Chip's financial background.

Of course, VMI's Ratline supposedly broke everyone down to an equal level, but money still talked inside Barracks at times, just like in real life. Just not for Chip.

At least not then. When he finally did let his wealth speak for him after graduation, he did it in quiet ways that helped others rather than producing cancerous cells or actions.

Of course, I'd heard of Chip and his family back in Richmond and recalled seeing him in tennis tournaments occasionally, but we were obviously in very different circles of society and life. Heck, I wasn't even in a circle.

Whether he liked it or not, Chip didn't have much of a choice in the matter. Chip's circle involved Monument Avenue and River Road addresses, second and third homes on the "rivah" or up in the Blue Ridge Mountains, private schools, and exclusive clubs with steep initiation and membership fees.

From the day we met and whether it was in our room, studying in Scott Shipp Hall, playing tennis, or drinking beers in Lexington or Richmond, our bonds would never be about money. It was obvious even during those early days at VMI that Chip knew there were many more important things than money.

—⁂—

In a strange twist of fate that I'm sure would make Pat Conroy and other southerners smile, our other roommate, Bradley Bell, was from Charleston. That's the pretty waterlogged city down in South Carolina surrounded by tannic rivers, rather than West Virginia's riverfront capital that's surrounded by black, coal-filled mountains. Like South Carolina, West Virginia was another state I'd grow to love later in life, but that's another story involving very different people and places.

Our Charleston roommate brought almost as much baggage to VMI as Chip and me, thanks to a long lineage of Citadel graduates who thought VMI should only be attended by Virginia boys.

Bradley's great grandparents had moved to Charleston from Poland in 1849. Bradley's father, a Citadel graduate who bled that particular shade of Citadel blue, had inherited a men's clothing store on King Street from his father. He'd fully expected Bradley to attend The Citadel, get his ring, graduate, and eventually take over the family's Bell's Menswear business with his older brother.

But Bradley had other ideas that stretched far beyond King Street and the rest of the Holy City. I wouldn't learn all of this about Bradley and his family until much later in my Rat year and during trips down to that special city when Bradley could finally bring himself to go home again.

When I first met Bradley, he'd just had his head shaved and he looked all of fifteen. The first thing I noticed about him were his piercing blue eyes. They were starkly contrasted by jet black eyebrows and, later, jet black hair that he still keeps well-trimmed to this day. He was — and remains — about one hundred and seventy-five pounds, while I entered VMI at one twenty-five and then surpassed the two hundred-pound mark soon after I left the army.

I remained skinny during my entire cadetship and most of my time in the army, though many filling German, French, and Italian meals did start catching up to me during my last year in Europe. Along with gaining weight, I also started losing my hair. I now actually wear my hair shorter today than it was when we were Rats more than thirty years ago. People tell me I now look like a chubby Anthony Edwards — Dr. Mark Greene of *ER* fame.

The three of us hardly spoke that first week, as we quickly moved from one task to another or collapsed onto our small metal cots — we'd later learn to call them racks or hays — for a few fitful hours of sleep until they kicked our doors in yet again. Once classes began, however, we started what would become an almost-nightly tradition in our Barracks room that first year and for the next three years and beyond.

With the playing of taps and lights out at eleven thirty, which we had quickly learned was 2330, military-speak, we would lay face-up in our racks and talk about the day behind us and our pre-VMI lives. That's when I learned about some of the parts of the privileged Monument Avenue life Chip was trying to escape and the King Street destiny Bradley felt he couldn't avoid — even with his flight to VMI and away from Charleston and The Citadel.

When I look back on those nights, I can't help but think how different my life at VMI and beyond would have been if fate hadn't brought us together in that stark room. In their own different ways, Chip and Bradley truly enabled me to survive Rat year with my life and mind relatively intact.

—m—

The three of us and many others attending VMI then will always remember the end of that first week once the rest of the Corps of Cadets returned as "Citadel Blouse Burning Day." I also vividly remember our first Honor Court drum out later that same night.

We'd just run back to our rooms following a sweat party in Cocke Hall and a quick herding through the steaming showers when our door was kicked in once again to say it was time to get fitted for our two matching grey wool blouses. As Chip and I started to run out the door, Bradley told a particularly harsh Third Classman ironically named Jackson that he planned to wear his brother's Citadel blouse that he'd brought from Charleston and only needed to be fitted for one VMI blouse.

Jackson immediately wheeled around at the door in disbelief, shouting, "Do you think you're too good to wear a VMI blouse, you Charleston pansy? I'll show you what Virginia men think of South Carolina boys and Citadel blouses."

Jackson then grabbed the Citadel blouse out of Bradley's trembling hands and stormed out our door without another word. After what must have been a minute or two, but felt like ten, another Third Classman kicked our door in and ordered us out onto the stoop just inside Old Barracks. We were ordered to strain and face the courtyard at the railing.

Within another five minutes, they'd kicked in all of the doors and had most of our classmates out on the stoop in Old Barracks screaming, "Brother Rat," in unison. Looking down I could see that much of the Corps on the other three stoops had come outside to the railings to see what was happening as well.

The RDC president, a muscular guy from Richmond with a crew cut who was appropriately named Crossley, came out into the courtyard holding Bradley's blouse in the air and yelled, "Shut up, Rats."

After our chanting quickly came to a halt, Crossley clambered up on the sentinel box in the center of the courtyard, took a lighter out of his fatigues pocket, and lit Bradley's blouse.

It had obviously been soaked with lighter fluid or something after Jackson took it down to Crossley because the wool quickly burned and practically disintegrated down to the zipper, with the ashes wafting into the air around Crossley and the sentinel box.

After throwing what remained down into the completely silent courtyard, a red-faced Crossley screamed up at us, "Some Rat named Bell from Charleston apparently thought a Citadel blouse was better than our VMI blouse. Maybe he doesn't deserve to wear the VMI blouse — or our ring. Maybe none of you deserve it. We'll find out soon enough, Rats!"

With that Crossley climbed down from the sentinel box and stalked back to his room, leaving a dead-silent Barracks in his wake. To this day I still get chills with what happened next.

Bradley was between Chip and me, and Chip started screaming the chant of "Brother Rat" again to the still-silent Barracks. After he'd yelled it alone three or maybe four times, other Rats on fourth stoop then joined him, and Chip's lone voice quickly became a thunderous roar heard throughout Barracks. With everyone staring up at us from the lower stoops, all of the Rats headed toward where we stood ten deep surrounding Bradley in support.

Tears were streaming down Bradley's face as he joined in the cacophony, but I could tell even then that they were tears of determination to prove Crossley — and his family — wrong. Looking down again I even saw Crossley back out in the courtyard, looking up with what I still swear was admiration.

—‹‹‹—

Later that night we had our first drum out. I'll never forget it. I guess that's the point. Our doors were kicked in at 3:38 a.m. I knew because I couldn't help looking at the clock on my desk while getting out of my rack. I recognized the guy who kicked in our door as an Honor Court prosecutor. He shouted, "Get up, Rats. Your Honor Court has met," and then told us to get into our gym clothes and go into Old Barracks on our stoop.

After we quickly dressed and stood straining at the rail, Cadre members yelled at us to look down into the courtyard. I stared down through the fog and saw Thirds, Seconds, and Firsts out on the stoop as well. They wore sweats, bathrobes, and blankets against the middle-of-the-night chill and fog sometimes found during Shenandoah Valley Septembers. The Rats were the only ones dressed the same — VMI red gym shorts and short-sleeve bright yellow t-shirts with red stripes at the neck and arms.

Someone was loudly playing a drum somewhere below, repeating a fast drum roll followed by a single loud beat. I can still recall thinking that it sounded like a car driving over those rumble strips they often place on the sides of interstates to warn drifting drivers. Those rumbling drum rolls kept ending in a crashing single drumbeat before being repeated for what seemed like an hour but was probably five minutes at most.

The drum roll stopped with a final bang, and I saw and heard the coatee-laden Honor Court march into the courtyard from Jackson Arch. The Honor Court president called them to a halt and then screamed out hauntingly similar words used by Honor Court presidents for decades in the past and in the future:

> *Tonight the Honor Court has met and found Cadet Funk, BR, guilty of making a false report. He has placed personal gain before personal honor and left the Institute never to return again. His name will never be mentioned inside the walls of the Institute again!*

The Honor Court president then quietly commanded, "Court, about face," and they marched back into Jackson Arch. The three of us silently returned to our room as many other Brother Rats and upperclassmen headed to the bathroom with full and now-awakened bladders.

As would be the case with most drum outs in the next four years, none of us said a word once back in our racks. But I know we all stayed awake for a long time contemplating what we'd just experienced for the first of far too many times.

We would later learn a few more details about the Funk drum out. He was a Third Classman but had actually been "rolled" for lying quite late in the previous semester. His dyke, who was now a fifth-year cadet, had turned him in to the Honor Court after learning he'd made a false report about his whereabouts while he was on confinement the final week of that past May. It would not be my last September drum out.

—ᴍ—

September quickly turned to October, with sweat parties, classes, and football games providing a mix of pain and limited pleasure, like when I aced a chemistry test or the football team won and we got to head uptown on Saturday night for a couple of hours and beers.

One of those Saturday nights was Bradley's eighteenth birthday. While many of Bradley's high school friends back in Charleston would have enjoyed their first legal beer at breakfast to mark the occasion, the day passed without him mentioning it to a single person.

Though they didn't even check his ID, Bradley told us that night at Spanky's that he was scared of the perverse ways some at VMI might "celebrate" a Rat's birthday. Bradley kept it to himself. He kept far too many things to himself for far too long. We all did, I guess, and some of us still do.

Parents Weekend in October would obviously prove another test for me, but I would find that each year it became less of an issue for my psyche. That first Parents Weekend and for many football games to follow, Chip's mother and father made up for the glaring absences of my parents and Bradley's family with a huge tailgate spread at their reserved Keydet Club spot out on the Parade Ground's grass.

That crisp and bright blue October Saturday would be the first of many I would spend with Chip's parents in Lexington, in Richmond, or at their river house on the Rappahannock down near Urbanna. Winston "Win" Charles Shields III and Sarah Shields would quickly become my surrogate parents, and Chip would eventually become the brother I never had.

Chip had inherited physical traits from both his father and mother. The first thing I noticed was that Win Shields had shared his gray eyes with his son, while Sarah had given her son an almost feminine face. They were also both tall, lean, and long-legged, just like Chip — and his sweet Virginia.

That long-ago tailgate was the first of many times I would share hamburgers and so much more with the Shields family. I can still taste that first bite and feel the greasy juices running down both sides of my mouth, with Sarah Shields smiling at me and making a motherly swipe at my mouth with her napkin.

Mid-November meant Ring Figure for the Class of 1982, and I honestly couldn't fathom the two additional years of VMI time it would take for me to earn that ring. Each class designed their own oversized rings, with an "Institute" side and a "class" side.

For '82 their Institute side featured VMI's founding year of 1839, Jackson Statue, and a Confederate flag. I often wondered what the few African Americans in their class felt about it. I never asked.

Watching the Class of '82 receive their rings in Jackson Memorial Hall and then enjoy a weekend they'd truly earned made me more determined than ever to get through VMI. The challenges would prove immense and it sometimes had very little to do with making it through the Ratline.

—⚹—

I returned to Richmond for the first time at Thanksgiving. Chip and I got a ride with a First who also lived in the Fan. Bradley had gone back to Charleston, where his family apparently hoped he would come to his senses, leave VMI, and apply to The Citadel. I'd gone back to Richmond to deal with the life — and death — I'd left behind.

I found the apartment just as I had left it back in August. I'd not stepped inside my father's bedroom since the day he shot himself down at VCU, though I'd looked through the door before closing it for good back in the summer.

Back then I'd seen that he'd left a paperback collection of Hemingway's Nick Adams short stories on his bedside table. I remember standing there and wondering what in the world could have driven these two men who so embraced life to take their own.

That first time home meant revisiting my father's ghost, which I'd physically left behind in August. Because he'd killed himself just before I reported to VMI, I'd honestly never really had the time to process what he'd done to himself — or me.

When I got back into the Fan on that Wednesday night, it was already dark. The woman I'd hired to check weekly on the apartment had apparently come in and turned a couple of lights on for me, but it didn't matter. The apartment still felt dark no matter how much artificial light was used to brighten it.

Everything was just as I'd left it in August. My dad's door was still closed and the refrigerator was still completely empty. The maturity I'd gained in the past three months quickly drained out of me as I surveyed what little was left of my life in Richmond. It literally brought me to my knees in our little living room, and I had to get out of there within five minutes of my return home.

Back out on Monument, I walked slowly down to Joe's for a plate of baked spaghetti, which was — and still is — much better than the mess hall's version. I ordered a couple of draft beers and ate my dinner at the bar, speaking briefly to the long-time bartender and a few veteran waitresses my dad and I both knew well. It was easy to tell by their faces that they all knew about him.

Mary, one of many veteran waitresses, did come over to the bar to give me a hug, saying she was sorry to have heard about my dad and that everyone at Joe's really missed seeing him and me there. She also pulled a folded up page of yellow legal paper out of her apron, saying it was the ingredients list for their spaghetti that my father had asked her to give to me when she last saw him in July. She was wiping a tear from her eye when she walked away.

12 cans of water
2 1/2 cases of Full Red tomatoes
1 case of tomato juice
1 1/2 case of tomato paste
3 hotel pans of minced carrots, celery, and onion
Season the above with 4 large handfuls of garlic, oregano
and 3 handfuls of black pepper and salt
4 1/2 cups of sugar

*4 large frying pans full of ground beef seasoned with 1
handful of garlic,
oregano, black pepper, and salt for each pan.
Fry until meat is crispy around the edges.*

I read the sauce-stained ingredients list while finishing the
last of my spagheti, thinking of my father asking Mary for this
when he knew I'd receive it after he was gone. I've never tried to
replicate the recipe, though another long-time waitress recently
told me that Joe's daughter still comes into the restaurant twice a
week to make these huge batches of tasty meat sauce.

I didn't linger long over the recipe and thoughts of my father
before heading back home. I did stop at the little market across
the street from Joe's for a six-pack of yellow Coors cans, hoping a few more beers would help me sleep. I also bought some
strong Colombian coffee to deal with a very likely hangover the
next morning.

Once back in the apartment, I went straight out to the balcony, where little traffic passed below, to sip my beers and assess
my situation. It only took two gulped cans to conclude that my
life as I now knew it was really no longer in Richmond at all.

My life was in Lexington now and would be for most of the
next three and a half years. And although I didn't know it yet, the
little life I seemed to have left in Richmond would take place up
the street at Chip's house instead of in the apartment where my
dad's distinct smells still lingered, from his books to his Aramis
cologne.

After a third beer back inside the apartment and collapsing
in my room's single bed for a relatively unbroken night of sleep,
I awoke early Thanksgiving Day to sparse traffic on Monument

Avenue. Even though it was in the fifties overnight, I'd intentionally left my bedroom door open, as well as the one leading to the balcony. I guess it served as some sort of strange assurance that nobody would be kicking my door in for at least one morning.

After making it in the French press my father loved, I carried my coffee onto the balcony to warm me against the early morning chill. Though we could occasionally gulp some thin coffee during breakfast in the mess hall, I enjoyed the first peaceful cup of coffee since the day I'd left for VMI back in August. I don't think I've ever appreciated a cup of coffee more than that Thanksgiving morning.

After that first strong cup, I grabbed a quarter to buy a *Richmond Times-Dispatch* from a machine down the street, thinking I'd read it over some more coffee and breakfast at Joe's. In retrospect, I was trying to think of anything to take my mind off my dad. But Joe's was closed when I got there, and I realized they were letting the wait staff and cooks enjoy the day with their families. Of course, that made me miss my dad even more.

Back at what I still thought of as "our" apartment, I made another cup of coffee and headed out to the balcony with the paper. There was still little traffic, and I enjoyed the most restful morning I'd had in months. That peace unravelled when I noticed *The Lords of Discipline* sitting on the balcony's painted wood floor, just where I'd left it in August.

How naïve I'd been less than four short months ago, reading that book and thinking it couldn't possibly be that bad. It had been that bad and worse at times for some others no longer at the Institute.

The jacket cover described the characters as friends, cadets, and blood brothers who survived their military school experience.

Good God, I thought, Bradley, Chip, and I had experienced some of that already, and we hadn't even made it out of the Ratline. I shuddered to think that the events Conroy had created in his novel were based on his experiences at The Citadel and that many had already happened to us and more likely would in the coming years before and after I earned the ring.

I couldn't bear to open the book again. I'd finished reading it when my father was still alive and sitting just inside the French doors. Back in August he was probably rereading a Nick Adams short story like the poignant "Three Shots" for the thirtieth time.

I really found it hard to believe that less than a half year had passed since that last peaceful period in this apartment. It felt like a lifetime to me and in many ways it had been.

I was a very different person that Thanksgiving morning, and it wasn't just due to my dad's suicide. VMI had also already changed me from a fatherless boy to a man-child who could appreciate a simple cup of coffee and have the discipline not to reopen Conroy's book or the cruel chapter of a life when a boy lost his father.

As I rose, I tossed the book back on the floor and the noise broke the morning calm as I headed inside to call Chip about Thanksgiving dinner plans at his house. While I dialed the number he'd given me, I found myself thinking that I should get the apartment phone disconnected. There was really little need for it anymore.

Though we'd just seen each other the day before when I was dropped off at my apartment by the First, it was good to hear Chip's voice. I'd heard nothing but my father's voice in the apartment since arriving the night before, and I knew I needed to get out of there.

"Mornin, BR," Chip replied when he heard my voice. "Is your coffee incredibly good or what?"

"Yep. It's the best damn cup of coffee I've had since August," cradling the phone into my shoulder and taking a sip.

"Well, head over here, and I'll make a new pot — or are you too much of a coffee snob to drink our simple stuff?"

"I'm on my way, BR, and I'm shakin a leg." "Shake a leg" was a term used back at VMI for the bugle call indicating you had two minutes to shake a leg and get in formation. Many VMI graduates still use the term today when they're in a hurry or need someone else to hustle.

The short walk west on Monument was one I'd enjoyed often, and I guess I'd passed Chip's house and admired the architecture many times without knowing who lived there. I found it somewhat funny to ascend those slate-topped stairs, smiling at the small distance between my apartment and his mansion and how far I'd traveled since leaving for VMI back in August.

Chip was at the door before I had a chance to find the bell, and we firmly shook hands and locked eyes. "Wake up and smell the coffee, Adams, you short-haired Rat."

"I've already been awake for hours," I said, scratching my shaved head. "I couldn't wait to get up late on my own terms without having some upperclassman kicking in our door and dropping us for push-ups, but I still couldn't sleep in very long."

"You're already getting soft and you just left Lexington yesterday. Seriously, wasn't it nice to sleep until we wanted, even if we both did wake up pretty early anyway?"

We were still standing in the big foyer when we heard Chip's father yell out to us from what was obviously the kitchen, "Shake a leg, get in here, and get to work, men!" Chip and I smiled at each other and then walked down a long hallway that led to a kitchen that was truly larger than our entire apartment.

Mr. Shields was sitting on a barstool at the shiny black granite counter cutting what looked to be about five pounds of large onions. "Don't just stand there, men," he said, looking up. "Both of you grab a knife so I can get Chip's general of a mother off my back for being behind on her minute-by-minute military cooking schedule for the day. You two can cry over these Vidalias now instead of your miserable existence back in Lexington."

After I shook hands and locked eyes with Mr. Shields, the three of us cut onions right on the counter, which was something I would never have done on our cheap laminate counters. Mr. Shields also showed me a great technique for chopping onions that I knew I'd go on to use for the rest of my life — and have.

While I was cutting, I said, "I can't believe you can cut stuff right on the counter."

"Yep," said Mr. Shields. "This Luck Stone granite is great. The Luck family has big-time VMI ties and they even gave us a nice little VMI family discount on these huge slabs from their yard out on Patterson Avenue."

When we were almost done, Mrs. Shields came into the room, saying, "It's about time those onions were chopped. The celery is next, and it's in the fridge. Oh, and welcome to our house Nick."

"Thanks, Mrs. Shields."

"I don't know what I was thinking when I let that nice man at Ukrop's talk me into a twenty-two-pound turkey for just the four of us," she said while standing in the doorway and staring at the huge turkey on the counter. "You'll be taking turkey sandwiches back to VMI on Sunday for sure."

"They'd never make it past the third stoop, Mom. We've learned that free food is fair game with upperclassmen as you make your way up to the fourth stoop. I'd rather throw leftovers away than give them to some Third threatening me with the RDC."

"You're talking gibberish that your mom can't understand, Chip," said Mr. Shields as he pulled the celery out of its plastic bag. "Stoops, Thirds, and the RDC bring back vivid memories from my days there, but your mother just wants to feed you boys."

"Thanks, Mrs. Shields," I said, grabbing a stalk of celery to cut. "Maybe Chip and I can sneak some sandwiches all the way up to our room for a snack Sunday night cause it's very likely we won't get much in the mess hall."

"Don't they let you eat in there?" she asked.

I smiled and said, "Well, let's just say some upperclassmen like to yell at us a bit during meals, and eating what they call a 'square meal' means it's sometimes a bit hard to get enough grub."

"What's a square meal?"

"Rats have to bring their food up to their mouths at right angles," I said, demonstrating with my knife and returning it to the counter in the same manner. "And we have to sit on the front three inches of our chairs."

"Well, that seems quite civilized to me — except for the screaming, squaring, and sitting parts," she said, smiling. "But I'll be sure to make enough sandwiches to feed an army. Or at least enough to feed you two and Bradley up on the fourth stoop or whatever you call where you live."

"There are sure to be less on that stoop come Sunday night," said Chip. "We started with more than four hundred back in August, but I heard we were already down to something like three forty yesterday. My dyke says we'll likely lose at least a dozen more by Sunday when it's time to head back."

"I think that's about the same percentage we lost back in my Rat year," said Mr. Shields as he finished off the last stalk of celery and scraped it into the metal bowl with our already-chopped chunks. "I think we're about done here, Sarah. Can we watch a little football now?"

"I'll take it from here, Win. Thanks for the help, and don't either of you two boys try to slip one of my kitchen knives into your duffel bag to use back in Barracks."

We all laughed as we headed out of the kitchen. But two of our laughs had a sharp edge to them that meant it was something we might actually consider someday.

—m—

Situated just off the kitchen and spanning the backyard, their TV room was most definitely larger than our apartment as well. A long bar made of what looked like some exotic wood lined one side of the room, a wall of windows lined another, and a huge TV loomed on a third wall, jutting three feet into the room thanks to a large television tube of yesteryear. Mr. Shields had already turned on the early NFL game, and I remember the Lions were playing the Cowboys.

"Is it too early for a beer or something stronger, men?" asked Mr. Shields as he headed behind the bar.

"I'll take a Bud, Dad. How bout you, Nick?"

"Um, what are you having, Mr. Shields?"

"I'm thinking bloody, but I have to warn you that my bloody marys can be quite addictive."

"That's hard to resist, sir."

"They are indeed, but let's do try to resist calling me 'sir.'"

"Ten-four, sir. Oops, sorry. That was the last time…Mr. Shields."

He pulled a brown Budweiser long neck out of the full-sized fridge for Chip and then proceeded to spend a good five minutes making a pitcher of bloody marys that seemed to have about a dozen ingredients.

He poured our two drinks over ice, added one of two celery sticks he'd pulled out of the refrigerator, and passed mine across the bar to me before adding a stalk of celery to his bloody and joining us in black bar stools emblazoned with the VMI logo. With two sets of piercing gray eyes on me, I took a sip and smiled. "Damn, that's good! What the heck is in this?"

"Well, let's see," he said, staring at the ingredients on the bar. "You probably saw all the obvious stuff like tomato juice, good vodka, of course, Texas Pete from down in North Carolina, lemon juice, and Worcestershire sauce. But I also like to add little nuances like cayenne pepper, celery salt, horseradish, and some Old Bay to spice it up even more. You won't find anything quite like it outside this house, though I will say I like the bloody they make down at Joe's Inn almost as well."

We swiveled around on our bar stools to watch the game, and I found myself marveling at this man and Chip's life on Monument Avenue. I vowed then that none of the Shields family would ever set foot inside my little apartment and that I'd certainly never tell them much about my father past the most basic details. In the years to come, I didn't keep either of those promises to myself once the Shields clan became my family in so many ways.

"The Cowboys are really going to miss Staubach at QB, aren't they?" asked Mr. Shields without taking his eyes off the TV.

"It must have been that Naval Academy training, Dad. I was surprised he retired so young."

"We'll never see the likes of him again, and I seriously doubt we'll ever see a VMI man playing QB in the pros, boys.

"The really good ones rarely come to VMI, and even when they do they will likely end up getting run down and eventually run out. I know. I watched it happen during my time there, and the same thing will happen at least once during your four years."

"How did you make it through there back then?" I asked. "I can't believe we're only at Thanksgiving. Even Breakout seems so far off to me and Chip."

"I know it's cliché to you two and all of your BRs, but VMI is truly a one-day-at-a-time kind of place. When you start thinking beyond the next day or week at most, you can get overwhelmed and just may decide to leave at the thought of so many things both known and unknown that are still to come.

"I can tell you that many of those things still to come will be quite bad, but a few are also too good to even fathom right now. Like this ring," he said as he held it up and then brought it down on the bar so hard that it made our glasses jump.

Chip smiled and said, "Right now I just want to keep from failing chemistry and calculus. It seems like the Ratline takes so much time and mental energy that I never have enough of either to study nearly enough. It's the same with Nick, even though he's a fancy pants English major in Scott Shipp Hall who has it much easier than me over in Maury-Brooke."

"Whoa, BR. I'm taking those same Rat chem and calc classes as well and struggling with choosing whether to study the periodic table or spit shine my shoes too."

"What you boys will come to realize this year — and the sooner the better — is that getting good grades makes everything else easier during all four years there. Cadre and all upperclassmen just don't seem to bother Rats with a 3.0 or higher nearly as much. Plus later you start getting more weekends away from the Mother I just for getting a good GPA.

"If you can stay away from the RDC as much as possible, keep your demerits down, and earn a high GPA, you'll actually find time moves much more quickly at VMI. Except for not having to worry about the RDC anymore, the same will hold true when you're a Rat with a radio, a Rat with a ring, and even a Rat with a Rat. And speaking of which, how bout another bloody, Rat Adams?"

"I need another one just thinking about going back to Lexington Sunday. I will say, though, that my apartment down the street is certainly lonelier than I'll ever be back on Post — or here. I really appreciate y'all having me over to your house today. I'm not sure I could have faced an entire day spent with the ghost of my father roaming around our little apartment and my head."

"I didn't lose my father until much later in life, and I can't begin to claim to feel your pain now, but please know that Chip, Sarah, and I can all be your family now. I've only known you a short time, but you seem to be quickly growing into the brother that Chip never had, and I'd be honored to fill in as your father in whatever capacities you need as you head down this road you've chosen over in Lexington and beyond."

"Thanks, sir. But you have to promise you won't make me reread a Hemingway novel a year like my dad did."

"That's a promise, Nick Adams."

—◊—

As I look back on that Thanksgiving Day long ago, I'm so thankful for being embraced by a family that hadn't even known I existed four months earlier. Though I thought dealing with the loss of my father and the stress of VMI would be the worst I'd have to face while in their embrace, I didn't yet know we'd all face much more, and that embracing other human beings was a two-way street I needed to travel often.

We finished watching the football game — the Cowboys won, I think — and somehow Sarah Shields timed the serving of food just as the clock expired. Like my dad and me in years past, the Shields cooked much more for Thanksgiving than was needed for a small family.

I can still picture their dining room table loaded with plates of food, and I know exactly what we ate because we'd enjoy many of the same things for many more Thanksgiving meals to come on Monument Avenue. The menu included roast turkey, oyster stuffing, homemade cranberry sauce, succotash, green beans with chestnuts, mashed sweet potatoes, and Sally Lund muffins from Sally Bell's Kitchen on West Grace Street. Sarah's homemade pecan pie using a recipe from *Southern Living* was for dessert.

I don't remember much about the conversation that afternoon or when we headed back to their sprawling TV room to watch some more football and continue talking about surviving VMI. However, I vividly remember the moment Mr. Shields casually told me I should spend the night there.

I initially said no, and he didn't mention it again. But later that night, without really discussing it further, Chip and I found ourselves walking back to my little apartment. He waited out on the front porch of our building while I grabbed some clothes and my shaving kit before heading back to their house.

It was the first of dozens of nights I'd spend in a house that was already feeling more like home to me than our apartment ever would again. In taking his life, my father had also taken the soul out of those little book-filled rooms just down the street.

Chip and I intentionally did very little on Friday and Saturday. We went for a run in the Fan on Friday just because we wanted to exercise and sweat without the constant screaming of Cadre. We even played tennis on Saturday in the crisp November air for the first of many times over at Byrd Park.

Within five minutes of hitting with him, I knew that Chip was a country club-trained player who could generally handle my public court game. He'd played fall tennis at VMI, which released him from some of the rigors of the Ratline, and it appeared he was going to make the team for the spring schedule against the likes of other country club players now attending UVA and W&L. He broke my serve once in the first set, I broke him once in the second set, and he returned the favor in the third to win 6-4, 4-6, 6-4.

Following two wonderfully peaceful days and nights immersed in the very different life the Shields led just down the street, I returned to my apartment Sunday after lunch and packed up what little else I'd need back in Lexington until Christmas. I then walked back to the Shields' house, where the three of them were waiting by the three-car garage in the alley behind their house.

Mrs. Shields hugged me like a son and then hugged Chip good-bye as well. After Mr. Shields backed their '74 blue Volvo station wagon out of the garage and I got in the back, the three of us headed up Monument Avenue to I-64 and the march toward Christmas.

—∽—

The weeks between Thanksgiving and Christmas would always prove to be one of my favorite periods at VMI all four years. The focus for the entire Corps seemed to shift to academics over many military obligations, making it easier on Rats that first year and for my next three years as a cadet.

We had our first snow the second week of December, and that layer of white added an austerity to Post when I didn't think the place could be any more grim. We formed up for breakfast and supper in the dark, with the snow muffling the shouts of upperclassmen and numbing our feet as we stood at attention and eventually marched down to Crozet Hall for yet another square meal. Memories of our Monument Avenue Thanksgiving feast faded quickly.

Except for some visits by screaming upperclassmen, our Barracks room remained a haven for the three of us. Soon after our return and during one of our talks after taps, Bradley told us his Thanksgiving in Charleston had not gone well, with his father still barely speaking to him for choosing VMI over his beloved Citadel. After hearing this Chip told Bradley that it was the last

Thanksgiving he'd have to spend in Charleston and that he was welcome at the Shields house anytime.

Exams started the third week in December, and I remember thinking then that VMI felt as much like a typical college campus as it could ever feel to me. Those exam periods each winter and spring would turn into my favorite days on Post, when studying generally took precedence over shoe shining, rifle cleaning, and listening to upperclassmen screaming.

All three of us were doing well in the classroom. Though Chip was majoring in chemistry and Bradley was pursing an economics degree, we all had to take core courses like English, chem, calc, and the dreaded Rat boxing or swimming down in Cocke Hall. It was better known to us as Rat Beating and Bleeding and Rat Drowning.

We all expected to get mostly A's and B's that first semester, which was better than a majority of our BRs. If the Ratline didn't chase enough of us off Post that first semester, failing grades and a sense of futility would also lead to even fewer fourth stoop residents come second semester.

I took my last exam on December 21, but we had to remain until the next day to be released for Christmas break. Chip's dad came to pick us up that afternoon, with Bradley considering but ultimately declining an invitation to join us back in Richmond for our three-week respite from the Ratline.

The drive up the Shenandoah Valley and then east on 64 was filled with talk of VMI among three people who knew the harsh realities of life there. Mr. Shields, as I still called him most times, regaled us with stories of his first semester back in the fifties.

Some upperclassmen had learned he was the son of a tobacco tycoon and had blown cigarette smoke in his face whenever possible as he passed in the Ratline. "If someone did that to Chip now, he'd be in big trouble, right?" he asked.

"Probably, Dad, if the brass learned about it. But that doesn't mean they haven't come up with creative cruelties of their own for me. Do you know that smelly snuff your company also makes? Well, it's quite popular in Barracks these days, and let's just say that the occasional chewing out by upperclassmen is sometimes laced with tobacco-filled spit. Believe me, they know my last name as well as they know the name of their beloved dip."

"Have you reported it son?"

"Are you kidding? I'd be run out of Barracks within days if I said anything. It might sound a bit like hazing, but I can handle some warm tobacco juice on my face and in my eyes. I'd honestly rather take that abuse than getting dropped for nose-numbing push-ups out on our icy stoop."

"I'm still not sure singling you out just because you have that last name is right," said Mr. Shields, turning around to look at both of us.

"I don't have to remind you that I've had to live with my last name for eighteen-plus years. I know that it's a personal choice to use your company's products, but a little tobacco juice in my eye is much easier to take than the occasional playground taunts I used to get about my family killing people and getting rich as a result."

"Let's not wash our family laundry in front of Nick now."

"As you can guess, Nick and I don't just sit around our Barracks room and talk about Hemingway all the time. He knows all too well that being a Shields isn't all about the big bucks I may someday inherit, whether I want them or not."

"Don't forget I was once a son as well, Chip," Mr. Shields quietly responded, eyeing Chip in the rear view mirror.

"You've reminded me of that many times," said Chip, locking eyes with him in the mirror.

"Well, we'll just see how you feel in a few years, son."

"OK, Dad, but I don't think anything will change."

We had thankfully reached the Broad Street exit near Monument Avenue by then, and I was honestly glad this conversation was forced to come to a close — though only temporarily. Back at VMI I often forgot about Chip's wealth, but it was hard not to notice it in Richmond.

They dropped me off in front of my apartment building, and I once again had to face my home — and my father. Everything was just as I'd left it, including the three empty beer cans still on the kitchen counter from the Wednesday night before Thanksgiving. I glanced out the French doors to the balcony and noticed *The Lords of Discipline* was still on the floor where I'd tossed it that night before Thanksgiving.

Each time I thought of that book and my father I realized how correctly Conroy had described military school life. I knew some of the upperclassmen at both schools took ideas straight out of the book, and much of that fiction had now become reality for me, many of my BRs, and those poor Knobs down in Charleston.

I threw my duffel bag in my room, walked past the closed door of my father's bedroom, and grabbed one of the three Coors cans left in the fridge from Thanksgiving break. After briefly wondering why I kept the fridge running at all in my absence, that first cold sip of Coors in almost a month gave me my answer. The refrigerator would remain plugged in and stocked with cold beers during my extended absences — and there would be many more of them even after I left VMI with my diploma.

After briefly giving the apartment a once-over, I went out to the chilly balcony. For the past month, I'd been thinking about doing something I couldn't do back in November.

I opened *The Lords of Discipline.* Even turning to the first page took me back to that hot mid-August day when my dad gave me the book after we got back from our cross-country trip tracing the ghosts of Steinbeck and his dog.

It was one of dozens of books he'd given me over the years, but this one was the last. He had never wrapped any of them but simply gave them to me, saying, "I think you might like this one, Nicky."

He'd had a wry smile on his face when he'd given me *The Lords of Discipline,* and he added, "This Conroy guy just might be the next Hemingway, Nick, and this one should particularly resonate with you right now." I remember I'd taken the book and gone out to the balcony, plowing straight through it in two long afternoons and evenings of reading.

"What'd you think?" he'd asked when I came back inside late that second night, looking up from a book of his own — a Jim Harrison novel or book of poems, if my memory serves correctly. My memory is serving me correctly less and less so as I age, but I distinctly remember it was something early in the career by the Upper Peninsula writer I've since grown to love as well.

"Well, I hope to hell half that stuff doesn't happen to me in the next four years," I said, as he put down his book on our coffee table.

"I thought the same thing when I read it last week right after I got the review copy in the mail. I've heard similar stories over the years from VMI and Citadel grads — and those who didn't make it — but I can't help thinking Conroy was exaggerating in spots. Especially that first year, huh, Nicky?"

"I guess only time will tell if he was exaggerating Dad. I sure hope so."

"It's probably the only criticism I'm going to include in the review I'm writing for the *Richmond News Leader*."

Time would indeed soon enough tell, and it was still shouting at me that Conroy had gotten much of it right — even the death parts. But rather than me losing a classmate like in the novel, I'd lost my father before I even got to my own all too real military school trials and tribulations.

As I leafed through the book, a piece of paper fell out of the paperback onto the balcony. At first I thought I'd forgotten a makeshift bookmark after finishing the book back in the summer. Both my dad and I liked to use random pieces of paper to mark our places in the various books we were reading at any given time.

But what I thought was a bookmark was actually a single piece of linen notepaper with what I immediately recognized as my father's meticulous block printing on it. I picked it up and slowly read it through increasingly tear-filled eyes.

My Dear Nicky,

When you discover this note, as I know you will before you leave for Lexington, I realize you will still be angry with me and wondering why I had to do what I did.

As with many things in life — and death — the answer is actually quite simple.

I did it because I was going to die within the year. They found an inoperable brain tumor in May. I did not want you to feel you should postpone your Rat year at VMI to be with me. Many may call my decision Hemingway-esque, but please know that I did it for you.

I was so very much afraid that staying home with me during my final months would lead to a different life for you, and I was determined that you head to VMI in August as planned.

I hope you will come to believe that I made the right decision, Nicky. Doc Old at MCV, who delivered you, knows he may hear from you someday to learn more about my fate and decision.

Remember our open fires, son.

With Much Love,
Dad

His father was with him…and always with open fires. — "Fathers and Sons," Ernest Hemingway, *The Nick Adams Stories*

After reading the letter and the Hemingway quote again, I slowly refolded it and put it back between the pages, taking a deep breath for the first time since starting the letter.

My father had placed the letter at the beginning of Chapter Eight in *The Lords of Discipline*, which starts, "So the fearful order lived again. From reveille to taps, the Barracks filled with the screams of the Cadre." How ironic, I thought, and I finally started to cry, wiping away the tears with the sleeve of the scratchy wool sweater I'd thrown on against the December chill. With a guttural scream of my own, I then picked up my half-empty can of Coors and threw it against our porch's brick wall, watching the beer and foam run down the wall through tear-filled eyes.

My months of questioning the specific reason he'd killed himself had ended, but other questions certainly still lingered — and I knew they would likely do so for the rest of my life.

Why the hell didn't he tell me about the tumor and ask me my wishes about staying with him and delaying my entrance into VMI? Why did he assume I wouldn't go to Lexington if I stayed home with him that fall and winter? And why didn't he leave the note somewhere he knew with certainty I'd find it before leaving Richmond to simultaneously battle the demons of his suicide and Rat year?

Though I now at least understood why he'd killed himself, all three of these questions and many more weren't answered by some damn note he'd written in August. Instead, my dad's note left me with a guilt he probably couldn't have foreseen. His desire for me to attend VMI had been so deep that he'd chosen to shorten his life so he knew with fair certainty that I'd at least head there in August.

The next thing I knew, I was walking up Monument Avenue onto the Shields' porch and ringing their bell. As soon as he opened the door, Chip saw my swollen eyes and came out on the porch to gently lead me down the stairs and across the street to the grassy median dividing Monument Avenue traffic.

He prodded me to the ground, where I sat against a big old oak tree, and he kneeled down right in front of me, saying, "Talk to me, Brother Rat Adams." And I did.

—m—

After gathering myself, I quietly said, "My dad left me a note in *The Lords of Discipline* that he assumed I'd find before leaving for VMI. It basically said that he had learned he would die within the year from a brain tumor and that he'd killed himself to make sure I went to school on schedule instead of staying back in Richmond with him and missing Rat year."

"Wow, man. Isn't that like Hemingway or something?" Chip asked, holding my tear-filled gaze.

"Yes. It most certainly is, Sherlock."

"Well, at least now you know, Nick."

"But what the hell good does that do me when Dad's dead and getting me to VMI on schedule was the reason he did it? I was living through hell enough there without knowing that, in a way, I'd helped cause his suicide. Now I have to go back there knowing this. I almost wish I'd never found that damn note or read that God damned Conroy book."

Chip didn't respond further to my rant. Instead he pulled me up from against the tree and started to walk down the median. We made it to Lee statue without talking and then sat back down in the grassy circle surrounding the fabled Confederate general. I lay back on the almost frozen grass, gazing up at the clear sky and then the statue.

—m—

Lee had died at sixty-three and probably dealt with death more than I'd ever experience. But I was just nineteen, and I'd already had enough of it.

"Nick, I think what your dad did was one of the bravest and most selfless acts a father could fathom for a son. Maybe we'll both come to realize that in coming years, when we get out of the Ratline, get our rings, and walk across that stage for our diplomas."

"Your father will be there for all that, so that's damn easy for you to say."

"You must know by now that he'll be there for you too. I think he's already coming to regard you as the second son they've told me they couldn't have, and this is no sentimental BS, BR. I couldn't think of a better brother."

"Thanks, man. Right now, I just need to get through this night — and then the next. I'm already looking forward to getting back to Barracks with you instead of living with the ghost of my father back in our apartment."

"Well, we can easily solve that problem. Let's run by your place and grab some clothes. You know there's always a bed back up the street at Chez Shields like we did at Thanksgiving."

We walked back up the median, crossed Monument, and I went back into my apartment so I could grab the duffel I hadn't even unpacked. I'll admit that I did glance at the book on the kitchen counter that still contained the note, but I decided to let that sleeping dog lie until at least May when I'd next be in Richmond. Chip, Bradley, and I had already talked about going down to Florida for some sunshine and spring training games over VMI's short spring break and now that plan sounded better than ever if it kept me away from Richmond and the apartment.

Back at Chip's house, I threw my duffel bag in the spare bedroom where I'd slept at Thanksgiving, planning to live out of it for the next twenty days until we returned to Lexington. This was the first of many Christmas and New Year breaks I would spend with Chip and his endlessly generous parents.

The two of us were inseparable then, relishing the freedom from the rigors of VMI and in our still-developing friendship away from Barracks. We were alike in many ways. Our minds were often too active for our own good, and we had a love-hate relationship with VMI — and our fathers.

We played tennis or ran every morning except Christmas Day, working up a sweat in the chilled winter air on the empty Byrd Park courts or quiet Fan streets. On the courts, his game showed more talent than mine, but what I lacked in skill I often overcame with sheer grit.

Whenever we decided to play best-of-three sets — and that was almost every time we played — it inevitably went to a close third set. Looking back on those crisp days in the bright winter sun, I remember not caring who won, and I still feel that way today when I play Chip's pretty daughter Virginia on those very same courts.

Christmas Day was much like Thanksgiving Day in the Shields house. We watched football, talked about VMI, and ate yet another wonderful meal prepared by Sarah Shields. She cooked a goose. It was the first of my life, though I've now enjoyed that delectable dark and fatty bird in Manhattan, Paris, and Shanghai.

Again it was just the four of us at their large dining room table. I found it odd then that they didn't have other family and friends over for holiday meals in their big house, and I would only later learn why that was usually the case.

Chip had lost all four of his grandparents in his teens, and his parents were their only children. He told me this some time later, along with revealing his mother and father had been unable to conceive again after he was born.

I'd also learn later that except for a few board positions and lots of cash donations, Chip's parents had somewhat isolated themselves from Richmond society because of their continued tobacco connections — and money.

However, on that night and many more to come, they embraced me like a son and brother, and I started one of our many traditions that day by toasting the three of them and thanking them for bringing this parent-less boy into their home. That toast had more meaning each holiday meal, though the specific Shields family members I toasted in person or vicariously on Christmas Day would change in ways I couldn't possibly have known back in 1980.

Another family tradition for this tight-knit trio that had adopted me as a fourth member was spending New Year's Eve at home, reminiscing about the previous year and voicing very specific plans for the upcoming year and beyond. Since that night and for the rest of my Decembers since, I have tried to be in Richmond on New Year's Eve as often as possible.

As a U.S. Army officer stationed overseas and then a far-ranging journalist, that's been difficult. I've been many places since I started an almost ceaseless worldwide search for a solace that I've eventually learned can't be found out in the world. It can only be found in the mind.

If I can't be there for New Year's Eve, I repeat the ritual wherever in the world I might be that night. There are four

Shields now who share this moment with me, and we're in different time zones more often than I wish was the case.

—⁂—

Chip and I returned to Lexington with equal doses of dread for the next two months and hope that we would be out of the Ratline by early March and one step closer to our rings and diplomas. Mr. Shields dropped us off at Jackson Arch, where we could already hear the echoes of upperclassmen yelling at Rats on the stoops.

After he shook Chip's hand and gave him what was obviously a hug of love and encouragement, he did the same for me. My father had never hugged me. Not once. I'm betting Hemingway never hugged his sons either. I hope I'm wrong.

After we marched up from SRC that evening, I followed Chip through Jackson Arch, assuming the all-too-familiar strain position and just hoping to get up to our room without being hassled. We made it up to the third stoop, and I was about fifteen feet behind Chip when he got stopped by a Third sitting on his room's concrete threshold spit shining his shoes.

"Whoa, Shields! Rack it in," yelled a skinny pimply-faced Third Class corporal named Wood. He put down his shoes on the stoop and got to his feet to face Chip just as I came to a quick stop right behind him. "Go around Shields, Rat Adams. I'll save you for later."

I hated to abandon Chip there but knew it would be worse for both of us if I didn't head up the nearby steps to the general safety of the fourth stoop, where Seconds and Thirds weren't allowed unless they were on official business. As I was running up the steps, Wood had already started laying into Chip.

I could still hear him yelling when I shoved open the door and said to Bradley, "Chip got stopped by Wood on third stoop, and I'd say he's going to be there a while."

"That guy's such a jerk. He wears those corporal stripes on his sleeve like he's the regimental commander and really seems to have it in for Chip. Just because he's apparently poor white trash doesn't make it right to take it out on Chip, who has never worn his wealth on his sleeve or anywhere else. Well, except for maybe those stupid Izod shirts he wears."

I had to smile at that. Chip wore his civilian clothes like they were uniforms as well — Bass Weejuns with no socks year-round, Duck Head khakis, and one of many colors of Izod shirts with the collar generally turned up in summer and down for the other three seasons. If it got below freezing, he might top this uniform with a colorful L.L. Bean crewneck sweater and maybe even some sort of boating jacket from Land's End as well.

Bradley wore similar clothes and shoes, though the brand names were sometimes different because of his Lowcountry lineage. He was always and still is a meticulous dresser, whether he was wearing a VMI uniform or his preppy uniform. I'd always been more of a faded blue jeans, worn Izod shirts, and scuffed tennis shoes dresser myself and still am.

"The funny thing is that I've seen Wood head out on weekends in pretty much the same getup," I continued. "But I'm thinking the shoes and clothes are from K-mart."

We were both laughing at that just as Chip headed in the door with a big smile on his face. "Welcome back to Barracks, boys," he said as he walked over to his desk and tossed his hat on it. "Wood hasn't lost his touch with me at all."

"Did he have anything new to say to you?" asked Bradley. "Or is it still the same old rich Richmond kid thing he used all of first semester?"

"Same stuff. I'm just glad he didn't stop us both, though I'm sure he'll have some prize words for you later, Nick. His whole 'fatherless' thing with you has also gotten pretty damn old. I'm betting he doesn't even know who his father is, and neither does his mother."

We all laughed at that once again, even though it had been repeated many times during first semester when we realized we were going to need to be able to laugh at the yelling when it got all too personal. Upperclassmen — and especially Thirds who still had the Ratline fresh in their brains — could get very creative with their screamed words when they learned something personal about you that they knew could get to your psyche.

I never learned how the upperclassmen heard about my father, but the grapevine in Richmond and all of Virginia was well-connected even back then. Today's Internet makes our gossip long ago seem so twentieth century. But there were and are still the same truths and falsehoods in both centuries' grapevines.

"Why are you staying in your blouse, Bradley?" I asked as I was removing mine.

"I forgot to tell y'all I had a note waiting on my desk to report to Mr. Mathis at 2000. I can't for the life of me think what the hell I could have done before we left or while I was back in Charleston for Christmas, can y'all?"

"Getting called to the room of a guy who's on both the Honor Court and the RDC isn't something I'd want awaiting my return, BR," I said. "But you shouldn't assume it's anything bad."

"I'm very much assuming that. Except for our dykes, I've never entered an upperclassman's room without it being something bad. It's mostly led to lots of yelling and more push-ups than I care to count, but this somehow feels different coming on the heels of Christmas break."

"Well, it's five of and you may get stopped out on the stoops," said Chip. "You better get going. If someone tries to stop you, tell him you have a 2000 meeting with Mr. Mathis and they'll likely let you move on."

"Thanks, guys. I'll hopefully see you two sooner rather than later."

Bradley headed out the door with a sense of foreboding for all of us. We wanted as little to do with the Honor Court and RDC as possible.

Chip and I finished unpacking our meager bags, took down our racks and mattresses, and lay down on them to await Bradley's return.

Less than fifteen minutes passed before he was back in the room, sweating in his blouse even though it couldn't have been more than forty degrees out on the stoops.

"So?" I asked as he stripped off his blouse.

"That was pretty weird. I knocked on his door in Old Barracks, and Mr. Mathis and his three roommates were all inside at their desks. I racked it in as one of them yelled for me to enter, and I kept straining during the single minute that I was inside.

"He asked me where I was at 2300 hours on the Tuesday night before we left for Christmas. Even though I was nervous, it was an easy question to answer. I had my chem exam the next morning, so I know I was in Scott Shipp in that basement classroom studying with Murray and Grainger who also had that exam the next morning.

"That's what I told him and he then — I swear to God — said, 'Thank you, Rat,' and told me in a friendly voice that I could leave.

"I actually would have been back here even sooner," Bradley continued. "But I got stopped by that damn Wood, who was still sitting there shining his shoes. He laid into me again about my Citadel blouse.

"I finally told that story to my family over Christmas, and they thought it was hysterical," Bradley said, shaking his head at the memory. "It's almost like my father and brother knew what was going to happen when they sent that blouse up here with me."

"I wouldn't put it past em," I said. "Your dad has probably already told the story to every Citadel grad who comes into his store to buy yet another pair of khakis."

"I'll bet you're right," said Bradley. "I told my father and brother that a VMI man would never have done what they did, and they just laughed some more."

"That's so typical of the way your family has handled your decision to come here versus The Citadel," I said. "I've never met your father or brother, and I'm not honestly sure I want to."

"Besides laughing at that whole blouse burning, you should have heard the other stuff they said over Christmas about how easy VMI was compared to The Citadel. How the hell do they know? Besides, I'm pretty damn confident they're wrong based on our first four months here."

"If they'd ever come to visit you, they might think otherwise. Chip's father told me that an employee of his who went to The Citadel and then sent his son here said being a Rat was much harder than being a Knob or whatever the hell they're called down there."

"Ten-four to that," said Chip. "My dad said they place more importance on what company you're in instead of your class. What kind of class unity is that?"

"What happened after that blouse burning would never have happened at The Citadel," I said. "I swear that it solidified us as a class in the very first week, and I honestly think it blew the upperclassmen away. They still give you grief about it, Bradley, but they know our entire class backed you that day and beyond as a Brother Rat and VMI man who just happens to have sissy Citadel grads for a father and brother."

"I'd love to see you either of you call my father or brother a sissy Citadel grad if you ever meet em."

"Maybe at graduation — if they come," I said.

"I've gotten to the point that I really don't care," said Bradley, frowning. "I am hoping my mother will come, but she's so influenced by Dad."

"Well my father will be there for all of us, just like football games and Ring Figure. He may have his issues as a tobacco pusher, but he'll be there for all of us the next three and a half years. You have my word."

I would come to value Chip's word in coming months and years, but my still-maturing nineteen-year-old brain could not possibly know that someone's word couldn't always control human nature, health, or sickness — and certainly not death.

We didn't revisit Bradley's strange summons to Mr. Mathis's room until the middle of the night just a week later. It turned out that a Brother Rat had told an Honor Court member that he'd been studying in the same room as Bradley, Murray, and Grainger on the December night in question.

He'd actually just looked in the door's window to see who was there before sneaking off Post to meet his girlfriend. A First Class Honor Court member who was heading out to dinner (a First Class privilege every night of the week) had seen him and later wondered why he hadn't boned himself when his roommate mentioned what time the nightly status check had been run by the officer in charge. The check was while he'd been uptown at dinner and seen our Brother Rat.

That's when the Honor Court got involved and our Brother Rat tried to cover his tracks. Bradley, Murray, and Grainger all confirmed he hadn't been with them, and he was quickly tried and drummed out of the Institute within the week. We wouldn't make the connection until the next morning, when Mr. Mathis called Bradley back to his room to explain what had happened so he understood how thorough the Honor Court was in their investigations.

Along with Breakout, one other event etched in my memory from that winter is the snowy inauguration parade of President Ronald Reagan on January 20. VMI had first marched in Taft's 1909 inauguration parade, as well as parades for Wilson, Truman, Eisenhower, Kennedy, Nixon, and Carter.

We'd taken well-heated buses to Washington, DC, but the waiting and marching in the cold and snow is what I remember most. For some reason I also remember seeing Vice President George H.W. Bush as we marched past their review stand. VMI would also march at his inauguration in 1989 and that of his son in 2005. I was on the streets of Washington, D.C. when the Corps sharply marched past President Barack in 2009.

We had another snow in late January that made Post seem even bleaker but somehow appropriate in what we hoped were the waning weeks of the Ratline. The sweat parties seemed easier in many ways, with our muscles and minds finally accustomed to the physical and mental stress. I can still picture running out of Cocke Hall after a pre-sunrise sweat party, yelling, "Brother Rat," as steam poured off our shaved heads when we ran toward still-slumbering Barracks.

I'd always look up at the Parapet as we started up the steps, and I can still recite from memory the classic VMI quote from Colonel J.T.L. Preston that was and is still inscribed there:

The healthful and pleasant abode of a crowd of honorable youths, pressing up the hill of science with noble emulation, a gratifying spectacle, an honor to our country and our state, objects of honest pride to their instructors, and fair specimens of citizen-soldiers, attached to their native state, proud of her fame, and ready in every time of deepest peril to vindicate her honor or defend her rights.

In days and decades to come, I'd often recall the "peril" and "defend" parts of the quote I memorized long ago and can still recite today.

—ɷ—

The time seemed to pass quickly as the seemingly endless routine of formations, meals, classes, parades, sweat parties, and runs turned packed days into passing weeks.

February brought rumors that we might break out of the Ratline later that month or in early March. This had been the Breakout timing the last few years, but many of the upperclassmen liked to joke that we didn't have a chance of getting out of the Ratline by then.

Unless we were studying late outside Barracks, the three of us would turn off the lights and hit the hay at taps. We'd exchange stories from the day, recall earlier Ratline episodes, speculate about Breakout, and then, one by one, fall asleep to the twenty-four-hour sounds of Barracks.

At least once a week in February, we'd have our doors kicked in by Cadre for a run, sweat party, or some other type of mental or physical test. However, one morning in late February, there was a different feel to the way we were awakened and what was to follow.

Instead of Cadre kicking in our door, it appeared the First Class was conducting our sweat party. In fact, a First we knew was an Honor Court prosecutor kicked in our door and yelled at us to get our blouses on and get outside.

They then herded us to Jackson Memorial Hall instead of Cocke Hall, and we all knew something unusual was happening. I found myself wondering if this was a different kind of drum out where they only included Rats.

Dressed in blouses, the entire Honor Court marched down the center aisle and up onto the stage, where they stood at attention as the Honor Court president strode to the center of the stage in front of them. We were all still standing at attention when he screamed, "Rack it in, Rats!" We hadn't been ordered to strain in Jackson Memorial Hall since early in the Ratline, so we all knew something bad was likely forthcoming.

"You're here tonight, Rats, because you are dishonoring VMI and the Honor System that these men on this stage cherish and uphold. This has to stop, and it has to stop tonight. If it doesn't, I don't give a damn if we drum out every one of you!"

"Each of you needs to reread every single word of our Honor Code and heed it. Numerous incidents since we returned from Christmas have shown your Honor Court that you brought society's supposed honor back with you to Post. That *will not* cut it. Now get back to Barracks and reread the Honor Code on your walls, or I swear I'll have many more of you leaving Lexington in shame before the week's out."

We all then ran back to the still-silent Barracks. There was no chorus of "Brother Rat" like there would have been after a morning sweat party. And more than three hundred of our Brother Rats stood in our Barracks rooms rereading the Honor Code yet again.

We couldn't help wondering if we'd inadvertently broken the Honor Code or if one or more of our Brother Rats had done so knowingly. I honestly expected a Rat to get drummed out the next night. We couldn't know then that the Honor Court president's dressing down of our entire mass was something repeated almost every year to remind a soon-to-be class that the Honor Code came before our classes, our roommates, and our friends.

We were silent in our room as we replayed the speech in our minds. We didn't have time to talk about it before the bugle signaled ten minutes until BRC formation and we headed down to each of our dykes' rooms to wake them up.

It was a Monday, so instead of rolling up their hays, we took them out on the stoop for airing. This was yet another age-old

VMI tradition that I'd always figured probably started after an outbreak of bedbugs in the 1800s or something.

At BRC formation it seemed like our corporals yelled a bit less than normal, and I figured they knew about the speech as well. They didn't even seem to bother us as much at the breakfast table as we quickly gulped downed tepid scrambled eggs and coffee. The march back up to Barracks was equally quiet, with the shouted cadence of the Rat Company commander the only sound in the early-morning light.

I didn't have an eight o'clock class, and neither did my dyke, so I hustled over to the then-quiet Post Exchange to buy both of us a cup of strong PX coffee. This had become a ritual for the two of us on Mondays, and I'd grown to treasure that time with him.

—w—

My dyke's name was Randy Armstrong, and it was sometimes hard for me to believe that he would soon be a VMI graduate. Randy was from the northern Shenandoah Valley town of Winchester, home of Patsy Cline. He had gone to John Handley High School, just like Patsy. He was a history major with great grades and had as little to do with the rest of the VMI experience as possible.

Randy had never held rank. His primary goal after getting out of the Ratline back in 1978 was to leave VMI as often as possible until he left for good after graduation in 1981.

He'd worn academic stars since the start of Third Class year, which was one of many ways he earned extra weekends away from Post. I rarely saw him except to wake him up and make his hay or when I returned with coffee on Mondays. I was lucky that I would never need my dyke to help me with any typical Rat issues, but I always knew he was there for me if I needed him.

Typically I'd have to awaken Randy again when I brought his coffee because he'd drop out of breakfast formation and head back to his room for another hour of sleep in his hay, which he just rolled out right on the floor after grabbing it from the stoop's railing on the way back into his room.

I'd already been awake more than three hours that morning when I held the steaming cup of coffee in front of his nose and said, "Wake up, sleeping ugly."

"Now is that a way to treat your truly handsome dyke, Rat Adams?" he asked while rubbing his eyes and sitting up from his hay to grab the coffee.

"It is when said dyke has drivel running out of his ugly mug."

Randy dramatically wiped his mouth with the back of his hand and took a tentative sip before getting up from the floor. "It's still good and hot, Nick. Thanks."

"Anything for my truly handsome dyke. Did you hear about our little meeting in J.M. Hall this morning?"

"I didn't hear the doors get kicked in like I sometimes do for sweat parties, but someone did mention it in formation before I headed back here for some more shut-eye. I honestly wouldn't take it too personally. They often do that to Rats early in your second semester to remind y'all of what's most important around here."

"Well, it certainly scared the heck out of me. Do you think there will be a drum out tonight?"

"Who knows? Sometimes those little meetings are precursors to some sort of Honor Court action, and sometimes they're just a wakeup call to what can soon be called a class. I wouldn't lose any sleep over it, though you just might in coming nights."

"Everyone was sure quiet afterward. I think I'd rather go to a sweat party."

"You'll have plenty of those in coming weeks."

"Do you think we're breaking out soon?"

"Now you know I'm the wrong guy to ask. I have as little to do with all of that stuff as I can. I will say that I've always thought y'all might break out earlier than normal ever since your mass did that Brother Rat business for Bradley and his Citadel blouse. It still gives me chills, and I thought I'd seen everything at this place."

"All I know is that I can't wait to become a Fourth instead of a Rat."

"I truly know how you feel," Randy replied, taking another sip of coffe before continuing. "But you and I also both know that there are many other milestones to be earned — and endured — here. As you'll soon learn, it isn't a cakewalk after Breakout. My most difficult time here was actually Third Class year when I found out that VMI was really still completely different and more difficult than any other typical college experience in the nation."

"I know. I know. But it's the milestones that keep you here, right?"

"My milestones now come pretty much every weekend when I get to leave. Heading up the Valley on Fridays or Saturdays is what keeps me going until graduation. We each have to establish our own ways of coping with this place, and I know you'll find yours."

"Well, it certainly won't be going back to Richmond."

"Do you still think about your dad much?"

"Every damn day. He haunts my every action and thought here, and I can't help but wonder how things would have been different if he hadn't killed himself."

"Didn't you tell me after Christmas that he did it so you'd come to VMI on schedule instead of staying back in Richmond with him?"

"That's what he wrote, and I guess it was a very brave thing in some ways, but I still question it every damn day he's not alive to share what I'm experiencing here."

"I know. I'm not sure what I would have done without my parents and fiancé back in Winchester or their many visits here before I could pretty much leave every weekend. I'm still amazed I didn't just go back home with them at some point my first or second year here."

"It's funny. I've often thought of leaving, but never of going back home. I'm not even sure what that is anymore. I'm pretty much staying at Chip's house when I go back to Richmond now, but I can't do that forever."

"The longer you're here, the more you'll develop your way of coping with being here — and being away. That may not happen til next year."

"I just want to get to Breakout, and we'll go from there. Speaking of going, we need to get to class formation, don't we?"

"Don't have a Rat shitty on me, Nick. We have two minutes to get out there. I wish classes were forming inside. It's cold out there."

We left the warmth of Randy's room for the freezing first stoop, and he let me out of the Ratline to walk with him out Washington Arch for our class formations down at Scott Shipp

Hall. Though I wasn't officially in the Ratline, I automatically saluted Washington's statue, and Randy laughed, saying, "Soon you'll be able to walk out of Barracks without saluting some statue."

"How soon?" I asked, smiling.

"I told you I'm the wrong guy to ask. The only dates I know for sure is graduation day and my wedding day back in Winchester a month later."

He headed off for a history class, and I got to my English 102 class formation just in time. I'd spend the next fifty minutes thinking and talking about Thomas Wolfe's *You Can't Go Home Again*, knowing he was right. But that knowledge wouldn't get me an A on the essay I had to write by the following week.

—m—

As February marched slowly forward, the Ratline actually seemed to pick up in intensity. We went through a four-day period where we either had a morning or evening run or sweat party every day and sometimes both. You could never plan your sleep or study times, and twice I found myself falling asleep while trying to study down in Scott Shipp Hall in the evening.

Rumors abounded that the increased intensity was leading up to Breakout, and our room buzzed with anticipation. One day in mid-February, Cadre woke us up Monday through Thursday for morning runs in the cold dawn. I can't for the life of me remember the distances we ran. I can only remember thinking how much easier the runs and the yelling had become since those early runs the previous August.

On that last Friday of February, we were awakened at six and told to get our sweats on for a visit to Cocke Hall. It turned into the longest sweat party any of us could remember, and all of us noted that it was run almost entirely by the Third Class.

We'd heard it was tradition to go through a sweat party run by each class before Breakout, and this made us even more hopeful. Late-night visits from several members of the RDC for room-to-room mental and physical challenges raised our hopes even further.

On Saturday morning we had a sweat party with the Second Class, and the fourth stoop was abuzz with rumors that we might break out early the next week. When nothing else happened Saturday or Sunday, though, we all started to get worried that we'd been through what the upperclassmen called a "false Breakout," which was designed to dash our hopes of finally becoming a class.

On Sunday night, right after taps, our doors were kicked in, and we were told to get into our sweats yet again. We quickly dressed and exchanged glances, noting that this sweat party was being run by the First Class.

For the first time the entire year, our three dykes had come to our room for a sweat party. Though they worked us out pretty hard and we did our share of push-ups (I recall us doing a total of eighty-one in unison to honor their class), it was probably the easiest sweat party any of us could remember.

After the sweat party ended, our dykes shook hands with each of us before sending us off to the showers, and we then collapsed into our hays, talking about the possibility of Breakout in the coming week. I felt like I'd barely fallen asleep when our doors were kicked in again before sunrise.

Cadre yelled at us to get back into our sweats, and I smiled to myself as I pulled the still-damp t-shirt and hood back over my aching shoulders. Even though we'd done thousands of them since August, the numerous push-ups the night before with our dykes still left us with aching reminders of the workout.

That morning the focus seemed to be more on our legs than arms. They had us form one big company that was ten across the front and must have been about thirty Rats deep. I don't think we'd lost a hundred from our class yet, but we might have by then.

We marched halfway around the Parade Ground and then headed down the steep "Supe's Hill" toward the tennis courts. When we got to the courts, Cadre yelled that it was time to run, and we took off at a slow jog toward the Chessie Trail.

We jogged out the trail for what must have been at least a half hour, and I swear I thought at the time that they were going to run us all the way to Buena Vista before dawn. But we finally turned around at two miles or so where rumbling I-81 towers over the trail and headed back toward Lexington and Barracks.

We trudged up the hill, and some classmates had to fall out to catch their breath, but when we got to the top of the hill and the Parade Ground, we stopped as a group and shouted, "Brother Rat," over and over again in unison until we were all back together and could run the final stretch to Barracks as one cohesive unit.

Once back to Barracks, they dropped us for a few more push-ups in the early morning light, giving us only twenty minutes to shower, get dressed, head to our dykes' rooms, and get out to BRC formation. But everyone had done all of that in less time by now, and we all seemed to have a spring in our step with Breakout seeming imminent.

—⁓—

When I think back on that day more than thirty years ago, I couldn't tell you what classes I had and certainly not what any of my professors might have said to us. I'd bet that was true for all of my classmates, in that all we could think about was getting out of the Ratline for good and becoming a class instead of a mass.

Our DRC formation for lunch was marked with the typical yelling, but they didn't seem to have their hearts in it. Corporal Jackson, who had seemed to have it out for all three of us and especially Bradley, seemed almost sad that the Ratline was apparently coming to an end and he wouldn't be able to bother us nearly as much.

"You think you're big stuff, don't you, Adams, just cause you've made it this far?" Jackson snarled just inches from my face. "Well, lemme tell you that it doesn't get any easier next year. In fact, I'd be willing to bet your roommate Bell won't even be back next year. Maybe he can get another one of his brother's blouses from The Citadel and go there instead. He'd fit right in, wouldn't you, Bell?"

Bradley was standing to my left in formation, as he'd done all year. "I'll be back here for sure, sir. But I don't think I'll bring another Citadel blouse."

"You're damn straight you won't. That's if you come back at all."

"I'll be back, sir. Will you?"

"Are you being a smart-ass, Bell?"

"No, sir. I honestly want to know."

"Of course I'll be back. I already know I'm going to be at least a sergeant and that I'll be back for Cadre. Care to join me?"

"No, sir. Brother Rat Adams and I think there are plenty enough Cadre members like you to handle the Rats next year."

"Well, don't forget that's still all you are — just Rats."

With that we marched down to lunch for what we hoped would be one of our last square meals.

—m—

Breakout for the Class of 1984 began in earnest on Saturday afternoon, February 21, 1981. We went for a twelve-mile march in the afternoon, and that was followed by yet another sweat party by the First Class on Sunday night.

The Second Class kicked in our doors Monday morning at five forty-five and then took us to Cocke Hall for a sweat party, while the Third Class got their chance back in our rooms for an unusual midday sweat party at twelve thirty just to keep us guessing. Later that day Cadre took us out on a two-mile run with our rifles. My shoulders ache at the memory. I think we had another sweat party that night as well.

The Thirds gave us a sweat party in Cocke Hall early Tuesday morning, and then we had another midday workout with the Seconds back in our rooms. Then the RDC and lots of Firsts took their turns with us that night. It was by far the most intense few days of workouts our class had ever faced — or would face.

They awoke us before five on Wednesday for yet another long run. Then, after an adjusted class schedule, our soon-to-be-class sat through a speech by the First Class president in Jackson Memorial Hall before being herded into New Barracks.

What came next was the new Breakout that the administration and First Class had concocted after years of having classes Breakout in Old Barracks — where broken bones and worse weren't unusual.

Our groundbreaking Breakout, which Virginia says is still generally followed today, started with a sweat party in New Barracks. Then groups of about a hundred at a time were quickly led down to the rifle range, where the Second Class played "King of the Hill" while the Rats charged the steep incline there.

After what seemed like an hour but was evidently just ten minutes, the Seconds allowed us to pass before then having to get through a muddy pit filled with Thirds trying to make our trip through the muck as difficult as possible.

Once everyone had passed through these trials, we ran back up to the Parade Field for a final workout before being herded into Barracks. There the Class of 1984 officially came into existence with our first old yell:

> *Rah Virginia Mil*
> *Rah Rah Rah*
> *Rah Rah VMI, '84, '84, '84*

It resonated through Old Barracks and was music to my ears. We then gave old yells for our dykes' Class of '81 and even for the classes of '82 and '83. By then I'd found both Bradley and Chip for well-earned muddy handshakes and hugs.

I don't remember much about the rest of that Wednesday evening, but I do recall we shared a steak dinner with our dykes down in the mess hall. Mine was overcooked.

I do know for certain that I had an eight o'clock English 102 class the next morning. I got a C on an essay I'd written about Wolfe's *You Can't Go Home Again*. It seemed fitting.

—⁂—

The three of us thought there would be a letdown after Breakout, but it certainly didn't happen my first spring in Lexington. Though we still had less than a quarter of the freedom they had over at W&L and every other college in the state, it felt like we were at a completely different institution after we became the Class of '84.

It was hard to pinpoint just one thing that made the difference, and to explain it to an outsider would have been and is still futile. But regaining small human pleasures and privileges made all the difference to us that spring.

The lack of large, time-consuming requirements like walking the Ratline, physical and mental Rat challenges, and eating square meals, as well as seemingly small things like being allowed to walk across the Parade Ground instead of around it all made the endless only-at-VMI things that remained seem easier to bear.

—⁂—

A wet March, when everything on Post remained gray — including our uniforms — finally turned to April. We returned to the white uniforms we'd worn when we first arrived in late summer, bringing back memories of that first week and the bleak period at the beginning of the Ratline when no end seemed in sight.

Since they'd never need them again, the Firsts burned their gray wool pants in the Old Barracks courtyard, and as the three of us watched from the fourth stoop, we couldn't help recalling the burning of Bradley's Citadel blouse during that first hellish week.

"Maybe when we're Firsts I won't burn my pants and I'll keep them for my son when he comes to VMI," said Bradley, smiling at us as we leaned against the railing up on fourth stoop in Old Barracks to watch the woolies burn.

"I really hope you're kidding, you son of a sissy tailor and brother of a wimp," I said, enjoying the play on words.

"Well, I can promise you no son — or daughter, for that matter — will be wearing my wool pants at The Citadel. I'll probably burn mine with the rest of our class. Besides, this son of a tailor will want his supposed children to head to whatever the hell college they choose."

"I feel the same," said Chip. "From the time I first remember coming to football games here with my father, I think it was assumed I'd be heading to VMI in his footsteps. I honestly never really gave it much thought, and I don't begrudge my dad for it. At least not for that.

"He really didn't even try to influence my decision," Chip continued. "But I think it was because we all assumed this was where I was heading. I didn't even apply to Tech as a backup, though I seriously think my dad would have supported me going there if I studied agriculture and somehow fell in love with growing and selling tobacco or something."

"Yea, right," said Bradley. "I can just see you walking the tobacco fields of southeast Virginia with a Camel between your lips," Bradley said as we walked back to our room just inside New Barracks while pretending to take a puff of a fake cigarette between his empty fingers.

"About the same as I can see you measuring some rich Charleston guy's inseam with pins between your sissy lips," I said as I faked a lunge at his legs. I was once again happy with my use of words to paint a picture and wished my English professors agreed.

—w—

The entire Corps of Cadets seemed to sigh a bit when we switched back to whites, but our class's journey through VMI and the lives that would follow was still just beginning. We couldn't have known in those first crisp clear days of April back in 1981 that an undercurrent was already underway that would change each of us in many ways — and also change the lives of those who would follow us at VMI some twenty years later and beyond.

My second semester classes had been going as well as those of first semester, and the same held true for Bradley and Chip. All three of our dykes, as well as Chip's dad, had planted the same seeds that good grades made almost everything easier at VMI — even after you got out of the Ratline.

I still enjoyed my second semester of Rat English best of all and even though we had different majors, the three of us were in the same English 102 class in Scott Shipp Hall. We even got to read some Hemingway short stories as an example of what our professor called "clean" writing.

Thankfully, they weren't any of those damn Nick Adams stories, and I didn't have to explain my name to everyone. That same professor, who knew the fictional Nick Adams all too well, would label my lame attempts at fiction critique "messy," scribbling in red that I was using way too many words to say much too little about what we'd read for class.

He also had us read Steinbeck's *Of Mice and Men,* and of course I couldn't help but think back to that seemingly idyllic summer trip with my father following the author's *Travels with Charley.* I also remember wondering why my father had gravitated toward Hemingway instead of a writer like Steinbeck, who seemed so much more in tune with America versus the more far-flung places, like Spain, Italy, and Africa that attracted Hemingway. Actually, maybe that's exactly what drew my father more to Hemingway.

Hemingway had wanderlust, and so did my dad. Though I didn't inherit their love of guns, I did develop their lust for travel. The last trip my father and I took together had ramifications I couldn't possibly have known at the time.

We'd already explored Hemingway's Michigan and Spain during previous summer trips, so the 1980 summer trip my dad concocted was to repeat the ninety-day cross-country trip John Steinbeck pursued the year before I was born. Steinbeck's trip led to his short travelogue, *Travels with Charley.*

When John Steinbeck set out on the 1960 journey that would lead to his best-selling book, he set out in search of America. He found it, and we did as well almost twenty years later when my dad and I retraced his trip and many of his experiences.

My father had always held a fascination for Steinbeck's journey and resulting book, as well as how we might someday repeat it. That "someday" happened the summer before I went to VMI.

Most people are generally familiar with Steinbeck's trip and book, but the brief summary my dad told to the many people who asked before and during our trip went something like this:

"Steinbeck left his home in Sag Harbor, New York, and then proceeded up to Maine before heading across the northern United States to Seattle. From there he went down the Pacific coast, including a stop in Salinas, where he was born and raised and where there's now the National Steinbeck Center. He then essentially raced through the Southwest across the Southern states before heading back to New York. He basically circled the nation in a counter-clockwise route," my dad would conclude.

—〰—

Although our journey followed his path, our trip had several differences. Many people wondered why we didn't take a dog, like Steinbeck. The answer was actually pretty simple. Our apartment didn't allow pets.

Another big difference with our trip was that we chose to borrow a friend's small Winnebago instead of taking a truck camper like Steinbeck's custom-designed one, which he named "Rocinante." We found ourselves wondering what Steinbeck would have thought of our modern Winnebago and many other things he couldn't possibly imagine finding in America just twenty years later.

After heading to Sag Harbor from Richmond, my dad and I basically followed Steinbeck's route whenever he provided enough details. Our occasional diversions came when we had the opportunity to go somewhere he mentioned wishing he'd gone, like a quick detour through Ontario, Canada, that Steinbeck couldn't pursue because he didn't have Charley's shot records.

The things I most remember about the trip were our fireside chats. We lit a fire almost every night of the trip on our way through Maine, across the north, and even on chilly nights late in the trip down in Texas.

I didn't connect the dots at the time, but — almost every night — my father would head back into the Winnebago for a few minutes. One night, after we'd grilled steaks on our fire's embers, I'd gone inside to get another Coke and found him leaning over the sink with a bottle of pills in one hand and a glass of water in the other. When I asked him what he was taking, he said his doctor down at MCV had given him some stronger antacid medicine because he knew we'd be eating differently on the trip. In hindsight, I guess they were pain pills or something else for his tumor.

I specifically remember a fire one night in Montana. Steinbeck had loved Montana, and we did as well. He'd said he would have moved there if Montana had had a sea, and my dad told me he felt the same. Steinbeck bought a hat in Billings, a jacket in Livingston, and a rifle in Butte. We stopped in all three of these friendly Montana towns, and my dad actually repeated Steinbeck's trio of purchases. I still have two of them.

The night we camped out and lit a fire outside Butte, my dad asked me if I remembered how Hemingway had killed himself, and I said, "Of course I do, Dad. I'm not quite the Hem buff you are, but I probably know more about his life than Steinbeck's, even with this trip and all the books you brought along for us to read or re-read."

"I thought so," he quietly replied over the crackling fire. "Do you think Hemingway's choice of suicide method was a good one?"

I can still remember not giving this more than a second of thought when I immediately replied, "I guess it's as good as any way of killing yourself. At least it's quick."

Oh, what I wouldn't give now to have taken more time to answer his question. He probably still would have killed himself, but I'll never really know for certain.

—∿—

The first week of May my first year at VMI was probably the best week I'd had at VMI thus far. The First Class had their eyes on graduation morning, and the three classes below them had their sights set on the new privileges they'd enjoy the following year.

We'd heard our class would get a taste of the new privileges right before graduation, and that proved to be true, with former Rats enjoying several Third Class privileges, like being able to move your eyes around while in formation instead of staring straight ahead like we had for more than six months. It all seems so trivial now, but back then it was a very big deal to gain those small, everyday privileges.

As with my first December at VMI, I really enjoyed the springtime exams period, when the focus became much more on the academic side of VMI versus the military. My enjoyment was enhanced by the May weather and the general mood on Post.

The end of the school year was approaching, and with it came the various life changes for everyone in the Corps. It meant graduation for some, Fort Bragg summer camp and other military obligations for others, and for more than a few a summertime decision not to return to VMI the following year.

Though I'd been to a few football games with my dad over the years, I'd never been to a VMI graduation and found myself looking forward to all of the pomp and circumstance. However, I'd spend all four years at VMI wishing I was a spectator instead of a participant in the various parades and other military spectacles meant mostly for the public. Well, maybe except for my own ring presentation and graduation ceremony.

Graduation was traditionally on a Saturday back then, and Post seemed packed with fawning family and friends. There was a formal dress parade Friday afternoon, and we watched in envy from the fourth stoop as the Firsts celebrated their last parade down in the courtyard. Some of them wrenched a fire hydrant open and flooded a quarter of the courtyard to make for a muddy slide in old pairs of white ducks that they'd never wear again. My dyke Randy had already told me he was keeping just a single starched pair for graduation the next morning.

The Class of 1981 graduated with 202 out of the 433 who had matriculated back in August of 1977. Randy strolled slowly across the Parade Ground stage, took his diploma from the dean, shook the superintendent's hand, and bounded down the stage's three steps while pumping his fist to his parents and fiancée somewhere out in the crowd behind me.

As I sat there, I found myself picturing that moment three years later, wondering who in the hell I'd have as a fist pump recipient. After a brief picture in my mind of my father, Win Shields immediately popped into my brain, and I had to smile at the thought.

Back in Barracks after the ceremony, I headed to Randy's room for some seriously heartfelt thanks, handshakes, and finally a sincere bear hug for my dyke. Though he hadn't been around most weekends, Randy had been a good dyke and a bit of the father figure I'd needed in Barracks the last eight months. Most importantly, he'd shown me how to take VMI's ups and downs with a grain of salt and to focus on what really mattered during my cadetship — and how to get away from Post as often as possible.

When I walked out of his room, the courtyard was filled with an unfamiliar sight: civilians. Mothers, fathers, girlfriends, sisters, brothers, and others milled around, talking to brand-new VMI graduates, none of whom seemed able to stop smiling.

I recognized most of the Firsts by now and typically knew who was going straight into the peacetime military and who would be starting civilian jobs spread throughout Virginia — and the world. Many of those entering the civilian world would be hired by VMI grads, who were taking care of the brotherhood I'd heard existed as soon as you left Post on graduation day.

I took the steps two at a time up to the fourth stoop to our room and found Chip and Bradley packing up their meager belongings to head back into the world for three months. None of us would be going far. Chip and I were headed back to Richmond as soon as his dad finished reminiscing with his own classmates down in the courtyard. Bradley, after a week with us in Richmond, was actually coming back to Lexington to get ahead academically for what we'd constantly heard could be a tough Third Class year in and out of the classroom.

"Hey, you two. What'd you think of graduation?"

"The three of us will be right there together in three long years," said Bradley.

"Hell, with summer school, you might get out of this prison even sooner," said Chip.

"Not a chance. I'm going to carry a light load next year so I can spend more time sitting around with you two whining about how hard we have it as Rats with radios."

"Speaking of which, who's bringing a stereo in August?" I asked.

"Why don't I get a new one at Circuit City this summer?" Chip volunteered. "You two can bring a bunch of albums as your contribution. We can always use some Stones or maybe that new Boston album that's always blaring in Barracks. Why don't we see if Skip Castro or maybe Robbin Thompson have something new out as well?"

Chip always had a way of spending money for us as a trio without it ever feeling like it was charity. I'd never had experience with seriously wealthy people, but Chip's generosity without attachments made this first exposure to the moneyed world better than I'd expected.

As we were finishing our quick packing job, Chip's dad launched into the room, dramatically sucking in deep breaths, followed by a rotund man who was breathing even harder and who apparently wasn't acting. "Boys," he said, "it's much farther up to fourth stoop than I remember it being a few decades back."

"I'll second that, you Thirds," said the man. "At least you will only have two sets of steps next year."

Mr. Shields fanned himself and said, "Nick and Bradley, this is my classmate, Sal Mosley. He's from Newport News. We roomed together Rat year and planned to do so as Thirds as well, but he somehow didn't quite make it back the following August, and I just had one roommate here in good old New Barracks that first semester."

"Yep, your dad's right," said Mr. Mosley, shaking each of our hands and saying it was good to see Chip again. "I bailed on him back then. That summer after our Rat year, I was taking a summer school class at ODU, met a girl, and thought a civilian school — and girl — were more to my liking.

"They were both still to my liking until about October, when she ditched me for a tall and good-looking basketball player and I realized I liked hanging around with this ugly red-faced mug of Win here more than I did kissing those ruby-red lips of hers.

"I came back for second semester as a Third," Mr. Mosley continued. "I had to spend some serious time in summer school right here in lovely little Lexington where the female form wasn't quite as prevalent, but walked across the Parade Ground stage with Win on a hot May day a long time ago."

"He's right about everything, including the red-faced mug," said Mr. Shields.

"Well, it's good to see you again," said Chip. "The three of us were just talking about walking across the stage three years from now."

"Are you guys rooming together again next year?" Mr. Mosley asked.

"Yes, sir," said Bradley. "That's our plan for the next three years, and we won't let any girl or some slack civvie school get in the way. We're actually trying to stay in this same room all the way down to one forty one for our First Class year."

"Good men," he said. "Being away that single semester made me realize just how special a diploma is from this place, and you three shouldn't forget it. Speaking of forgetting, Win, I told our

BR Calvin I'd meet him downtown for a beer in fifteen minutes. Can you four join us?"

"I'm afraid not. I promised Chip's mom we'd be back in Richmond this afternoon. We're taking Bradley back with us for a week before he comes back here for summer school."

"Trouble with Rat English, Bradley?" asked Mr. Mosley.

"Oh, no, sir. I'm just getting ahead for Third Class year."

"Well, that's smart. Just watch out for those uptown girls this summer."

"I will, sir," responded Bradley as Mr. Mosley smilingly saluted us and headed back out our door toward a rendezvous with another BR.

"You boys packed?"

"We're all set, Dad. We don't have much."

"You don't need much. I'm driving, and I have a cooler full of ice cold Coors for you three to enjoy on the ride back to Richmond. You deserve it."

—⟡—

I remember that drive to Richmond like it happened yesterday — though I certainly can't imagine heading down the highway today with an open can of beer, even if I'm not driving. My license is way too important to me to lose it over a beer.

Chip sat up in front with Mr. Shields, while Bradley and I sat in the spacious backseat of Mr. Shields's blue wagon. The promised cooler of gold cans sat right behind me in the back of the wagon, along with our half-full duffel bags.

We mostly talked about our exam results, the coming summer, and rings and graduation. Mr. Shields let us babble, while occasionally tossing in a memory from his four similar years at the Institute.

"You boys have it so easy now. Back in the old Corps, the military side of things didn't let up a bit during exams. They didn't let us study past taps, so we often found ourselves huddled under our blankets with flashlights to get in more study time."

Chip laughed, saying, "I'm so tired of that 'back in the old Corps,' crap, old man. That's what every VMI graduate has been saying since the mid-eighteen hundreds. You know it's all relative, and that it's as hard as ever back there today."

Mr. Shields smiled back at Chip across the front seat, gave us a knowing nod in the rear view mirror, and said, "I'm just giving you grief. It's simply one VMI man to another — or another three VMI men, as the case may be. Speaking of cases, why don't you open this old grad one of those cold beers for the homestretch, Nick?"

Times were different then. We didn't think twice about drinking a beer while driving, though we did try to keep from driving drunk whenever possible. That was sometimes hard back in Lexington, when you had to return to Barracks by a certain time and you couldn't always count on the timeliness of Lexington cabbies or the reliability of so-called designated drivers.

I'd learn that the hard way the following year, when a couple of classmates rushing back to VMI before Saturday night taps didn't make it past one of those tight turns on the road from the Maury River through Goshen Pass.

But back on that clear May day, we headed down Monument Avenue with four open cans of ice-cold Coors and a summer of supposed freedom. I knew that trying to find freedom from my father's memory just down the street — and throughout the Fan, really — wouldn't happen that summer or with help from the temporary buzz of a few beers.

Mr. Shields didn't even ask if I wanted to go back to the apartment, and we headed straight to their house, parking in the garage out back. We grabbed our three duffels and went through the kitchen and up the stairs, where I again took the room next door to Chip, and Bradley took the slightly smaller one across the hall from us. I hadn't thought of it before in this way, but I found myself wondering if we were providing the Shields with the additional children they'd obviously planned to have when they bought the huge house.

I threw my bag on the floor and went next door to Chip's room, finding Bradley already sprawled on one of the room's two single beds. "What's next in your big city, boys?" Bradley asked.

"Well, that Coors my dad brought tasted damn good," said Chip. "Why don't we walk down to Tex-Wis, get a pitcher, eat a late lunch, and talk about a week of freedom for the Three Musketeers?"

"I'm in," I said from the door, and we quickly headed downstairs and onto Monument Avenue.

We walked a block east on Monument when Chip said, "Hey, let's hang a right here and weave our way over to Main. I like the architecture of the smaller houses on the Fan's side streets anyway."

Before we turned I gazed further down the street but couldn't quite see my apartment building. It was then that I realized Chip really didn't want to see architecture at all; he wanted to avoid passing by the apartment for my sake. It was stuff like this that made me realize Chip was a very special person to have in my life.

We ended up on Hanover and walked past John & Norman's, with Chip saying we would get Bradley there for breakfast sometime that week. "You'll never want breakfast in Crozet Hall again after you eat there," Chip said.

"I already never want breakfast in the mess hall again, but I gotta eat somewhere."

I smiled and asked, "Do you think we can go just ten minutes without talking about VMI, guys?"

We turned right on Shields and walked past Joe's Inn to West Main Street and then down to the beloved Texas-Wisconsin Border Café. It was packed with many others our age who'd obviously returned to Richmond for the summer from college as well. It was standing room only, but we found a space at the corner of the bar just inside the door. The cool blast of spring air whenever others entered actually felt good as a contrast to the hot, dry, and smoke-filled air inside.

Max, one of the regular bartenders, headed over to us with napkins, saying, "Hey, Chip. Hey, Nick. I didn't know you two knew each other."

Chip smiled at Max, put his arm around my shoulder, and said, "We really didn't until we ended up as roommates at college."

"Those don't look like college haircuts, guys. You're both at VMI, if I remember, right?"

"Yep. And so is our roommate here, Bradley."

"Nice to meet you," said Max, shaking Bradley's hand across the bar after wiping his own with a white bar towel. "What'll it be, you three?"

"Is a pitcher of Lone Star OK, Brother Rats?" asked Chip.

VIRGINIA'S RING

"Yep, but enough with the Rat stuff, Chip," said Bradley, as
Max headed over to the taps with an empty pitcher. "We're just
three college students on summer break like everyone else."

"We're most definitely not just like everyone else, Bradley,"
Chip laughed. "Do you see anyone else in here with heads like us?
And, man, I completely forgot to grab three R-Braves hats for us."

"Yea, we'd fit right in then," I laughed. "Three cue balls with
Braves ball caps."

Max brought our pitcher and three frosty mugs just as three
guys sitting catty-corner from us headed out the door. We took
their barstools, and Chip, ever the host, poured our beers.

"Here's to a week of freedom in Richmond, boys," he said,
holding out his glass to the two of us. We clinked glasses, and
each of us downed the entire mug in a couple of quick gulps.

"You sure drink like VMI guys," Max said, laughing. "I'll
start pouring another pitcher soon, given that demonstration.
I'm assuming you're eating?" he asked as he threw down three
tattered menus onto the scarred bar.

"Bradley here's never had the Widowmaker Chili, and I've
been thinking about it since Christmas," said Chip. "I don't think
we even need the menus, Max, pushing them back to him. Is it
cool to go with three bowls of Widowmaker, guys?"

Bradley and I nodded as Chip poured three more beers and
Max grabbed our pitcher to start a refill.

Our food arrived about five minutes later, and the chili was
piping hot and seriously spicy, as always. After his first bite of
chili, Bradley dramatically fanned his mouth and said the chili
chased by a cold gulp of Lone Star was just as we'd described the
combination so many times back in Lexington. "Can we come
back tomorrow?" Bradley jokingly asked.

Chip laughed, saying, "Nick and I have a few other favorites we want you to try as well. We know it's not classy Charleston dining, but we eat pretty well up here in the Old Dominion as well."

"If the other restaurants serve grub like this, I'm never going back to Charleston. Not that I planned to anyway."

"You're going to have to go back sometime, BR," said Chip, staring intently at Bradley. "You can't go to summer school every year."

"Wanna bet? I'm already planning to go to both sessions next summer as well, and then we have ROTC obligations after Second Class year. I've got it all figured out, especially if you'll let me crash here when I'm not at VMI or elsewhere as far away from Charleston and my family as I can get."

"You know you'll always have a bed here, man, but you can't avoid your family forever."

"Well, I'm going to give it the old college try. Or should I say old Veemie try?"

"You can try all you want, Bradley, but family is family — even if your dad and brother are both Citadel sissies. You only get one father and one brother."

As soon as he'd said it, I could see Chip realized I didn't have either, and he immediately put his right arm around my shoulder and said, "That didn't come out quite right, Nick. You know you have a brother and father in me and my dad, right?"

"Thanks, Chip," I said, staring into my beer glass. "It's not the same, as you know, but I can't tell you how much I know and appreciate that you both feel that way. If it hadn't been for the two of you — and you too, Bradley — I'm not sure I could have made it through this first year."

"Well, just three more years to go boys," said Bradley as he held up his glass. "Here's to the three of us making it three more years." We clinked glasses again and dove back into our bowls.

It was around five when we finally left Tex-Wis and our late lunch, heading west on Stuart instead of Hanover to make our way back to Chip's house. We were just coming up on Buddy's when Chip suggested we head inside for another pitcher at a place Chip and I had both frequented, but never together.

"Man, the Fan has a ton of spots like Tex-Wis," said Bradley. "So you guys could drink at bars like this even before you were eighteen?"

"They rarely IDed us," I replied. "And when they did, fake driver's licenses were a dime a dozen."

"Isn't it funny? We'd never dream of doing something like that now. The Honor Court would roll us out of VMI before we'd downed our first beer."

"Well, we don't have to worry about that now that we're all men of drinking age," said Chip, opening the door to Buddy's for us to enter.

Buddy's was as packed as Tex-Wis, but we found a spot to stand at the bar and ordered another pitcher — Bud this time. A guy our age walked up behind Chip, tapped his shoulder, and said, "Nice haircut, Shields."

Chip smiled and turned around, shaking the outreached hand. "Hey Hank. I could say the same thing about that long-haired mop of yours."

"Yea, yea. The haircut policy at UVA isn't quite as stringent as VMI, huh?"

"I think we're safe in agreeing nothing is as stringent in Charlottesville, except for maybe the unwritten rules about drinking a certain amount of beer every weekend. Speaking of which, have a beer, Hank," Chip said while pouring an extra glass he'd grabbed from across the bar.

"It looks like you haven't lost your touch with the beer either. Thanks, Chip," he said, holding up his beer to him. "Who are these two marines with you?"

"These are my roommates, Nick Adams from here in town and Bradley Bell from Charleston."

"Where'd you go to school here, Nick, and why the heck didn't you go somewhere sensible in South Carolina, Bradley?"

"I went to TJ," I said, knowing he'd probably gone to St. Christopher's with Chip.

"And I actually wanted to get as far away from South Carolina as possible, and VMI certainly achieved that," said Bradley.

"Is it as bad at VMI as I've heard?"

"Let's just say that Junior ROTC routine we did at St. Chris didn't exactly prepare me for the Ratline," replied Chip.

"No question. Didn't Drew Robinson from our class go there too?" asked Hank.

"He left the first week, and I heard he attended J. Sarge the rest of this year and plans to head back to Lexington in the fall. To W&L."

"I thought he was a stud and could hack it."

"The last time I saw him, he was doing some seriously slippery push-ups in the steaming showers," said Chip, who hadn't even told us about Robinson. I vaguely remembered him as being from Richmond, but didn't know he went to St. Chris with Chip.

"Well, I haven't done a single pushup since tennis season back at St. Chris last spring. Are you playing at VMI, Chip? I didn't have a prayer at making UVA's team and didn't even try out."

"I made the cut and played in a few doubles matches this spring, but nothing special. It's incredibly hard as a Rat. You're already so tired by the time you get to practice that the upperclassmen have a leg up on your aching limbs and forehands, so to speak."

"How are your parents, Chip? My dad just asked about them the other day when he picked me up at school."

"Same old, same old. Dad still makes his millions off those killer sticks, and Mom still makes a mean meatloaf."

"Well, please tell them hello for me. Speaking of moms, I gotta get going, guys. I was supposed to run out for a quart of milk down at that market on Shields and somehow ended up here. Thanks for the beer, and give em hell next year at VMI."

We finished the pitcher and started making our way back to Chip's house again, with the sun sinking lower in the sky over the West End. "He seemed like a nice guy. Did you know him that well at St. Chris?" I asked.

"We ran in the same circles both in and out of school, but I never really got that close to him. Hank was destined for UVA and that life, while I knew my college experience was going to be slightly different. Unless we both end up working and living back in Richmond — which I don't plan on happening for me — we will definitely continue to go our separate ways."

"What does his dad do?" I asked.

"He's a broker at Wheat First, which is ironic cause it has more VMI grads than from any other school. Hank's dad went to UVA, of course. I heard he's a really good broker and has half of CCV's members as clients."

"What's CCV?" asked Bradley.

"It's the Country Club of Virginia, and you have to sacrifice your firstborn as the initiation fee," joked Chip.

"Assuming your parents are members, wouldn't that have been you?"

"Yep, and I can tell you I've felt like the sacrificial lamb for my father in this town more than once."

"What do they do at CCV?" asked Bradley. "I think we have similar clubs in Charleston, like the Carolina Yacht Club down on The Battery. My parents don't even like the water all that much, but they're members anyway."

"It's similar at CCV," said Chip. "But instead of sailing the men play golf and the women hit tennis balls and pay big bucks for lessons from tan young guys in short shorts. But I'd say both places are more about doing lunch, drinks, and deals. More businesses — and daughters and sons, now that I think about it — have been brokered at CCV and down at the Commonwealth Club on Franklin than anywhere else in Virginia."

"I've never set foot in either place," I said, not sure I was proud of the fact or actually hoping Chip would take me to CCV sometime to hit tennis and maybe even have lunch surrounded by all those rich daughters.

"Well, we'll solve that someday," said Chip. "In fact, why don't I get dear old Dad to take us to lunch at CCV sometime this week?"

"As long as he'll pay, I'm in," said Bradley. We headed down the alley behind Monument Avenue to the back gate and found Chip's mom sitting by their pool in the small patch of sunlight still remaining in their yard.

—ᴍ—

I can honestly say I
was so male-centric
mind and body could
, as well as lingering

ere was little time or
yond the typical teen-
few of the cheerlead-
r football and basket-
d to think and talk of
times in quite creative
my classmates would
en. I see two of these
sionally return to the

o stare at Mrs. Shields
e looked darned good
ly forties then and was
highlighted her mature,
e way. At least to this

nd me into my left ear.
grill up some burgers
rea. You in Nick or do
you just want to keep ogling my mom?"

I laughed and muttered my agreement, trying to shrug off
Chip's comment. But Mrs. Shields held my gaze for a moment
before smiling, turning to Chip, and telling him that the ground

beef was in the refrigerator and that he should light the charcoal soon so we could grill while it was still light outside.

Chip threw his arm around my shoulders and we headed into the kitchen, where he got the beef out of the fridge and started pulling potatoes from a bag his mother had left on the counter. I didn't say a word after he handed me a knife to start slicing potatoes.

Chip said, "It's OK, Nick. You aren't the first of my friends to stare at my mother like that. It's a little creepy, but I'll admit she does look pretty good, even if she is my mom. I was beginning to think you two were gay with your lack of interest in the opposite sex back at VMI.

"Who has time for girls?" asked Bradley. "The last thing I need is some Southern Sem girl messing with my head."

"What you need is exactly that — some girl messing with your head. And I'm not talking about the one on your shoulders."

We both laughed at that but I knew there was some truth in what Chip was saying. He'd told us he'd reconnected with a former girlfriend named Becky a few times when he'd been back in Richmond, claiming it had helped get it out of his system.

"Why don't I try to set you both up with some good ol Richmond girls this week? I'm sure Becky and I could come up with a couple of loose ones looking for a roll in the hay without any commitment afterward."

"No thanks, BR," said Bradley. "Don't you remember you tried to do that for me with some Richmond girl who's down at Hollins now? I know that school is known for attracting the wealthy horsey crowd, but that girl truly had a face like a horse."

"That girl was hot to trot, and you knew it."

—w—

Since I'd left for VMI that past August, I can honestly say I hadn't thought about women much. VMI was so male-centric back then, and I'd generally found that my mind and body could really only handle the male-on-male stress, as well as lingering thoughts of my dad's death.

I'd dated a few girls back at TJ, but there was little time or space at VMI for thinking about females beyond the typical teenage daydreaming when looking at a select few of the cheerleaders who came from Southern Seminary for football and basketball games. Of course, other cadets seemed to think and talk of little else than the female form, and sometimes in quite creative language. I will say, however, that three of my classmates would even go on to marry Southern Sem women. I see two of these couples at football tailgates when I occasionally return to the Institute on Saturdays.

But I can still remember trying not to stare at Mrs. Shields in the late sun long ago and thinking she looked darned good for someone's mother. She was in her early forties then and was wearing a tight white one-piece suit that highlighted her mature, womanly curves in a Mrs. Robinson-like way. At least to this nineteen-year-old.

"Earth to Nick," Chip said from behind me into my left ear. "My mom just asked us if we wanted to grill up some burgers tonight, and Bradley and I already said yea. You in Nick or do you just want to keep ogling my mom?"

I laughed and muttered my agreement, trying to shrug off Chip's comment. But Mrs. Shields held my gaze for a moment before smiling, turning to Chip, and telling him that the ground beef was in the refrigerator and that he should light the charcoal soon so we could grill while it was still light outside.

Chip threw his arm around my shoulders and we headed into the kitchen, where he got the beef out of the fridge and started pulling potatoes from a bag his mother had left on the counter. I didn't say a word after he handed me a knife to start slicing potatoes.

Chip said, "It's OK, Nick. You aren't the first of my friends to stare at my mother like that. It's a little creepy, but I'll admit she does look pretty good, even if she is my mom. I was beginning to think you two were gay with your lack of interest in the opposite sex back at VMI.

"Who has time for girls?" asked Bradley. "The last thing I need is some Southern Sem girl messing with my head."

"What you need is exactly that — some girl messing with your head. And I'm not talking about the one on your shoulders."

We both laughed at that but I knew there was some truth in what Chip was saying. He'd told us he'd reconnected with a former girlfriend named Becky a few times when he'd been back in Richmond, claiming it had helped get it out of his system.

"Why don't I try to set you both up with some good ol Richmond girls this week? I'm sure Becky and I could come up with a couple of loose ones looking for a roll in the hay without any commitment afterward."

"No thanks, BR," said Bradley. "Don't you remember you tried to do that for me with some Richmond girl who's down at Hollins now? I know that school is known for attracting the wealthy horsey crowd, but that girl truly had a face like a horse."

"That girl was hot to trot, and you knew it."

"That's a nice play on words, Chip," replied Bradley, smiling at the memory. "But I wasn't going to do any trotting with her unless she put a feedbag over her head."

"Well, what about you, Nick? Want me to set you up with some girl from St. Catherine's?"

"I'm with Bradley. My life at VMI is complicated enough without having some girl messing with my mind. I would, however, like to mess around with another beer. Can I grab some out of the fridge behind your dad's bar, Chip?"

"Of course. Our beer is your beer. But girls don't have to mess with your mind if you don't let them, Nick."

"Maybe later in the summer, man," I said as I poured our beers into mugs from the freezer. "I just want a simple summer to make a little money and forget about VMI for a couple of months. August will be here before we know it, and I want to go back to Lexington with a few bucks in my pocket. Going out with some girl from St. Cath's isn't exactly in my budget or brain."

"OK, guys, I get it. But Becky is most definitely in my budget, my brain, and elsewhere."

"Go for it," I said. "You've got the girl, and you most definitely have the budget."

"Hey now. I didn't mean it that way. They get on me enough back at VMI about my stinking rich parents. I don't need that stuff from you two as well."

"Sorry bout that. You know Bradley and I are always amazed when we remember you're a bazillionaire heir. You most definitely don't wear it on your sleeve, and that's always impressed us."

"Thanks. I hated it this year when I got singled out cause of my family and those damn tobacco bucks. I'd give anything to have parents who aren't rich."

"I'm thinking Nick here would give anything to have parents at all, Chip."

"Oh, shoot, Nick. I'm sorry. I just wasn't thinking...again."

"It's OK," I said. I generally forget you're rich, and you two seem to forget I don't have parents. In a way the two of you have become brothers to me, and Chip, both your dad and your mom have filled in for my father in so many ways."

"You'd most definitely want Chip's parents in that role," said Bradley. "I think my folks now believe they only have one son, and it ain't me."

"So you don't plan to head back to Charleston at all this summer?" I asked.

"Not if I can help it. When I talked to my mom on the pay phone down in the concourse right before school ended, I told her I was coming to Richmond with y'all for a week and then heading back to VMI for summer school. She didn't even ask about me heading home and didn't mention my father or brother at all. She did say she'd make sure Dad at least paid the summer school bill."

"That stinks about your dad. But you know you will always have a place here, right?" asked Chip.

"Yep. Thanks. I'm already starting to feel more at home here than in Charleston. I haven't spoken a word to my father since Christmas furlough, and then it was barely courteous conversation."

"Do you think they'll ever come around?" I asked.

"I honestly don't think so. I actually think the longer I stay at VMI rather than attending The Citadel, I'll become more and more estranged from my entire family."

"Well, when we graduate, my parents will see three of their sons walk across that damn stage."

"That's a deal," said Bradley. "By the way, and speaking of stinking, I heard before we left that they were thinking about removing those nasty cigarette machines from down in the concourse before next semester."

"There goes my inheritance," Chip joked.

While we'd been talking, the three of us had pattied up a dozen differently sized burgers and cut the potatoes into wedges for the grill. Mr. and Mrs. Shields came into the kitchen from the backyard, and, thankfully, Mrs. Shields had thrown on a cover-up. "Hey, boys. The fire Mom lit is looking perfect, and so are these burgers and potatoes," said Mr. Shields, surveying our work. "Why don't you go get refills, Chip, and grab one for me as well?"

Chip quickly grabbed four bottles of beer from the bar's refrigerator, came back into the kitchen, and passed them out at the counter. He then picked up the plate of burgers, tilting his head toward the potatoes and buns for me and Bradley to bring out to the patio. "Want to supervise the cooking, Dad?" Chip asked as he headed out the door.

Mr. Shields walked outside with us, taking a seat by the pool while the three of us worked on getting everything on their black Weber domed grill. The raw, red, and fatty meat sizzled as soon as it hit the metal, and that familiar smell of summer immediately wafted through the air — charcoal and grilling meat, along with the faint hint of lighter fluid.

"What did you three stooges do on your first afternoon of freedom?"

"I took them to Tex-Wis for a late lunch and then Buddy's for some more beer. We actually ran into Hank Lowry at Buddy's, and he asked about you two."

"I haven't seen him or his folks in ages," said Mr. Shields. "Did he say how George and Nora were doing?"

"Nope. We mostly talked about the differences in our first years at school. The typical UVA versus VMI banter that always leaves me feeling like a loser."

"You'll get used to it," replied Mr. Shields. "That first year, with your hair and all, makes it all the more obvious that you're not going to some normal college."

"I guess I don't mind too much," said Chip. "If I learned one thing as a Rat this year, it's not to worry about what other people think."

"That's a damn good lesson to learn at your age. I'm still learning it at forty-two."

Chip flipped the burgers and potatoes, and the smells further permeated the air around the four of us. He then added a slice of American cheese on each burger, as well as placing some lightly-oiled bun halves on the outer edges of the grill. "I'm thinking that in another three minutes, dinner is served. Bradley, can you run inside and let my mom know that we're ready and maybe also grab the plates and other stuff I'll bet she's probably pulled out by now?"

Within minutes Bradley came back outside with Mrs. Shields, and they started setting the large table under the arbor just as strands of twinkling lights seemed to magically appear on a trellis above us and running along the top of the fence separating their yard from the equally large one next door.

"Wow, this is like some fairytale out here," said Bradley, gazing upward.

"It's definitely an oasis, isn't it?" Mrs. Shields asked as she too peered up at the lights. "I'm betting the atmosphere in the mess hall isn't quite the same, so y'all should enjoy these evenings while you can. I'll take that small burger without a bun, Chip."

Chip served everyone, with the three of us serving ourselves two burgers each and Mr. Shields saying he was good for just one. "You know you're eventually going to grab a second one, Dad. Why don't you just take it now?"

"We'll see. Your old man has to start watching his girlish figure."

"Speaking of girlish figures, Nick couldn't keep his eyes off Mom in her bathing suit when we got back from Buddy's."

I could feel everyone looking at me — including Mrs. Shields — and I can still recall having no idea what to say or do. I just stared at my plate.

Mr. Shields tried to lighten it up again by saying, "Uh-oh. Competition for the old man, huh, Nick?"

"You got that right, Dad. Nick had those Southern Sem girls beating down our Barracks door once we got out of the Ratline. He's a real ladies' man."

I finally got my voice back, but I still couldn't look at Mrs. Shields. "Yea, right," I said, staring at Chip. "The only female in my life since last August has been Virginia Woolf, and I plan to keep it that way."

"Well, I'm still afraid of the competition from anyone who likes Virginia Woolf, Nick. I landed this pretty woman here when I was about your age, and I won't give her up without a fight — even if you did pass Rat Boxing. Do they still call it Rat Bleeding or something like that?"

"It's still Rat Beating and Bleeding, and Nick here barely passed," said Chip. I think you could easily take him in three rounds and protect Mom's honor. Nick got a C in boxing"

"Well, I'm definitely going to keep an eye on him."

"I'm actually going to try to set him up with one of Becky's classmates from St. Cath's or maybe even someone from Hollins, where she's supposedly going to college," said Chip.

"Hey now, Chip," said Mrs. Shields. "Several of my friends sent their daughters there this year, and I've heard it's a good school."

"If you like to ride horses and find husbands, it's a quite good school," I said, trying to shift the subject away from Mrs. Shields and me.

We finished off our burgers, making more small talk about our first year at VMI and the summers ahead for each of us. Mrs. Shields went back into the kitchen and brought out an apple pie she'd made for us that afternoon. "It's my mother's handwritten recipe, though it's incredibly similar to the one that seems to run every year in the *Southern Living* cookbook."

We all added a scoop of Ben & Jerry's vanilla ice cream. This was the first of many times we'd spend an early summer evening in their backyard enjoying that luscious apple pie and some of the ever-changing flavors of Ben & Jerry's. It would be many years before I would come to truly appreciate the taste of that simple pie and the simple company of the people with me that sultry May evening.

—⟋ఱ⟍—

We spent the next few free days showing Bradley some more of the Fan that Chip and I both knew well, but in our own distinct and different ways. We definitely found that Chip's life growing up in the Fan and out in Richmond's West End had been quite different from my version nearby.

Chip's experiences revolved around rich sons and daughters on Monument Avenue and out in the West End, private clubs and schools for the well-heeled, and restaurants and wines where money wasn't an issue.

My life and relationships — at least before meeting Chip — had mostly centered on my father. I hadn't made many friends going through Richmond's public schools and had tended to spend more time with my father, his VCU students, and books. And our idea of eating out revolved around the tastiest, cheapest, and most filling meal we could find in the Fan — with leftovers, if at all possible. Admittedly, this often led to Joe's Inn and other similar haunts.

Along with sleeping in most mornings and lounging poolside in the sun most afternoons, the three of us also roamed the Fan, with Chip pointing out details about the houses, history, and architecture along Monument Avenue.

When I look back on those walks and several stress-free runs we took together on the grassy Monument Avenue median, I'm quite certain that Chip didn't say who lived in any of those huge houses we passed. I now realize he probably knew a majority of the inhabitants, but he was already well on the road to distancing himself from his Monument Avenue life in so many ways.

Our week as modern Three Musketeers passed all too quickly, which was the opposite of how I wanted the rest of the summer to go before we had to head back to Lexington in August. Chip never brought up finding dates for us again, and he didn't even go out with Becky that week. He also never mentioned heading to the Country Club of Virginia with his dad.

The three of us were essentially inseparable. Except for two more backyard barbecues and leftover apple pie, we walked to a different restaurant in the Fan every night. Though I'd been to a few of them with my dad, Chip usually chose the restaurants that week and paid in cash without a word when the check came.

Chip said his dad had told him that he'd pick up all of our dinners out that week, evidently giving him a wad of cash, and we certainly didn't protest. I'm not sure I ever thanked Win for those particular May meals. I can't thank him enough for so many things that have nothing to do with money.

I didn't think about it at the time and would never have imagined it would evolve the way it did in coming years, but my career as a restaurant critic began in many ways during those meals with Chip, Bradley, and sometimes his parents. Of course I'd pretty much eaten three meals a day with Chip and Bradley since the previous August, but the mess hall's square meals sitting at attention on the front three inches of your chair didn't exactly make for culinary conversation.

During those cool May days out in the streets with the two of them, Chip went about choosing restaurants like he was planning a military invasion. As part of our long daily walks, we'd head by various places of his choosing to look at dinner menus. I'd swear he timed our walks to coincide with our noon hunger because two or three times that week he talked us into eating in a restaurant for lunch as well.

In all I think I recall eating out at least a half dozen times that week. Along with Tex-Wis that first day back, I can remember having lunch back at Buddy's and over at the New York Deli in Carytown, plus dinners at The Robin Inn, Bogart's, and Athens Tavern. There was also a late breakfast at John & Norman's at least once.

I didn't realize it at the time, but I was developing an almost photographic memory when it came to eating. Chip had an analytical way of restaurant dining that I now realize I've emulated in many ways.

Even if he'd already practically memorized the menu earlier in the day, Chip made us go through the entire list of appetizers and entrées again, discussing the pros and cons of various order combinations. Whether it was an appetizer, entrée, or even dessert, Chip had a steadfast rule that none of us could order the same thing, and each of us had to try everything that was ordered by passing plates back and forth.

I'd grown up mostly eating at a table for two at home or in a restaurant with my father, where we rarely discussed what we were eating. Both of us typically even read a book propped up against our iced tea glasses. His tea was heavily sweetened, but I always drank my iced tea unsweetened and still do. Attempting to order any sort of iced tea outside the United States has always been a cultural experience that still makes me smile every time I'm lonely for the South.

During one of our dinners that week, Chip said his parents had well-honed palates. I didn't admit that I didn't know what the word "honed" even meant and I wasn't exactly sure about "palate" either. He told us between bites that his love of eating out had developed over many meals in restaurants with his parents in the Fan, the West End, Manhattan, San Francisco, and even across the Atlantic in Europe.

Besides eating our way through the Fan, Chip took us to the Virginia Museum on the Boulevard, where his mother sat on the board, as well as the Virginia Historical Society next door. Mr. Shields was involved with the Society as well due to some VMI classmate connection. It would be almost a decade before I told Chip that I'd never set foot in either place before that week.

My father believed literature was the most important art form, and I'd honestly never questioned it. However, hearing Chip passionately talk about art like the Virginia Museum's famed Faberge egg collection right when we were looking at the treasures certainly made me question my father's belief.

Of course, I couldn't help but think of my dad as we roamed the Fan. We passed by his old office several times when walking through VCU's urban campus, but I couldn't bring myself to go inside to see who was in his space now.

I thought I recognized several of his students who must have already been in summer school, but I quickly looked away and hoped they hadn't seen me. They probably wouldn't have known what to say if they had. I certainly wouldn't have had the words.

I didn't go back to our apartment that week, and neither Chip nor Bradley ever pressed me on it. Without saying a word, we avoided my old block of Monument Avenue the entire time.

Sunday came all too quickly, and Bradley came down to breakfast with his duffel bag packed. "You ready to hit the books again, BR?" Chip asked.

"You two'll be jealous when I'm only carrying fifteen hours this fall."

"It's going to be strange living in Barracks on first stoop but not having to do any of the VMI stuff, isn't it?" I asked.

"I actually wondered about that. I think it's going to be hardest when we're back to the same VMI grind come late August — especially after I've had a taste of more normal college life, like going to Spanky's any time I want this summer. Well, within reason, given my meager funds."

Mr. Shields came into the kitchen and asked, "When do you want to head west, young man?"

"I'm set anytime, Mr. Shields."

"How bout we start out around ten and go to Spanky's for lunch before I drop you off at Barracks? I'm buying."

"In that case," Chip said. "Nick and I will come along for the ride — and the free lunch."

"That's a deal, boys. Lemme just let Mom know our plan. We're going to miss you around here, Bradley, but you know you're always welcome. Unlike those Citadel boys, VMI men stick together."

"Thanks, Mr. Shields. And thanks to both you and Mrs. Shields for letting me crash here with these two hoodlums this week. It was a nice break."

"Come any time, Bradley. I'll be ready in about ten minutes, if you want to throw that bag in the wagon."

You would have thought the three of us would run out of things to talk about after our week together, but the drive back to Lexington was still filled with chatter about VMI, as well as the rest of the summer ahead of us. As he often did those days, Win Shields would occasionally chime in with his own VMI and summer experiences.

We went straight to Spanky's, and each of us ordered our favorite sandwiches: Dicky Moore for me, Babe Ruth for Chip, Buffalo Boo for Bradley, and Julius Caesar for Mr. Shields. We split a pitcher of Heineken and an extra basket of those salty chips we all loved — and still do at their other far-flung locations in Virginia, West Virginia, North Carolina, and even Tennessee, I think. The restaurants are now all called Macado's, though I still often refer to their new two-story Lexington location on Main Street as Spanky's. Sadly, they now bring out their still-salty potato chips in single-serve bags.

After lunch Mr. Shields drove up to Post and pulled right in front of Jackson Arch, where other summer school students were dropping off their bags as well. I noted several of them were upcoming Firsts who were probably behind on grades and hours and still hoping to graduate on time. There were a smattering of our BRs, but I knew most of them were actually retaking classes they'd failed Rat year instead of getting ahead like Bradley.

"Well, Bradley, this is probably a little easier this time than when your parents dropped you off last August, isn't it?" asked Mr. Shields.

"Actually, a high school classmate drove me up here. My family hasn't set foot in Lexington yet, and I don't picture a familial visit on the horizon."

"That's pathetic, son. I have a mind to head down to Charleston and knock some sense into your father and brother with this ring," Mr. Shields said, holding up his right hand.

"That's OK, Mr. Shields. They're both too hard-headed, even for that ring."

"Well, I'll pick you up and drop you off anywhere and anytime you need, son."

"I appreciate it, Mr. Shields. Why don't I let y'all get headed back to Richmond for another one of those great barbeques? I need to go nab the best spot for my rack. It's going to be really weird living on first stoop this summer and especially without you two as roommates."

We all shook hands, with Bradley saying, "I guess we'll see you two in August."

"I'm betting it's sooner," Chip said. "We're bound to head over here once or twice or talk you into catching a ride back to Richmond sometime for a weekend."

"You boys can borrow the Volvo anytime you want this summer to do just that."

"We'll see. Thanks again for the ride, Mr. Shields."

It was funny watching Bradley walk through the arch without a uniform. We jumped back in the car, with Chip sitting up front with his dad again and me sprawled in the backseat.

We got back to Richmond around five and Mrs. Shields was thankfully already in the kitchen instead of out by the pool sunbathing. She told us she already had big rib eyes marinating for us in their refrigerator. I learned that night that Mr. Shields had taught Chip to grill a steak to medium rare perfection. I miss those nights, those steaks…and Chip.

—⟋⟍—

My summer with Chip and his parents was exactly what I needed in so many large and seemingly small ways. Chip and Win and Sarah Shields kept me too busy to dwell on my empty apartment just down the street. Chip and I taught tennis for long hours over at Byrd Park for a little spending money, though Chip didn't really need it. We also played one or more sets almost every day, went for occasional runs, and ate our way through Fan restaurants and the Shields' kitchen and backyard.

Bradley got a ride to Richmond for two weekends, but we never went back to Lexington that summer. Though Bradley said he was happy to get ahead academically, he felt that he hadn't gotten enough separation from VMI and that it would make Third Class year seem even longer. His insight made me more determined than ever to graduate on time without attending summer school.

Before we knew it, Chip and I were packing up the same small duffel bags we'd brought from Lexington in May. I can remember now thinking that heading back to VMI didn't feel nearly as hard as it had been in January when we were returning to the Ratline.

In many ways I was wrong. If I'd known that hot August day that Third Class year would have as many trials and tribulations as Rat year, our return to Lexington might have been more fraught with foreboding.

Again Mr. Shields drove us back to Lexington, with our conversation carried forward by his memories of a Third Class year decades earlier. He said there had been five Third Classmen drummed out in the first semester alone and that the Honor Court had made their point with his class. He didn't lose another Brother Rat the rest of his cadetship — at least not to the Honor Code.

"You boys and Bradley should be more careful than ever starting today. The Honor Court watches Thirds especially closely, and I guarantee you'll lose a couple of your BRs this semester. They rolled a star football player my Third Class year, and that guy ended up on scholarship at UVA. He's in Richmond now, and I still can't bring myself to speak to him when I see him out in public. I know it's been drilled into you, but don't forget that ignorance truly is no excuse — with the Honor Court...and life, actually."

We pulled up to the familiar scene at Jackson Arch, and we could hear the yelling inside Barracks as soon as we opened the car doors. I was glad Chip and I had not pursued rank and didn't have to come back for Cadre. Bradley was a private as well but had volunteered to help Cadre that first week to earn a free weekend. All three of us planned to remain privates throughout our cadetship and leave the Rats alone. There were enough people to make that first year as hard as it had been on us.

Bradley had been looking for us out our third stoop window just inside New Barracks and came down to say hello to Mr. Shields. We said our good-byes quickly, and Mr. Shields' firm handshake was followed by a fatherly hug that I was finally allowing myself to start appreciating.

The three of us walked up to our new room on third stoop. It had the exact same layout as our previous year's room just above us, but it felt better being closer to the lower two stoops — and our rings and graduation. We placed our racks in exactly the same spots we had on the fourth stoop the past August and took the same desks as well.

"So did you pass that English class?" I asked Bradley.

"Yep. I got a B. You two shouldn't have any problems with it, but I'm still glad to have it out of the way. There's a ton of reading."

"Well, you know Chip and I don't mind that. Reading was the easiest way to get my mind off the Ratline last year, and I'm betting it will do the same for these three Rats with radios. Speaking of radios, let's hook up the stereo and those rockin speakers Chip got at Circuit City."

We spent the next couple of hours moving into the room, knowing we'd soon be putting on our uniforms for the first of more than a hundred supper formations before Christmas. Though we had the stereo cranked up high to Robbin Thompson's "Sweet Virginia' Breeze" and then Skip Castro's "Boogie at Midnight" album, we could still hear Cadre yelling at Rats above us. That yelling would soon become white noise in our room, since it wasn't directed at us like it had been the previous year.

Clad in white pants and his blue blazer, the seemingly age-less Bill the Bugler sounded the five-minute call for supper formation, and we headed down the concrete steps as the Ratline rushed by us. They had just completed what had been the worst and hardest week of their lives — and it was really just the beginning in so many ways large and small. Bradley told me he'd heard eleven Rats had already left, and the addition of academics to the mix would mean many more would depart Lexington in coming days and weeks.

We were all in the same company again for Third Class year, and a Richmond friend of Chip's was our company commander, so we hoped the military side of things wouldn't be too bad. We wanted to keep demerits to a minimum so we could take advantage of Third Class privileges, including at least several weekends away from the Institute each semester.

The Corps of Cadets marched down to the mess hall, and I can remember comparing the food — it was spaghetti that night — to the meals we'd enjoyed in Richmond all summer. "This isn't exactly like Spaghetti a la Joe, huh, Chip?"

"And I can promise you that what they call steak on the menu tomorrow night won't exactly match my medium-rare rib eyes hot off the grill back in Richmond," he smilingly replied while forking soggy noodles into his mouth.

"I wonder if we can talk your folks into grilling steaks before a football game this fall?" Bradley asked.

"Are you kidding? Dad would jump at the chance. "Maybe when we play App State in a couple of weeks for Parents Weekend."

We walked back up the hill to Barracks as a platoon of Rats marched past us. I'm betting they hadn't spent supper talking about the food they were gulping between Rat Bible questions from Third Classmen. I recall just being happy to get something in my stomach that first week or two — as well as Cadre's constant concern that everyone have a bowel movement. Those first few weeks could even cause tension when it came to bodily functions.

—⟋ϾϾ⟍—

That first semester of Third Class year was much easier than either semester of my Rat year at VMI. We had more freedom and privileges, but both seemed comical when compared to other normal colleges. It was all relative to other people and places — and still is. I certainly learned that lesson each year as I gained and lost freedoms and more at VMI and in life.

The first two months back in Barracks were marked by Honor Court issues, just as Mr. Shields had predicted. We lost four Brother Rats in the middle of four eerie September and October nights, and all were for cheating. The pressure of passing grades had taken its toll and their honor. They'd never wear the ring. I think they were all civil engineering majors, where the classes seemed the most difficult.

I don't recall there being a general fear in our class about the Honor Court singling out Thirds, but I do think the Court had made its point with us. We didn't lose another BR to the Honor Code the rest of that year. I just wish I would have been able to say that two years later, when the price of getting drummed out as a First was even higher than for a Rat or a Third. We lost one Brother Rat a week before Ring Figure Second Class year and another just five days before our graduation.

My life at VMI continued to revolve around my classes in Scott Shipp Hall, my room, and my roommates. Of course, the background music of daily life at VMI continued to play, and I continued to march to the now regular beat as best I could (with a little Skip Castro thrown into the mix). Except for getting good grades, I tried to fly under the radar as much as possible.

For all three of us, our big goal for Third Class year was to earn academic stars, which you wore on the sleeves of your blouse and the collar of your coatee the year after achieving a cumulative GPA of 3.5 or more for the year. All of us had come close Rat year, but each had fallen short. We'd all heard classes were actually more difficult Third Class year.

Our football team that fall of 1981 did provide another nice diversion for the three of us and the entire Corps. When the team won on Saturdays, it typically meant extra privileges for us that night, like getting to stay off Post an extra hour. A win also seemed to lighten the mood for everyone — at least until early Monday morning when the drudgery of VMI returned in full force.

Win Shields did indeed grill rib eyes for us before the App State game. He told us he'd marinated them overnight in French red wine, extra virgin olive oil, and lots of coarsely-ground salt and pepper. I guess that technically marked the first — but not the last — time I would imbibe alcohol on Post.

We could smell his grill as soon as the three of us walked out of Jackson Arch after the morning parade, and I still think that this first of frequent pre-kickoff steaks was the best single meal I've ever had at VMI. There would be several good meals at VMI, but never in the mess hall. I hear that has changed.

I can still taste that steak. We didn't, however, get a taste of victory that day. It ended in a tie with App State.

The football team finished with six wins that season, including an away win over Army that was a Corps trip and my first visit to West Point. I've since been up that way many times when pursuing stories or taking classes at the pretty Hyde Park campus of the Culinary Institute of America.

We also beat Virginia Tech down in Blacksburg that year. Really. The score was 6–0.

—⁓—

What a game. I think it was the last time we beat a big-time college football team, and I'm pretty sure that 1981 was the last time we had a winning record. That's the kind of thing Chip would have known.

Several members of our class contributed in a big way on the defensive line and a Second Classman caught a crucial pass near the goal line that led to the only score of the game. We muffed the extra point kick, and I can still remember why it happened.

It was incredibly cold that day, and the kicker's feet and holder's hands were surely even colder than our own appendages up in the stands. We were in our thick gray overcoats, black gloves, and extra socks, but our extremities stayed frigid from kickoff to the final play when we all rushed onto the field to celebrate as a Corps with that 6–0 win.

We went wild that day in a way I'd never witnessed at a home or away VMI football game. It seemed like an even bigger win than when we beat Army up at West Point, where we also swarmed the field. For the Class of 1983, it must have made getting their rings even more memorable. Their formal dinner that night was at the Hotel Roanoke, a place I would grow to love in coming years.

During several defensive stands, many from '83 took their gloves off and banged their new rings on the metal stands in unison, starting a tradition that's occasionally revisited for big plays and wins during VMI athletic events to this day. That banging of VMI rings would also become one way of dealing with death, but that would come later and would involve wooden coffins instead of metal bleachers.

VMI football was so different back then, and VMI was able to compete with much larger schools like Tech. Now that it's mostly about big money in college football, VMI's smaller players rarely stand a chance against the likes of their big-time — and just plain big — scholarship players who are often on their way to the NFL instead of Afghanistan.

For Thanksgiving the three of us got a ride from a First back to Richmond and Bradley joined in the Shields family traditions just as I had the previous fall. Bradley hadn't been back to Charleston since the previous Christmas, and I don't recall him returning to the Holy City and his less-than-holy family the rest of his cadetship.

After Thanksgiving we hit the homestretch for another round of exams, and yet again I enjoyed the period when academics seemed to take precedence over the military at VMI. The three of us did well on exams, and we all finished the first semester with GPAs above 3.5. I'm fairly certain there wasn't another room on the third stoop who could have said that.

Bradley came to Richmond for Christmas as well, with Mr. and Mrs. Shields now treating us both like sons. In a sense both Bradley and I were parentless, and Chip's folks seemed to thrive on helping us with a wide variety of things big and small as we transitioned from boys to men without the presence of true parental guidance.

I still couldn't bring myself to walk the few short blocks to our old apartment. I'd asked a pretty VCU student across the hall if she'd occasionally check around inside to make sure everything was OK, and I assumed that no call or letter from her meant that everything was fine.

Mr. Shields never asked me about going back to the apartment, and neither did Chip or Bradley. Looking back on it, I think I'd almost gotten to the point by then of thinking that the Shields' mansion was as much my Richmond home as the little apartment Dad and I had once shared down the street.

Since he'd already paid the rent for another two and a half years, I guess I should have considered subletting it for some extra money, but the thought never crossed my mind. It would have meant going into his bedroom. It would be several years before I crossed that threshold both literally and figuratively.

—∿—

That Christmas and New Year's was also the first time I can remember not absolutely dreading returning to Lexington. Though I enjoyed being embraced by the holiday spirit and Chip's parents, I sometimes found that the ghost of my father in Richmond had become somehow even harder to bear than much of my life at VMI.

When Mr. Shields dropped us off at Jackson Arch, we could hear the yelling inside. Mr. Shields said, "It's a little easier coming back from Christmas this year, isn't it, boys?"

"You got that right. They're going to be in the Ratline for another couple of months. I did hear that they're going to adjust Breakout again this year after that first attempt with us outside Barracks. Everyone from '83 still says their Breakout was much worse than what they concocted for us."

"Like I keep telling you, boys, it was so much harder back in the old Corps."

"Oh, come on, Dad. Back in the old Corps you didn't have snuff spit in your face."

"Nope, just smoke blown into my eyes," he replied, looking through the arch and into Barracks with still-lingering memories from his time inside those thick walls. After the requisite hand-shakes and hugs for the three of us, we headed through Jackson

Arch with our duffels and walked up the two flights of concrete steps to our third stoop room just inside New Barracks. Several Rats had made the mistake of getting back in their uniforms before they were required to and were paying the price out on the third stoop.

One of our BRs had stopped a poor Rat and was drilling him on what he'd done over Christmas break, screaming, "I'll bet you didn't even have a date with that haircut and ugly mug on top of those pathetic shoulders."

Looking back on stuff like that, I hate to admit that all three of us had smiled at that seemingly creative tirade and many others. We didn't participate, but we also didn't stop any of the same verbal, mental, and physical pressure we'd experienced firsthand the previous year. Ironically, two of us would have another opportunity to experience the Ratline again vicariously with Chip's daughter, Virginia, when the words weren't not nearly as crass and the hair of Virginia and her female Brother Rats not so closely shaven.

In many ways, the second semester of our Third Class year went much like the first semester. We embraced our routines to give some semblance of order to the sometimes overwhelming academic and military requirements of our days and nights, when every minute seemed accounted for before we even heard reveille. The classroom was still my haven during the day, as was the little study room down in the basement of Scott Shipp Hall at night.

I continued to especially thrive in my English classes. I even started doing some writing for *The VMI Cadet*, our weekly newspaper.

Articles that I would pen during our First Class year two years later actually led me across the Parade Ground to the superintendent's office once for the only time I exchanged words with him until saying, "Thank you, sir," when he handed me my diploma. It seems so silly now when I reread those words complaining about the food in the mess hall, but it certainly got the supe's attention back in the spring of 1984.

As with almost every day I spent at VMI, the semester wasn't without angst. Two more Rats were drummed out in January and another one in March just before what we thought was a much easier Breakout than we'd experienced.

While our four BRs had been drummed out for cheating back in first semester, all three honor code violations by the Rats were for making false official statements. The pressure of avoiding military penalties like confinement or penalty tours by lying could sometimes become just as hard as that of academic pressure that led to cheating.

Either way, a middle-of-the-night drum out still put the Honor Code's ultimate priority in perspective for me. After every one of them, we returned to our dark room and quietly vowed to each other that we would never leave VMI in that manner.

—◆—

Not long after Breakout for the Class of 1985, the three of us went down to Florida as planned for Major League Baseball's spring training. This was my first experience with this rite of spring.

We rented a silver Honda Civic hatchback in downtown Lexington and drove through the night after we were released for the break. We split up driving duties three ways, downed a quick supper and breakfast at McDonald's, and arrived in West Palm Beach exactly at noon.

There's no longer spring training there, and I think they tore down West Palm Beach Municipal Stadium, but that little ballpark was the first of what would be dozens of spring training games for me, Bradley, and Chip in the coming decade. After graduation, rather than driving through the night, we'd fly into Florida and even Arizona for our traditional week of spring ball.

Back then, along with finding cheap eats, we camped in a green, four-man Eureka! tent. On later trips we'd hit a hotel, still hurting from our spring sunburns and one too many afternoon beers at various stadiums in West Palm Beach, Vero Beach, Fort Lauderdale, Miami, and more. We also didn't eat at too many McDonald's on those later trips, opting instead for places like Joe's Stone Crab.

There's no longer spring training in any of those four cities, with modern spring training and Florida State League stadiums now drawing thousands of fans throughout Florida compared to the hundreds we sat in the sun with back in 1982.

Though my father wasn't much of a baseball fan, I'd grown up an Atlanta Braves fan. It was mostly due to having the Richmond Braves AAA minor league baseball team less than two miles away at old Parker Field, which was replaced by The Diamond back in 1985 and no longer even houses the R-Braves. I still take a march down memory lane occasionally when I go to a Richmond Flying Squirrels AA game out at The Diamond.

Chip also followed the Braves, and Bradley was just along for the ride and company, so we'd made their spring home in West Palm Beach our spring home that first trip to Florida. Back then, the Atlanta Braves shared the ballpark with the Montreal Expos, so we were able to see a game there every day. After that first game — which I think the Braves lost to *les* Expos — we found a nearby campground, pitched our tent, and then headed straight to the beach for some more late-afternoon sun and a swim in the Atlantic. We bought a bucket of Kentucky Fried Chicken and took it back to the campground that night, along with two six packs of PBR cans.

For the next four days, we essentially repeated the same routine — and would for years to come. We'd sleep in until the tent got too hot, catch a spring training game, eat ballpark peanuts and dogs for lunch, drink beer, go to the beach, eat a cheap dinner or maybe even grill something at the campground, drink beer, and go to sleep.

—w—

Back at VMI for the homestretch run of Third Class year, April and May were again my favorite two months in Lexington. We switched to whites for most of our daily activities, making Post seem brighter and happier compared to the gray days and dark nights of winter.

It didn't feel quite so bright and happy inside Barracks when less than two months before graduation, four Firsts were dismissed. Two had too many demerits, one was caught uptown in Lexington drinking at Spanky's in civvies while on confinement, and the fourth, who I still see sometimes in the Fan, was drummed out. I can remember lying in our bunks after the drum out and talking about all of the ways it was possible not to make it to graduation — even when you were as close as that First had been that spring.

Graduation on another sunny May day out on the Parade Ground wasn't quite as big a deal to us as the previous year when our dykes were graduating, but it still brought thoughts of our own graduation that much closer. Two more years to go, we thought and even said aloud several times.

A First, now a VMI graduate, gave the three of us a ride back to Richmond, where we essentially pursued the exact same summer Chip and I had enjoyed after our Rat year. We knew this would be our last full summer break; we were all slated to head to "summer camp" between Second and First Class years. Chip and I would be going to army ROTC's fabled summer camp in the sand and sun down in Fayetteville, North Carolina, or "Fayettenam," as U.S. Army ROTC cadets liked to call it back then. Bradley would be going to sea with the U.S. Navy for his summer ROTC commitment.

—⟋⟍—

For three months that summer of 1982, we again avoided walking by my apartment or even talking about it. Each day I spent in Richmond without stepping foot in that apartment would make it even more difficult to ultimately do so. I knew I would have to someday, and I did go back there eventually.

Chip went out on a few dates with various girls from his high school days who were now going to Southern Sem, Hollins, and UVA, but Bradley and I never took him up on his repeated early-summer offers to double- or triple-date. I remembering telling Chip that I thought it was the lack of a strong maternal presence in our lives that had something to do with Bradley and me avoiding female relationships. I'd learn later that it wasn't the case for Bradley.

Win and Sarah Shields still often acted like they were the proud parents of three young men, instead of just one, and we fully embraced it. I think Chip appreciated it most of all, in that the pressure of being the only child of a tobacco millionaire seemed to be lifted for a time — even if we all knew that he'd someday have to deal with his role as sole heir.

While Chip and I taught tennis from Monday to Friday over at Byrd Park, Bradley worked as a waiter at Joe's all summer, pulling lunch shifts when he was needed and working every night except Sunday to save as much money as possible. His parents were still paying his tuition and all of the basic VMI fees, which were higher for out-of-state cadets, but Bradley was paying for everything else during his cadetship and summers away from VMI.

I think if he could have done it, Bradley would have paid for everything. He told me years later that, in 1989, he sent his father a check for more than $30,000 after researching how much his family likely paid VMI during his four years there.

Bradley's summer job location and hours did make for some late-night sessions sitting at the long wooden bar at Joe's. We'd wait for his last table to leave while downing a pitcher or two of beer and then walk back through the summer's late-night heat and humidity to Chip's house. I can't remember much of what we talked about now, but I'm sure it revolved around our next two years at VMI, our rings, the following summer at Fort Bragg or at sea, graduation, and our post-VMI lives.

If I knew now what would pass during each of those various stages in our lives, I likely would have paid more attention to the words of my friends regarding their plans and passions. We were barely out of our teenage years but talking of adult things, even if we didn't really know we were. At least I didn't then.

—⚬—

Mid-August came, and the countdown for our return to Lexington began yet again. The VMI experience was filled with many Post arrivals and departures, and I suspect all three of us had it easier than most. We were together when we left and still together upon our return. Somehow the times at VMI and the times away were not as dramatically different as I knew they were for many of our classmates.

Once again Mr. Shields drove us back to Lexington and right up to Jackson Arch. As soon as we opened the Volvo's doors, we could hear the yelling inside Barracks. "I'm so glad none of us came back for Cadre," Chip said.

"Maybe there's some Citadel grad's son or brother here again this year and he brought a blouse," Bradley joked, smiling as he watched a Rat in fatigues head straining and sweating through Jackson Arch into the Ratline that would be part of his life for at least six long months.

"You should be so lucky," laughed Mr. Shields. "I'm sure you'd yell at him just like they did with you."

"You should know better than that by now, Mr. Shields. The only people I yell at inside Barracks are these two heathens when they use the sink as a urinal and don't even turn on the faucet afterward. Or when we get boned for hairs in the cracked porcelain sink we'll likely have in our room again this year."

"I didn't know y'all still used the sink like we did back in the old Corps."

"I promise I'll run some water after using it this year, Bradley," I deadpanned.

"Yea, right. Just watch those hairs when I'm responsible for the room inspections."

With a knowing smile and nod, Mr. Shields then shook our hands and hugged us, looking each of us straight in the eye when pulling away. He knew that in some ways, Second Class year wasn't any easier than the first two. But he wore the ring, and we didn't — yet.

As he did a U-turn in front of Jackson Statue and guided the rusting old Volvo back toward Richmond, we grabbed our duffels and walked up a single flight of stairs to our new room, 241. It's funny now how something so small like one less flight of stairs could feel like such a big deal back then. It's still two flights up to my Richmond apartment and I don't have the spring in my step that I did back in 1982.

Moving into our room had become routine, and we already knew who took each desk and the location of our racks for yet another year. The routines of VMI actually made it easier to bear the non-routine things — like a drumming out or unwarranted demerits or confinement that kept you from a planned weekend away from those routines. We were lucky in that we'd roomed together the last two years and didn't have to get used to new roommates and their ways. And we were determined to keep it that way for two more years.

Our first SRC formation that night felt like we'd never left Lexington. Second Class privileges at meal and class formations allowed us to turn our heads and talk, so the three of us immediately set about catching up with the few other classmates and Firsts in our company that we'd become somewhat close with our first two years.

As in years past, we sat together down at the mess hall and continued talking to BRs and Firsts about their summer, including learning that two guys in our company had not been allowed to return due to their grades. Both of them would eventually return to VMI and graduate just a semester late. Coming back to VMI like that was something I thought had to be harder than leaving at all.

We fell asleep that night to the sounds of yelling up on fourth stoop, but we were one more set of steps removed from the life of a Rat. That night, like many of the nights in the coming couple of months, we talked about rings.

We agreed that the four defining moments of our VMI experience together would be that very first day and long night in Barracks, getting out of the Ratline, getting our rings, and graduation. We'd completed two of the four steps, and we were less than three months away from the third seminal moment.

Our rings had been designed by a committee of our classmates the previous semester, and we'd voted as a class for the top design for each side. There was traditionally a "class" side and a "VMI" side to rings, and each of us could then choose the metal (most chose gold), the stone, and any enhancements, like the small diamond inset I chose to have embedded in the VMI logo above my garnet stone.

I recall we could pay for the ring in three installments, but I'd paid for it in full when we ordered them back in May. I'd decided to use some more of the money my father left me, which I'd thus far just used for tuition, some other expenses at VMI, and my summers back in Richmond when I didn't make enough money teaching tennis.

I thought and hoped my dad would have seen using the money in this way as fitting. I did, and so did Chip and Bradley when I told them about my decision. The past May Bradley had used most of the money he'd saved working the summer before coming to VMI to pay for the first installment and planned to pay off the rest with the money he'd earned at Joe's that summer.

That summer we'd all shared our ring choices with Mr. and Mrs. Shields as if they were our own parents and not just Chip's. I can still remember Bradley saying he wouldn't wear his ring around his father or brother when he next saw them. And he didn't.

"But I sure as hell will wear it when I return to Charleston someday," he'd said. By then I think it'd been more than eighteen months since Bradley had seen his family or returned to South Carolina. I guess the same could be said for my apartment back in Richmond. In some ways I guess we were avoiding facing the same thing: loss.

—w—

The fall was as uneventful as any season I can remember during our four years at VMI — or at least as uneventful as any time at the Institute could be. As Seconds we enjoyed more weekend privileges. That often meant that whenever we could, the three of us returned to Richmond.

It was always a great feeling to change out of our uniforms and into civvies, but in retrospect, we were really changing from one uniform to another. Though our polo shirts were always a different color, all three of us inevitably changed into khakis or jeans, Topsiders or Weejuns without socks, and a polo, most of which was purchased from Alvin Dennis at the corner of Washington and Jefferson downtown. Bradley had already stopped wearing anything he owned from his father's shop in Charleston.

Though we wore civvies back to Richmond, it was still easy to tell we weren't going to a normal school. While we could grow it a little longer, our hair gave us away anywhere we went. By then we didn't really even care. There were so many other things about our unique college experience that made us different. But as I recall, it was typically just the three of us, along with Chip's parents sometimes.

On one of the weekends back in Richmond — I think it was in September — Chip ran into a girl named Beth who had gone to St. Cath's and was now a junior at UVA. She sat with us at Joe's, had a beer, and then left with friends. "I always had a crush on her back in high school," Chip said as he watched her she walk down the narrow lane between the bar and dark wood booths.

"But Beth's dad is an attorney here in Richmond who likes to pursue cancer death lawsuits against tobacco companies. My folks would kill me if I even asked her out, much less went on a date or something."

"I can picture your dad welcoming her into your house right now," I laughed. "He'd probably offer her a cigarette."

"I always got the feeling that she was interested in me back in high school, but I could never pull the trigger and ask her out. I came close once and had even gone so far as looking her number up in the phone book. But I knew it couldn't go anywhere once my parents learned about it. Especially my dad."

"You should ask her to come down to VMI for Homecoming weekend and not even tell your parents, since your dad said they couldn't come this year." Bradley said. "It might get it out of your system without any harm being done back in Richmond."

Before we left the city that weekend, Chip called a high school friend of Beth's who he thought would have her phone number over in Charlottesville. "Just in case I finally get the guts to go for it," I recall him saying with a smile after hanging up the phone in his upstairs bedroom.

He did ask Beth Sherman out for Homecoming, and she said yes. She came down to VMI and spent Friday and Saturday nights, staying out at the Keydet-General on Route 11 west of town.

Neither Bradley nor I had a date that weekend, and we didn't see much of Chip or Beth, but I didn't think much about it until Sunday night when we were lying in our hays and I asked how the weekend had gone. Chip said, "We had a great time, and we even finally talked about both of our fathers when we had lunch at Spanky's today." Chip said that night he planned to ask her to Ring Figure. Of course we didn't know then that this simple decision, like many, would change everything.

Our Ring Figure weekend started on a crisp November Friday morning. By Second Class year, we'd learned to awaken as late as possible, get dressed quickly, and just barely make it to BRC formation before the last long note of the bugle sounded. On that morning, however, we were all awake at six and talking about the weekend ahead.

That was also the first morning I saw a cardinal, Virginia's bright-red state bird, sitting atop Stonewall Jackson's head on VMI's iconic statue of him. Bradley and Chip saw it as well and Virginia says she caught a cardinal sitting in the exact same spot during several winter mornings her Rat year. I'd like to think that particular cardinal carried the spirit of her father, making sure his girl was surviving another harsh VMI winter.

We had to attend classes like any normal day at VMI, which still included Saturday morning sessions back then as well. However, I couldn't take my mind off the ring ceremony that afternoon in Jackson Memorial Hall.

In many ways it would really be the first material recognition that I was becoming the VMI man that my father had envisioned. There'd been landmark events like matriculating and getting out of the Ratline, but getting *the* ring was something we'd have for a lifetime — assuming we graduated.

The ceremony was midafternoon, and the entire Corps was in attendance, as were most of the officers, faculty, other VMI staff, and a smattering of parents I recognized from football games. As he'd promised, Mr. Shields was standing by the cannonball, which had been made to look like a hand with our ring on it. He actually saluted us with his ring-laden right hand as we passed, and I would swear I saw a tear in his eye as he watched us walk single-file past him and Mrs. Shields.

Once we were inside and seated, the superintendent came walking down the center aisle and the Corps rose to attention. When he was behind the podium, he said, "Take your seats, gentlemen."

I can't remember a word of the speech that followed or that of our class president. I could only think of taking off my white glove and placing the ring on the index finger of my right hand. Our class stood one row at a time and walked across the stage to receive our rings, which were in black velvet boxes with the Jostens logo on them.

When the last name was called, the supe said a few closing remarks, and we filed out of J.M. Hall, wearing big smiles and knowing we'd be wearing our rings once back in the courtyard.

Mr. and Mrs. Shields had followed us into the courtyard and easily found us as planned by the sentinel box. After old yells led by our class president for our dykes and our class, it was time to wear the ring.

With me going first and Chip last, we each put on our rings, shaking Mr. Shields's hand and then shaking each other's hands and locking eyes in turn. Heartfelt hugs inevitably followed all around with each other and with Mr. and Mrs. Shields.

There was a sense of pride that day when I put on the ring that I've never quite matched — and that honestly includes graduation and a number of journalism honors I never thought I deserved. Except for when I slept, I would wear that ring every day forward for the next eighteen months of VMI, for four years in the army, and for a decade or so more before it would no longer slide onto my ring finger.

Our rings would have a very different meaning to all of us in coming years and for reasons we could never have guessed that bright November afternoon. Now when I put it on my finger, the initial pride is joined by a flood of memories directly related to everything that came before and after that day.

One of those memories occurred soon after we left the courtyard that afternoon. When we got back to our room, Chip went straight to his rifle and detached the bayonet. He then went back to sit at his desk and proceeded to prick the tip of his now ring-laden finger with the sharp point of his bayonet. His finger immediately started to ooze a bit of blood.

I was still standing nearby and he passed the bayonet to me with an unsaid request to repeat his bloodletting. I quickly followed suit and then passed the bayonet to a silent Bradley to repeat what Chip and I had done. After Bradley had also pricked the tip of his ring finger, Chip stood back up, walked over to the two of us, and held out his bleeding finger for us to mix our blood with his.

Locking eyes as we joined our three ring fingers, not a word was spoken. Words weren't needed.

—∭—

We had a formal dance in Cocke Hall that night, and Bradley and I took two girls Beth had known back in Richmond. Bradley's date was a cute, short-haired girl from Hollins. I escorted a petite blonde who was also a high school friend of Beth's. She was in her second year at Southern Sem and was a cheerleader for VMI's football team. I couldn't tell you her name today and would likely not recognize her on the streets. I'm betting Chip would remember. I wish I could ask him.

Though it was difficult to keep them from crossing paths, Chip and Beth thought it was best that they didn't introduce her to his parents that weekend. It might have tainted an otherwise perfect weekend and, in any case, that time would come more quickly than they could have predicted or wanted.

I also can't recall the name of the band that played Friday, but you can bet I still remember the one that played for our informal dance at the Richmond Hyatt Saturday night.

After the formal I slept with my ring on, and I remember waking many times to feel its weight on my hand. I even hit my head with it when I tossed and turned with the nightmares that had started haunting me at VMI. I haven't slept with it on since that night, but those nightmares — ranging from memories of my father to being late for a formation — certainly persisted long after leaving Lexington.

We awoke Saturday and for once didn't mind the early BRC formation — especially after we spotted the cardinal sitting atop Jackson's head and traded smiles. Most of us fell out after roll call and headed back to bed if we didn't have classes. Every single Second Classman I saw seemed to walk a bit differently with that ring on his finger.

Chip drove us all to Richmond after the football game, which I think we actually won. Win had bought him a dark green 1978 Volvo four-door and Chip had talked a high school friend of his who was a junior at W&L into letting him keep it at their frat house in town.

Beth sat between Chip and me in the front, and the other three sat in the back seat. I can still picture Chip driving up 81 and on 64 with his right hand at the top of the steering wheel so he could constantly stare at his ring as he drove.

Rather than the formal coatees we'd worn on Friday night, we got to wear civvies for Saturday night's dance. The Skip Castro Band played for us that night, and they rocked the Richmond Hyatt like they would for decades to come throughout Virginia and even further afield.

Some of my classmates — like dear old preppy Chip — danced to every song with a variety of girls, including my date. But he mostly danced with Beth. Skip Castro played "Boogie at Midnight" at the stroke of twelve and even I, who rarely danced, went out on the floor with everyone else, shuffling to the beat.

Later that night another class tradition got its start when a football player still smiling from the afternoon's win came barreling into the ballroom from the hallway and performed what we called an "aircraft carrier landing." After his running start, he belly flopped onto the floor at full speed and slid another twenty feet on the slick wooden dance floor before smashing into the far wall.

Other delirious classmates soon followed suit. Incredibly, many of these same BRs would do it again at a reunion twenty-five years later — and the Skip Castro Band would still play for us at the Lexington Country Club. But then they played "Boogie at Midnight" around ten, as those of us still around to dance headed toward our own twilights. We dubbed it "Boogie at Midlife."

The three of us had booked one hotel room at the Hyatt, and our dates had two rooms on the floor below us. We dropped them off and then collapsed in our own room about one, but Chip said he'd forgotten to tell Beth and the other girls the plan for Sunday, so headed back down to Beth's room to let her know. I don't know what time he returned — the weekend's adrenaline couldn't keep Bradley and me from quickly falling asleep.

There was a class brunch in the hotel the next morning, where I was surprised to see most of my class and their dates up early and devouring it. I don't think any of us wanted to miss anything, storing it in our memory banks as one of those purely good moments during our VMI experience. It would be used on the scales when the bad moments of the past and still to come sometimes seemed to easily outweigh everything else during our cadetship.

The six of us spent the morning walking around the empty streets of downtown Richmond and down in Shockoe Bottom, which is an area of the city I'd later grow fond of thanks to a tasty restaurant scene and a thriving farmer's market filled with local meats and produce. That morning, over bloody marys at The Tobacco Company, we were just happy to be dressed in civvies and frequently admiring our rings, thinking and talking about what it would be like to wear the ring without a uniform all the time.

The drive back to Lexington was relatively quiet after all of the weekend revelry. We dropped the three girls back at the cars they'd left at the Keydet-General, said our good-byes and thanks, and watched them — and our weekend — disappear.

The natural letdown that one would expect after a momentous occasion like Ring Figure set in for all three of us Sunday night. It was still VMI after all, and we still had more than a year and a half to go until graduation. Like life for most, the good and great could sometimes be followed by bad and worse. I already knew that, and it always tempered the good things with the bad that happened at VMI — and later.

The rest of November passed quickly, with each day seemingly colder than the last. Mid-December again brought that period when academics seemed to take on more importance than the military in VMI's long days and nights. There were many nights in a row that I would find myself rushing up the hill from Scott Shipp to be back in my Barracks room by one — the cut-off for being outside of Barracks studying.

Exams went well for all three of us, and looking back I'd swear we'd gained an inner confidence in ourselves thanks to those big hunks of gold on our fingers. When I occasionally put it back on today, I do somehow again feel a strength that I no longer seem to have on a daily basis. That sometimes false sense of confidence can be both good and bad. I've seen it work both ways with VMI men and women who wear the ring.

The three of us returned to Richmond again for Christmas. It had been just Chip and me for Christmas our Rat year, with Bradley joining us during Third Class year and again in 1982 and into 1983. We followed the same general theme, with late nights at Joe's and other Fan bars and restaurants, crisp morning runs and tennis over at Byrd Park, and some more memorable meals and all of Christmas Day with Mr. and Mrs. Shields.

That sunny day included presents for all of us and a Christmas dinner that featured a wild turkey that a friend of Mr. Shields had recently shot down near Appomattox. I can't remember the name of my Ring Figure date, but I can recall the entire menu that day. And that Sarah Shields made a Virginia Gentleman bourbon sauce to serve over her apple pie.

The day after Christmas, we met Beth for a beer one night at Joe's, but she just ordered iced tea and seemed distracted during the half-hour she stayed with us. She left with our second pitcher still half-full. "More beer for us, guys," Chip said with a smile at us as he watched her walk out the door.

Returning to VMI for second semester was difficult, in that we didn't have Ring Figure to look forward to anymore. The phrase "Rat with a ring" resonated with the three of us, especially when Chip's Richmond friends told us about their freedom and experiences at the likes of UVA and Hampden-Sydney. We were still Rats in many ways and would be for another sixteen months.

The rest of January was wet and cold, with several snows turning Post's grayness into a hazy white for far too many days. Except for Rat year when we seemed to be the target of every snowball thrown in Barracks, I always liked snow at VMI. Thinking back, I seem to have enjoyed anything that got us out of our routines. I still do. I think that's why I travel so much, with time on the road becoming more routine than my time back on Monument Avenue.

On the first Sunday night of February, Chip received what we called a "status slip" from the Guard Room with a note saying that Beth had called and asking him to call. He didn't seem to think much of it and didn't even call her back from the bank of pay phones down in the Barracks basement concourse until the next evening after SRC.

Chip returned to our room as white as his ducks, which was and is the long-time nickname for our starched pants. Beth had told him she was ten weeks pregnant.

Beth had not related to Chip what she planned to do with the baby, and he hadn't asked. "It was a really short conversation guys, and I said I needed some time to think about it. Beth told me she understood and would wait for a call from me later this week."

The three of us stayed in the room that night to study, which was very unusual because we all found it hard to study in Barracks. I think Bradley and I felt like we needed to be there if

Chip wanted to talk it through, but he didn't say a single word about it until after we'd turned the lights out for taps.

He found his voice in the dark. "What the hell am I going to do, guys?" he asked in a quiet plea.

"Did she give you any feel about keeping the baby?" Bradley quietly asked.

"Not at all. I guess she's waiting to see what I'm thinking, and I have no clue. At least not yet."

"Are you thinking about leaving VMI?" I asked him.

"I don't think so. Not after I've come this far. But the thought of an abortion is even worse than thinking about telling my parents. I've despised abortionists as long as I have cigarette makers. They're both murderers."

"I wonder if Beth feels the same way."

"I have no idea, Nick. I honestly barely know her."

"I think you need to go see her, Chip," said Bradley.

It's hard to believe now, but that's exactly what Chip did. In fact, he jumped out of our second stoop room about an hour after Bradley gave him the idea. There honestly wasn't a huge chance he'd get caught before returning by BRC; we'd heard them run an accountability "stick check" on the doors soon after taps, and that was likely the only one they'd run overnight.

Chip had changed into some civilian clothes he kept hidden in our room, jogged uptown to get his car, and then called Beth from a pay phone at White's Truck Stop up on 81. He later told me he'd heard relief in her voice when they talked and he told her about his plan to come to Charlottesville right then.

She was living off campus just west of Charlottesville in Crozet, and Chip got to the rented house she shared with two other Richmond girls just before two. I would only learn about their entire conversation many years later, but I can still remember lying on our hays back at VMI and saying to Bradley, "I guess he's talking to her right now. The only thing I hope is that they're thinking the same thing about what they should do — whatever that is."

"Me too. I just can't imagine Chip leaving VMI, can you?"

"No, but he may not have a choice."

—⚒—

Chip got back to Barracks and our room a little before five, slipping quietly into the room in case we were asleep. We weren't.

"You OK?" I asked.

"I'll tell y'all about it after BRC formation. Let's try to get a little sleep before that damn bugle."

I guess we all may have slept a bit, but it seemed to take forever for the first bugle call to come at quarter to seven. We dressed quickly, without talking, headed to breakfast formation, and then fell out with the other upperclassmen who were also skipping breakfast — or at least the one served down in the mess hall, since the Post Exchange was also popular for quick breakfasts for a few bucks.

We walked back into our room together and went to our desks for the conversation I knew was coming. Looking back on it, I wouldn't even call it a conversation. It was a short monologue from Chip, and we just listened without interrupting him.

"Here's the deal, guys. Beth's going to have *our* baby," he said, emphasizing the word 'our.' "We both agreed it's the right thing to do. We're going to get married as soon as possible, she's going to finish the year at UVA, and then she's going to move back to Richmond and live with my parents. If they'll have her. I know they will. And with your help, I'm going to try to make it to graduation as a married man with a kid."

Chip looked to each of us in turn for a response. It was me who eventually spoke first. "I can honestly say that I don't think either Bradley or I saw that plan as a real possibility. But I am certain we both agree that it's the honorable thing to do and that it's worth a shot. You know you can count on us to keep it in this room."

"Agreed," said Bradley. "Rumors fly quickly around here, and they don't always stay in Barracks. This needs to stay right here in our room."

"Thanks, guys. On the drive back down here, I kept thinking that you two would support this plan. I hope my parents — and particularly my father — will as well. I realize I hardly know Beth, but that's really not the point now.

"Dad always says that the honorable and right thing is usually apparent," Chip continued, looking at each of us in turn. "And I think it really is in this case — especially with how I feel about abortion. Beth briefly brought up adoption, but I could tell her heart wasn't in it."

"Well, starting now, we'll be there for you and Beth and then the baby, once it's born," I promised, with Bradley nodding in agreement.

—w—

Chip and Beth married a month later in a civil ceremony in Charlottesville on a cold Saturday afternoon. Bradley and I got a weekend pass and stood beside them at the very short affair in the Albemarle County Courthouse. The two Richmond girls who shared Beth's house were also there in a show of support.

So were Chip's parents. Chip had called them the morning after he'd made the plan with Beth, and though he could tell they were shocked, disappointed, and worried, they'd immediately agreed with Chip and Beth's decision and request for Beth to live with them before and after she had the baby. Mr. Shields stood by Chip at the wedding, and Mrs. Shields stood by Beth.

Beth's parents were not there. The weekend after Chip's middle-of-the-night visit with Beth in Charlottesville when they'd made their decision, they'd driven to Richmond together to tell her parents. Though I've never been a parent, how Beth's parents responded will always boggle my mind.

Quite simply, they disowned her as a daughter and never spoke to her again, as far as I know. I've never seen her attorney father in Richmond since. We don't run in the same circles — or courtrooms.

Except for Rat Boxing, he'd be the first man I'd punch if I did. I'm surprised Win Shields didn't, but I suspect he correctly figured that Beth's father would sue him. So it was just Chip, Beth, me, Bradley, and Mr. and Mrs. Shields for the baby to come. And we would be all she needed.

—◊—

March and April brought warmer temperatures and leaves back to the trees. The three of us had accumulated enough weekend passes to head back to Richmond practically every Saturday afternoon and sometimes even on Friday evenings. We stopped in Charlottesville to visit Beth two of those times, but she never went to Richmond with us.

Though there was always the shadow of Chip's situation, we tried to make the most of our short time in Richmond whenever we were there, with beers and meals in various Fan restaurants and back at the Shields house. Those meals with Mr. and Mrs. Shields continued my palate's education, as they enjoyed seeing me try things like foie gras, sweetbreads, and caviar for the first time. With their very different upbringings from my own, both Chip and Bradley had already enjoyed these delicacies with mixed reviews.

When we were there, we never spoke of Beth and the baby. However, I'm sure Chip must have made plans with his parents for the summer to come.

Graduation for the Class of 1983 was next, but — though unspoken — the only thing the three of us could think about was making it to our own graduation together a year hence. We'd heard about cadets being secretly married and still graduating in past years but really didn't know if it was possible, especially with a baby involved.

—⁂—

Right after 1983's graduation and finishing her junior year at UVA, Beth moved in with Chip's parents. They didn't give her "my" room and made a point of telling me so.

As we'd known when we enjoyed the previous peaceful summer in Richmond, the months between our Second and First

Class years were destined to be quite different. All three of us had our summer ROTC commitments to fulfill.

Because of the timing of our summer training, we each took a summer school class right after '83's graduation so our course load would be even easier for First Class year. By then I was taking mostly English electives and scheduled another English lit course. Chip took the Shakespeare course I'd really enjoyed our Third Class year, though the joke within our room was that he should have repeated the family planning course VMI's beloved chaplain taught and that we'd all already passed the previous semester.

Bradley got his final required econ course out of the way as well, completing it with four guys from the Class of 1983 who had failed it the past semester and hadn't graduated. He passed the class, and so did three of the other four, but that fourth guy would probably only get one more try to pass it before losing his chance at a VMI diploma.

Our experience at Fort Bragg was typical for VMI cadets. All of those gung-ho ROTC guys from civilian schools took the marching and other military stuff so seriously because much of it was generally new to them. In contrast, most of the VMI cadets just went through the motions of having to march in the hot summer sun on scalding pavement and sand after we'd already been doing it in and on all kinds of weather and surfaces for three years.

Chip and I bunked together in those weathered World War II two-story gray wooden Barracks, some of which I hear are still standing. I was in the top bunk, and we likely would have talked about the situation with Beth every night, but we knew we couldn't. He occasionally brought it up when we shared a tent during our frequent overnights in the woods and on the sand. Then he usually just said, "I'm not sure how I'm going to do it, Nick."

I'd always respond with something like, "It's not how *you're* going to do it, Chip. It's how *we're* going to do it. It's mere months, and you're doing the right thing. We can do it." And we did.

Our six weeks at Fort Bragg actually passed pretty quickly. Beth and her two former Charlottesville housemates came down to Myrtle Beach for a week, and Chip and I actually got permission to head down there one Saturday night.

By then Beth was seven months pregnant and clearly blossoming into her pending motherhood. Thinking back, I really don't believe she'd thought about the consequences of Chip being caught back at VMI, and I'm also not sure she'd thought about life after graduation if Chip did make it to graduation.

On the morning we were released from summer camp, we drove up 95 back to Richmond in the red Volkswagen Beetle I'd bought with some more of my dad's money.

Bradley finished his summer commitment with the navy the next day in Norfolk, so Chip, Beth, and I went down to pick him up and then continued on to Virginia Beach, where Beth had a high school friend who was renting a little beach house in Sandbridge for the summer while she waited tables, partied half the night, and chased boys. For the record, Chip, Bradley, and I bunked together, and Beth had her own room.

We swore Beth's friend to secrecy about her pregnancy and she kept her promise once back in Richmond. I saw her the other day on Cary Street and she introduced me to her teenage daughter, Carolina, whose father is a UNC grad and evidently bleeds baby blue.

We spent three blissfully free days and nights at the beach, though I could tell that Chip was anxious to get back to Lexington to start — and finish, if at all possible — our final year. Back then I'm not sure that Beth or the baby was his focus. He just didn't want one mistake — though he never called it that as long as he lived — to risk wasting the previous three years of his life or his possible post-VMI future.

We drove back to Richmond for a week there before we needed to be back in Lexington and continued the traditions we'd created for our time there — but with the addition of Beth.

Chip, Bradley, and I went for runs west along Monument Avenue and through the Fan and Byrd Park, played tennis, and then joined Beth and Mr. and Mrs. Shields for more Monument Avenue meals.

Mr. Shields seemed to particularly enjoy this time with me, Bradley, and Chip. He said several times that we were in for the best year of our cadetships and that we would remember things about this year more than any other period at VMI.

Chip also spent a lot of time alone with Beth, who was due in two weeks when we'd already be back in Lexington. The plan was for her to have the baby at Stuart Circle Hospital and continue living with the Shields until our graduation. I wonder what Beth did with all of her time in that big house before the baby was born.

After saying our good-byes with hugs, handshakes, and even a chaste kiss on the cheek for Mrs. Shields from all three of us, Chip and Bradley took Chip's Volvo wagon, and I drove my Beetle alone back to Lexington. The normal dread I felt when returning to Lexington from Richmond had been mostly replaced this time by the excitement about being a First, though this was tempered with the constant fear that Chip would get caught.

We went straight to Barracks to unload our cars and then drove over to the First Class parking lot behind the Marshall Museum. As I walked past the museum honoring perhaps VMI's most famous and important alumnus — though many might vote for the actor Dabney Coleman — I realized I hadn't stepped into the ode to the man and Marshall Plan since my Rat year. I promised myself I'd make a list of things to do before I left VMI and Lexington in May, including re-visiting the VMI Museum in the basement of Jackson Memorial Hall and visiting Stonewall Jackson's gravesite uptown in Stonewall Jackson Memorial Cemetery. Incredibly, until then, I'd failed to visit the grave of VMI's beloved professor — and I've read he was as tough in the classroom as he was on the battlefield.

We'd come back for Cadre to perform various duties big and small, but mostly to earn another free weekend away from the Institute. The new Rats, including our dykes, were reporting that day, and it was easy to pick them out, along with their parents.

I couldn't help but picture that August day three years ago when I was dropped off at Jackson Arch by a high school buddy and feeling very alone while surrounded by other boys and their parents.

With the thought of that day still in my mind, we headed through Jackson Arch to our first stoop Barracks room. We'd had to move all of our stuff out of Room 141 after the first session of summer school because some other cadets had used it for second session, but it had still been fun to preview our First Class room experience back in May.

We picked up our uniforms from storage, smiling at the three thin black First Class stripes on our grey blouses and coatees, but ribbing Bradley half-heartedly about losing his academic stars for First Class year. I also couldn't help reminding him about his Citadel blouse from Rat year. In many ways the Class of 1984 had been born that hot August day three years earlier — thanks to Chip. It had been a typical VMI combination of something bad becoming something good.

—⚊—

Though there were certainly occasional exceptions on Post, most of the good times occurred away from VMI, and a large majority of the bad things happened inside Barracks or elsewhere on Post. Of course, many of the things we did or said in coming months hinged on keeping Chip and Beth's secret that long year.

One of the very good things for me was having a dyke and treating him the way I swore I'd treat my Rat when I got the chance. Though I tried to get away from VMI every chance I got — just like my dyke back in 1980 and '81 — I attempted to be completely present in the moment anytime I was with my dyke my First Class year.

His name was Clifford Shelton, and he was from Bristol, Tennessee, just across the state line from the Virginia town of the same name. He often joked that if his parents had known he'd want to go to VMI, they would have moved across the state line before he matriculated so they could pay cheaper in-state tuition.

That first afternoon back at VMI, the three of us put on our uniforms and headed to fourth stoop to find our dykes. I'd

looked Clifford's assigned room up in the list of Rats, and —
incredibly — he was in the same room that I'd been assigned
with Chip and Bradley back in 1980.

Heading through the door through which I'd last passed in
May of 1981 brought back a flood of memories and the same
old fears. How many push-ups and sit-ups had we done on that
worn floor until we were too worn out to pull down our racks?
How many nights had we lain awake in our hays wondering if
they'd be kicking in our doors for a sweat party or a run the next
morning?

I quietly opened the door, but a Rat standing at the sink just
inside saw the door open in the mirror and immediately yelled,
"Room, attention!" They all stopped what they were doing and
jumped to attention, straining with all their might and wondering
what bad thing was about to happen to them with some First
they'd never seen before entering their room.

"At ease, guys," I quickly said. "I'm one of the few nice
upperclassmen who will ever step inside this door. Which one of
you bald boys is Shelton?"

"Me, sir!" yelled the tallest Rat in the room as he quickly
went back to attention and started straining again.

"Take it easy, Clifford. I'm your dyke, Nick Adams," I said as
I walked across the room to shake his hand.

His sweaty palm was still shaking, and I held it tightly, looked
him in the eye, and said, "You have nothing to fear when I'm in
the room, Clifford. I'm going to make your Rat year a lot less
shaky than that right hand of yours."

"It's nice to meet you, sir."

"I'm not 'sir' in here to any of you. It's Nick."

"Yes, sir," they all yelled at once.

"We'll have to work on that," I laughed. "I know that 'sir' stuff is getting drilled into you."

"That and a lot of other stuff, sir," Clifford said, with the first hint of the smile that I would grow to love in coming months.

I sat down at what appeared to be Clifford's almost bare desk. It would be filled with books soon enough, but the only thing there now was his little Rat Bible, which was open to the list of the ten cadets who died at New Market in May of 1864. And yes, I can still recite their names to this day:

Corporal Atwill
Private Haynes
Private Jefferson
Private McDowell
Private Stanard
Sergeant Wheelwright
Sergeant Cabell
Private Crockett
Private Hartsfield
Private Jones

One of the cadets, First Sergeant Cabbell, was from Richmond. He's buried at Hollywood Cemetery. Chip and I found his gravestone on a hilly run there long ago.

"Is everything all right with you three so far, beyond the normal stuff they're putting you through?"

"Yes, Nick," my dyke quickly answered for the room. "I don't think we're getting it any worse than any other room. By the way, I went by Cliff back home in Bristol."

"Good. I can't help you, Cliff — or any of you — unless you're being singled out without reasonable cause. If that happens to any of you, let me or your own dykes know, and we'll solve it."

"Thanks, sir," said one of the other Rats.

"Well, Rats, I need to head back down to do some work on the school paper. It's called *The VMI Cadet,* and you'll see my name in there somewhere most weeks. Any of you ever heard of a fictional Ernest Hemingway character named Nick Adams?"

They all shook their shaved heads from left to right, and as I started to head out the door, I said, "Well, you have now."

—⚏—

I headed down to the *Cadet* office in the basement of Barracks and quickly typed up the short column I'd already written in my head. It would run in the second issue of the new VMI year, and I wanted to relate what it felt like to be a First and reminisce a bit about what it had been like to get a VMI ring, be a Third, and experience Rat year. I can still recall the feel of the keys on the *Cadet's* tan IBM Selectric and the smell of that little container of Wite-Out when I made a mistake.

There were many mistakes back then. There still are. They're easy to erase on my laptop today. They're much tougher to erase in life.

I had to hustle back to our room to throw on my blouse for SRC and our first supper as Firsts, so I didn't have time to talk to Chip and Bradley about their dykes. I knew that would come soon enough and we would begin sharing stories about our dykes' many failures and successes those first few painful months as Rats and cadets.

That first SRC at the mess hall as a First was anticlimactic, as happened many times when you regained simple privileges you'd lost when you came to VMI. As Firsts we were able to walk around the mess hall at will, allowing us to check on our dykes or get extra food for ourselves or other lower classmen.

My meals with the Shields family and elsewhere in the Fan had made me somewhat judgmental on the food front, and the mess hall's offerings hadn't improved much. As Firsts we were allowed to go uptown to eat almost any night we wanted to, and though money would be tight for me and Bradley, I knew the three of us would be heading up to Spanky's many evenings.

We used the next day to finish organizing our uniforms, military gear, and room for the coming year, with classes starting the following morning. I'm sure Chip felt it the most, but the pressure of keeping his marriage and impending fatherhood a secret added an extra burden to what should have been our easiest and best year at the Institute. However, we all knew that it was a burden well worth it if we could somehow get Chip to graduation.

Virginia Elizabeth Shields was born on August 20, 1983. Chip didn't get to see her for the first time until more than a week later during the first weekend we could leave VMI. Bradley and I finally met her two weeks after that when the three of us went back to Monument Avenue once again. We would go to Richmond as often as possible that fall.

Virginia had Chip's dark hair and sparkling gray eyes, along with Beth's pretty and petite face and high cheek bones. She was a happy baby from the start and seemed to revel in an essentially secluded life on Monument Avenue with Beth and her grandparents. Back at VMI we joked that she probably wasn't sure who her father was, with Win, Chip, me, and Bradley all playing that role at times in the coming months.

Other than the constant weight of Chip's secret, first semester went well. As Firsts we had many more privileges and quite a few less commitments, leading to more time than ever to hang around Barracks, help out our dykes, and talk about what we'd be doing after graduation.

That long-ago fall our post-graduation plans seemed pretty simple. We'd all graduate, go to our branch's officer's basic school, and then head off to our first assignments. Back then you took a commission if it was offered and committed to at least three years of service in the army and typically more in the other branches. I didn't think about the concept of "service" much back then. I do now.

Beth and Chip's plan was to reveal their marriage and baby the day of graduation and move on with their lives. At least that was the thinking that fall many years ago.

We had more weekend passes as Firsts, and the three of us spent most of them back in Richmond. Our weekends with Mr. and Mrs. Shields were better than ever in many ways. I didn't think it was possible, but they treated Bradley and me more like sons than ever. And now they had a daughter and granddaughter as well.

It was difficult, but Beth and Virginia essentially stayed sequestered on Monument Avenue. We knew it was best, given Richmond's well-known and often correct rumor mill.

One Saturday Mr. Shields took Chip, Bradley, and me to a reception at the Country Club of Virginia, and we even drank Virginia Gentleman with Mr. Shields and several of his VMI classmates down at the Commonwealth Club once as well. Though I see Win Shields often now, I haven't been back to the CCV or the Commonwealth Club since my First Class year at VMI.

Again the three of us spent Thanksgiving weekend back in Richmond, eating almost the same exact meal we'd enjoyed the previous three years. Sarah Shields seemed happier than ever during these times, when the house was filled with vibrant young men, a blossoming young woman and mother, and a grandchild. All of us appreciated her cooking and motherly love, her son and her husband, and the home she'd originally created for just the three of them.

I'll say I still had a bit of a boyhood crush on Sarah Shields. Win, Chip, and I never spoke of it, but there were times when Sarah gave me a look that said she knew. Decades later, I will admit that I can still have a Mrs. Robinson moment when I see her after one of my many long absences from Monument Avenue. I know Win and Chip would forgive me.

—◊—

Back at VMI after Thanksgiving, our three dykes seemed to be handling Rat and class pressures well. We'd all sworn we'd do anything we could to get them through Rat year, but they had only encountered the typical Rat issues thus far. As I'd advised and prodded him like my dyke had done with me, Cliff was getting pretty good grades and generally avoiding the problems that could get Rats run off Post without a chance af ever wearing the ring.

I'd told Cliff and his roommates that they'd appreciate the time right before and during exams, when some of the pressure on Rats — and cadets in general — lessened. "This almost feels like a real school, Nick," I remember him telling me in mid-December down in our room.

"Tell me that again in January when you've lost at least twenty more of your BRs over Christmas and certain guys are determined to get rid of at least another twenty more before Breakout."

"When do you think we'll get out of the Ratline?"

"I'm not the guy to ask, and I guarantee you'll hear plenty of false rumors before it happens. However, I wouldn't plan on getting out any time before March."

"That seems forever from now."

"It'll seem like it's gone quickly once it happens. Most things here — and in life, apparently — seem to work that way. At least that's what my dyke and grads like Chip's dad told me. In some ways I couldn't believe how quickly we got our rings. But it also seemed to take forever as it was happening to the three of us."

"Well, there's nothing that will keep me from getting out of the Ratline — and getting a ring," Cliff half-convincingly said, echoing words I had spoken back in 1980.

"Oh, there are plenty of people and things that can do just that," I retorted with conviction. "If someone in Barracks really wants to keep you from getting a VMI ring, they can likely do it one way or another. Didn't you read *The Lords of the Discipline*?" I asked half-jokingly.

"Don't you remember you made me read it over Thanksgiving? Is that really true that someone can get rid of you if they really want to?"

"I've seen it happen, but typically the ones who leave wouldn't have made it anyway and didn't deserve to wear our ring."

"That won't happen to me. You've taught me well."

"Well, we can only do so much. You're still the one doing the push-ups and taking the exams. Speaking of which, why don't we both get back to studying."

—⁓—

Exams that cold December of 1983 went well for the three of us, as well as our three dykes, and all six of us were one step closer to a VMI diploma. Our room had made it through first semester without anyone learning about Chip and Beth as far as we knew, but we were determined not to let our guard down.

—⁓—

My fourth time back in Richmond for Christmas and New Year's with the Shields family was perhaps my favorite during my cadetship. We pretty much did and ate the same things we had the previous three years, but I think I'd grown a much greater appreciation for what Mr. and Mrs. Shields had done for me and Bradley. It was also wonderful having Beth and little smiling Virginia in the mix, and it was obvious Mr. and Mrs. Shields had grown very fond of the two of them during their time together.

We ate and drank well. We talked of large and small things, and — again — spent New Year's Eve talking and dreaming of the coming year and beyond. Back then I think I still believed that talking and dreaming about things could and would make them all happen.

We drove back to VMI in my Beetle because we'd left Chip's car in Lexington over the break. Much of the talk during that drive revolved around graduation in May. Even when it was just two or three of us, we rarely spoke of Beth and Virginia at that point. But it was always in the background. One small slip by any of us, and Chip's life would be changed forever. It already had been, of course.

While we talked of graduation back in Barracks, our dykes spoke of little but Breakout. Rumors swirled that they would get out of the Ratline in late February, but I tried to keep Cliff from getting his hopes up too much. Our class had been fooled several times back in 1981, and it would likely happen to Cliff and his BRs as well.

They did, however, get out of the Ratline the first Tuesday in March. It was a long and cold day for them, but the elation on their faces as they made it to the top of that muddy hill made the months of pain somehow seem worth it.

After they'd showered up on fourth stoop, Cliff and our other two dykes came down to our room to revel in their new-found freedom. I didn't have the heart to tell them that although this was the end of one difficult period at VMI, it was simply the beginning of another of many trials that wouldn't stop until graduation and beyond.

March and April flew by, and with each passing day of successfully keeping Chip's secret, we gained confidence that we could all make it to May. However, we never let our guard down, and Chip still rarely saw Beth. He did continue calling her almost daily from the pay phones down in the Barracks basement, using many rolls of quarters.

"She's the real trooper in all of this," he said many times that year. "And so are my parents."

—∿—

Looking back it now seems inevitable that we'd have a scare concerning Chip, Beth, and little Virginia. Our careful planning couldn't possibly prevent a chance encounter and it finally occurred one April day. Virginia was actually there when it happened, but obviously doesn't remember a thing. But it's really her story more than mine and I'll let her tell it as she learned about it when she was a cadet.

—∿—

By early May and with that scare still weighing upon us, we had to gear up for exams, graduation festivities, and our lives to follow. Many of my BRs would report for active duty in all four branches of service the week after graduation, but Bradley, Chip, and I all had until July to head to our officer basic schools.

We'd gone into our whites in late March, and the weather by May was picture perfect. We had warm days where we could go for runs in shorts and t-shirts, while the nights were crisp for our almost-daily walks to and from Spanky's for pitchers of beer and sandwiches.

They had this sandwich for four called a Hindenberg, with a loaf of French bread piled high with ham, turkey, salami, melted provolone, lettuce, tomato, onions, and sauce, for something like fifteen bucks. It had become our sandwich of choice Third Class year, and the three of us still easily finished one.

The seven days preceding graduation brought exams and a general slowdown in military requirements for the entire Corps. I took an exam a day for five straight days and then had two days off before graduation. Chip and Bradley did the same, and we actually went back to Richmond for one night, with Mr. Shields breaking out some seriously smoky eighteen-year-old scotch from a distillery called Glenmorangie that I didn't appreciate then but do now.

He also dramatically pulled out four Cuban cigars for us to enjoy with our scotch. Only three were smoked. Chip never let a cigar or cigarette touch his lips. I haven't touched tobacco in more than two decades either. Not since we lost Chip.

Back at VMI the day before Saturday's graduation, Bradley got a message slip from the guard room saying that his parents and brother would actually be attending the ceremony in Cameron Hall. He called them to tell his mother that it really wasn't necessary, but she said they planned to drive up from Charleston and stay at the Hotel Roanoke the night before graduation, attend the ceremony, and then head back to South Carolina.

"I can't believe how many nights I spent in Lexington the past four years, and they will not have spent a single one in this pretty town. Of course I haven't been back to Charleston since Rat year either, so I guess we're even."

"You're not even at all," I said. "What the three of them — and especially your dad and brother — did to you is still hard to fathom. I'm not sure I'll be able to shake their tainted Citadel hands if I even walk up to them Saturday."

"Well, you're going to have to because I want both of you at my side when I see them after graduation," Bradley said firmly, staring at both of us to confirm his wishes. "You two are more my brothers than my actual brother is, and I wouldn't mind introducing your dad to mine, Chip. He's more my father now than my own dad for sure."

"My father would probably love that because he knows what they've put you through these past four years. I can't promise he won't punch your dad in the jaw and lead with his ring. Wouldn't that just be a fitting end to our cadetship?"

"Man, I'd love to see it," said Bradley, smiling.

"Me too," Chip said. "We'll see what happens, but know we're by your side long past Saturday."

We had the final parade of our cadetships on Friday afternoon, and Letcher Avenue was as packed as I recall ever seeing it for a parade. The three of us marched together one last time, and the band played "Shenandoah," a song that can still bring a tear to my eye whenever I hear it. I guess it's the Virginian in me.

We marched through Jackson Arch, where I couldn't resist looking up at that Jackson quote, "You may be whatever you resolve to be." How many other VMI boys becoming men had stared at that quote and questioned their resolve to become a VMI graduate? I certainly had at times, but I'd made it, and so had Chip and Bradley, who I saw were already breaking ranks and heading to our room to shed everything but ducks and t-shirts for the courtyard mudslide we knew was next.

Someone had opened the fire hydrant, and a corner of the courtyard was flooded and muddy. Our well-liked First Class president, who would eventually follow in his father's and grandfather's footsteps as the president of a multimillion-dollar Fortune 500 business back in Richmond, was the first to take a running start and do a belly flop into the mud, sliding a good ten feet before coming to a sloppy halt near the first stoop's rusty railings.

When he jumped up with hands held above his head, his face was covered in mud, and you could only see the whites of his eyes and teeth as the Second Class banged their rings on the railings up on second stoop, the Thirds jealously watched, and the Fourths gave the Class of 1984 a final Old Yell.

A bunch of our classmates went next, and that corner of the courtyard quickly became filled with Firsts in and around the mud. Bradley, Chip, and I ran side by side toward the mud, nailing our belly flops and slides simultaneously and then rolling around in the mud like the three happy pigs we were at that moment.

We got up laughing and simultaneously saw Mr. and Mrs. Shields standing with some other people over by the railing in the corner of Barracks down by our room. They were laughing and waving at us, but the other couple and younger man didn't seem to be enjoying our fun. "Those are my parents and brother," Bradley said softly from behind to the two of us. "They must have decided to come early or something."

Covered in mud and still beaming, the three of us walked over to the railing, and Mr. Shields gave us each a white hand towel he had grabbed from our room. Thankfully Mr. Shields was the first to speak, saying, "Bradley, we've just met your parents and brother. They came in early from Charleston to see your last parade."

Bradley didn't move or say a word. He just kept staring directly at Mr. Shields. Chip stepped closer to the railing and stuck out his hand to Mr. Bell, saying, "Mr. Bell, I'm Chip Shields. Sorry for the muddy hand. I've been Bradley's roommate all four years. This is Nick Adams. Same with him."

"Hello, Chip and Nick. This is my wife, Margaret Bell, and my son, Scott. He's Citadel Class of 1975, and I'm '53."

"I'm VMI '60, and these three are about to be 1984 Virginia Military Institute graduates," said Mr. Shields. "You should be very proud, Bob."

Mr. Bell didn't say a word but simply stared at Bradley, who continued to look straight at Mr. Shields.

"We were going to take these young men up to Spanky's tonight for supper," said Mr. Shields. "Can you three join us?"

"I'm afraid we can't. One of my Citadel classmates teaches army ROTC here, and we'd planned to take Bradley out to dinner with him. We're spending the night with him as well."

"I'd rather go with the Shields and my roommates, sir," said Bradley to his father, though he still wouldn't look him in the eye.

"OK, son. I didn't expect a warm welcome from you here in Lexington. We'll just see you tomorrow morning after graduation to say good-bye before we head back to God's country."

With that Mr. Bell led his wife and son out Jackson Arch. No one in our now smaller group said a word until Mr. Shields quietly said, "How bout this VMI family finds Beth and little

Virginia and heads uptown for a Southern family celebration at Spanky's where a Hindenberg just might be in our future?"

Bradley audibly breathed out a sigh of relief and seemed to thank Mr. Shields with his eyes before looking around at all of us and saying, "I'd like that very much."

After we found Beth and Virginia by Jackson Statue we all packed into the Shields Volvo for the short drive uptown. We had to wait for a table at Spanky's but enjoyed what I thought might be our last beer for some time at their weathered bar — or in Lexington, for that matter. We'd discussed bringing Beth and Virginia earlier and had decided it would be OK at that point. In retrospect I guess Chip still could have been caught — again — but he wasn't.

The four men shared a Hindenberg, while Mrs. Shields and Beth picked at salads with grilled chicken breast. Perched on alternating laps, Virginia noisily nibbled on anything we gave her.

Of course Mr. Shields paid, saying, "Once you three start making some money as junior officers, I'll expect you to pick up a tab or two."

"No amount of money could repay you and Mrs. Shields for what you've done for us these past four years," Bradley said. "There's no place I'd rather be than with the five of you on our last night in Lexington."

"I wish I'd said that first, Bradley. Here's to the three of you, Shields family of Monument Avenue. Thank you for letting these two family-challenged boys and this mother and child be a part of the extended Shields clan."

"It's been our pleasure and honor," said Sarah Shields, looking at each of us in turn before turning to Chip. "I know Chip has been thankful to have two brothers — and for us to have two more sons and a daughter and granddaughter we couldn't have imagined four years ago."

The seven of us piled into the wagon to head back to Post. I'm not sure they'd even invented child safety seats for the likes of little Virginia yet, so she squirmed in my lap in the back seat for the short drive back up Letcher Avenue.

Back in front of Jackson Arch, we all hugged Beth, Virginia, and Mrs. Shields good night and shared yet another firm handshake with her smiling husband, who knew all too well what we were feeling at that moment. As I walked through Jackson Arch for one of the last times for many years, I wondered if Win and Sarah could even begin to know what they'd done for me and Bradley — and even Beth and Virginia. I hoped so.

We talked late into that cool May night, with each of us lying face up on our cots and reminiscing about our four years at VMI and the years to come. We'd already discussed getting together after graduation but knew military commitments would make it difficult. In fact, I would not see Bradley or Chip again for almost five years once we went our separate ways after graduation.

Saturday morning was crystal clear, and it would have been a perfect day for graduation on the Parade Ground like they once did when weather permitted. Graduation was now always held in Cameron Hall, our basketball facility that had opened a couple of years earlier. In a typical example of VMI alumni success and loyalty, Cameron Hall was mostly funded by the Cameron brothers of Wilmington, North Carolina — 1938 and 1942 graduates.

Decades later the sparkling new baseball diamond would be funded by two other VMI grads from Richmond, and I still get back there for several games a year. I sit in almost the exact same location I once did as a cadet, but the stadium chairs are much more comfortable — as is my much more ample natural cushioning.

Cameron Hall didn't provide the same atmosphere as the Parade Ground, but none of us really cared when we walked across the stage to receive our diplomas.

In some ways that singular moment went way too quickly. I was certainly glad when my name was called and I took my diploma from the dean before shaking hands with the supe and saying thanks, but I had to grab the railing on the way down the steps because my legs were so shaky.

Both Bradley and Chip followed minutes later, with Bradley finding me for a fist pump as he headed offstage and Chip doing the same after acknowledging his parents, Beth, and Virginia with his raised diploma. I can still picture the moment we threw our white gloves into the air to signify the end of graduation and the beginning of our post-VMI lives.

Outside of Cameron Hall on North Main, Mr. and Mrs. Shields, Beth, and Virginia were standing with Bradley's parents and brother. "Congrats, VMI men," Mr. Shields yelled, stepping forward to share handshakes and hugs with Chip and then Bradley and me in turn. Mrs. Shields and Beth, with Virginia in her arms, came next, with hugs for each of us.

Bradley's father walked up to him and awkwardly stuck his hand out to him without a word. Bradley quickly shook his father's hand and then walked over to his mother for a brief hug and another stiff handshake with his brother.

Mr. Bell then said, "Well, it's a long drive back to South Carolina, and we should get going. Congratulations to each of you, and best of luck in the future. Good-bye, Bradley."

With those brief words and another quick and awkward handshake between father and son, the three of them walked away without another word or show of emotion. Mr. Shields, however, didn't miss a beat, saying, "Well, you five, what's next? Want to introduce Beth and Miss Virginia to the supe?"

"Come on, Dad," Chip laughed. "How bout a big lunch at the Southern Inn once we get into civvies and grab our gear?"

We all nodded in agreement and took the steps back up the steep hill one final time to Barracks. We'd already packed up everything back in our room, leaving virtually anything related to VMI behind. Each of us had decided to keep a single pair of cadet cufflinks. I still have mine.

We took the Shields wagon downtown again because we knew parking for two cars might be difficult, but we ended up getting a spot right out front. We hadn't eaten at the Southern Inn very often during our cadetship. Spanky's was more our style.

I can still remember several details about lunch that day. Mr. Shields ordered a bottle of Bordeaux — 1981 Lafite Rothschild to honor our dykes. The four of us then ordered steaks, while Mrs. Shields had a Caesar salad with just a bite of Mr. Shields' rib eye. Beth had salmon, which she shared in nibbles with Virginia.

"Here's to you, men," Mr. Shields toasted us. "May you wear the VMI ring proudly and never forget the friendships and bonds you've forged here."

The six adults clinked wine glasses, with each of us also tapping Virginia's plastic cup of juice. We lingered over lunch, and Mr. Shields ordered another bottle of the same '81 Lafite.

I can still taste that second bottle, but I can also hear what Bradley told us while we shared it. I'll leave it to Virginia to say what Bradley revealed, but know that the only thing it changed for any of us was just a new way to look at some of our many memories of our time at VMI together.

Afterward we drove back up to Post so Chip and I could get our cars behind the Marshall Museum, which I'd finally revisited the week before graduation. Bradley and I drove back to Richmond in my little Beetle, the Shields took their Volvo and all of our stuff, and Chip, Beth, and Virginia took his wagon. That day, I wasn't sure when I'd return to Lexington or to VMI. I'll let Virginia tell the rest of our story.

Part Two: Virginia
2000–2001

My name is Virginia Shields, and I wear the ring. This is my story and the story of several other Brother Rats and VMI grads — male and female — who also wear what I like to call "Virginia's ring."

I'm a VMI woman, standing in tight ranks with several thousand men and now a few hundred women who have come before and after me. My mother, grandparents, and close friends call me Ginny or simply Gin. Call me a Shedet instead of a Keydet if you will. I've been called much worse.

I'm often introduced as the daughter of Chip Shields, but he died years before I would become a Rat, get my ring, and graduate from VMI. I'm also the daughter of Beth Shields, who drove me to VMI in August of 2000 with a man I've called Uncle Nick since I can remember speaking.

They brought me to VMI in mid-August because I was on a cross country scholarship through VMI's Keydet Club. I'd just turned seventeen — I skipped a grade — and thought I could outrun anyone or anything. I quickly learned I couldn't.

I came to VMI a week earlier than all of my Brother Rats so I could start practice with the team. Yes, we all called each other Brother Rat — male or female.

Uncle Nick and others like Pat Conroy have explained the military school experience more eloquently than I will be able to, but all of us who wear the ring have similarly shared experiences. The initial haircut. The yelling. The straining. The push-ups. The sweat parties. Breakout to become a class. Third Class doldrums in the classroom and in Barracks, despite being allowed to have a radio. Getting our rings. And graduation for most — but not all — who earned their rings.

But these are just words written more than a decade after I graduated from VMI. All of these shared experiences with my Brother Rats were intertwined with very personal experiences, both good and bad. My mother and dear Uncle Nick are the only two who know most of what I went through at VMI — but not everything. I still have trouble putting some of it into words and may never do so.

I was in the fourth group of women who entered VMI. Some of those groundbreaking women who came before me had actually already graduated from VMI by the time I arrived because they were transfer students and only needed two or so years at VMI to earn their degrees.

Those I admire the most, however, spent all four years at VMI and walked across that Cameron Hall stage with more than two hundred men in 2001. There were just two handfuls of them. They were my dyke's class. Laura Reilly, VMI Class of 2001, was my dyke.

Before the women of 2001 arrived back in 1997, the administration tried to rid Barracks of long-used words like "dyke," "period," "raped ducks," the F-word, the P-word, and many others. They even tried to stop the decades-old use of "Brother Rat," a reference to classmates that's repeated hundreds of times during a cadetship and at VMI reunions ten, twenty-five, and even fifty long years after graduation.

But those early females, like my dyke Laura, wouldn't and didn't let that happen. From their first day at VMI, they screamed, "Brother Rat," as loud as they could — and never stopped. Three Augusts later we did the same.

I know it's a cliché, but I came to VMI very much a girl and left as a woman. Each of my four years at VMI shaped me in many ways I didn't recognize at the time. This was especially true my Rat year, thanks to Laura.

The very best thing that ever happened to me at VMI was lucking into getting Laura Reilly as my dyke. She helped me navigate the very rough waters of the Ratline and life well beyond Barracks. I owe her much. Our country owes her even more.

Laura came up to the fourth stoop to find me the day the Corps returned to Barracks, which also marked the end of our Hell Week. My room of four females jumped to attention and strained when she entered the room, but she quietly said, "At ease, Rats," and asked which one of us was Virginia Shields.

I immediately shouted, "Me, ma'am!"

She came over to me, stuck out her right hand, and said, "I'm Laura Reilly, and I'm your dyke. You're safe with me, Virginia."

"Yes, ma'am," I yelled.

"None of you need to use 'ma'am' around me, Rats. Those of us still in the Class of 2001 — especially the few of us females

— are your friends. We'll help you make it through the Ratline to your rings and your diplomas," she said firmly, holding up her large chunk of gold for all of us to see.

"Thanks, Ms. Reilly," I said. "We haven't had too many friends this past week, female or male. They all seem to hate us — even the women upperclassmen — and want us to leave."

"You'll see that's mostly just a show," Laura responded. "It's what was done to them, and they're just continuing the tradition to quickly weed out those who should never have come here in the first place. Did you lose many Brother Rats yet? I haven't checked."

"We've heard ten have left, including two girls, Ms. Reilly," I said.

"Don't call me 'Ms.' in here, Virginia. I'm Laura to all of you in this room and down in our room on the first stoop. But don't forget that Mr. and Ms. or sir and ma'am pretty much everywhere else for everyone but your BRs."

"Thanks, Laura," I said, smiling for the first time in days.

—⟋⟍—

I'll always remember the day I met Laura. She seemed so self-assured. Maybe it was the uniform, but I think it was much more than that.

I saw her in civvies several times that year when she was heading away for a weekend. She had short blonde hair, a mouth that always seemed close to a smile, and sky-blue eyes that seemed to give her an air of assurance. Just by her looks and bearing, it just seemed like she would succeed at whatever was at hand and so would the people at her side. I was one of those people for too short of a time.

Laura left us after telling me her Old Barracks room number down on first stoop and that I should be in her room the next morning no later than ten minutes before breakfast formation. "We'll get it down to five minutes within a week," she said as she closed the door behind her.

"Wow, she's impressive," I remember one of my roommates saying — the one who didn't return after first semester. "I wish our dykes would come find us."

"I'm sure they will, Brother Rat. But I do feel lucky getting Laura. She didn't say it, but her younger sister and I ran against each other in high school. That's how we connected and I became her dyke."

"Well, I just hope our dykes are half as nice," my other roommate, Patty, said. She'd be my roommate all four years at VMI, surviving the constant, "Patty is a Patsy" comments — and another word starting with P when officers weren't around to supervise male cadets — and even a few females who often rivaled the guys when it came to foul mouths.

—⚹—

We formed as a full Corps of Cadets for the first time that night, with the Rat Battalion out in front of New Barracks and Marshall Statue and the rest of the Corps outside of Old Barracks facing Jackson Statue and around the corner at Washington Statue. As I stood there with more than a thousand cadets on that hot summer evening, I couldn't believe this was only the start of the second week of the Ratline. My mother and Nick had prepared me well, but the lack of sleep and constant pressure of possibly making a mistake — and paying for it mentally and physically — had already taken its toll.

As Nick had predicted, going to classes proved to be a relief from the Ratline. Like him I'd chosen English as my major. I even planned to write for *The VMI Cadet* if they let me as a Third.

Academic time provided a creative release to be as singular as was possible at the Institute. The Ratline was meant to mold us into VMI cadets that were as similar as possible — at least in appearance and most group actions. That was certainly true of our uniforms and general bearing on Post, but there were still differences.

Laura's hair had been shaved just like the boys when she matriculated in 1997. They'd eased up on that in following years, and we'd been allowed to get our hair shorn just above our ears and collars for Rat year.

In attempting to be as much like the boys as possible, some of the girls in my class had requested that their heads get shaved as well. They ended up getting even more grief from the male cadets — and some upper class female ones — and I was glad I'd gone with the more feminine haircut VMI required of female Rats that year.

I have my father's hair. It's dark and thick and I always think of my dad when I run my fingers through it. He'd had that same thick hair shaved off as a Rat, but it had returned as thick as ever. As he aged his hair never thinned like Uncle Nick's. Well, at least until he lost it all.

My mother tells me he loved running his fingers through my hair when I was a toddler. On many early mornings during the Ratline, when we'd heard they'd be kicking in our doors for yet another run or sweat party, I thought of him lying awake in Barracks awaiting the same fate back in 1980. He couldn't run his fingers through his hair like I did as a Rat on many mornings, but I'm betting he rubbed his head's stubble and dreaded the kick on the door that every cadet remembers the rest of his or her life.

I also have my dad's gray eyes and couldn't help but notice the resemblance in color when I looked in the mirror the first time I tried on my blouse. Though I'd been told by Nick about the coincidence, it was still startling how my eyes seemed to perfectly match the gray of my blouse.

—m—

Of course Rat year was difficult physically and mentally, but I'd been prepared on both fronts by my mother, my grandfather, Uncle Nick, and even by my father in some ways years before I knew I was going to VMI. That was before he left us.

My Ratline's late summer and fall was as unremarkable as possible, and I tried to keep it that way. Sure I got yelled at daily and did thousands of push-ups, but I never got the sense that anyone was trying to run me out of school like they seemed to be pursuing with a few select Brother Rats, both female and male. We had the usual attrition those first few months, but I don't think anyone in my room seriously thought about leaving. At least not then.

In many ways I still believe it's harder to leave VMI than it is to stay. I know it would have been nearly impossible for me to call my mother — or Nick — to say I wanted to come home. Leaving wasn't really an option, and I think it was and is best that way. Once you started thinking about leaving, you had one foot out your Barracks door, and it got much easier to take the other step toward Jackson Arch and change your life forever.

We had one girl in our class from Waynesboro who took that first step early one October morning when they had us out on the fourth stoop doing push-ups. The Cadre's plan was that a group of about a hundred Rats had to do a total of 2001 push-ups before we could go back to our rooms.

The girl from Waynesboro had come to VMI totally unprepared and couldn't complete three push-ups in succession. Our group had gotten to a total of 1999, but Cadre wouldn't let any of us go back to our rooms until she had completed the final two push-ups.

While they pushed her physically and mentally to complete those two pushups, they drilled all of us on Rat Bible knowledge. The previous summer, Uncle Nick had given me his Rat Bible from 1980, saying there were a few things that would likely still be in my Rat Bible come August. He assured me that one of them was knowing the ten cadets that died at New Market in 1864 and he was right. I'd memorized them by July, along with other minutia, and that was just what I found myself reciting for Cadre while my Brother Rat from Waynesboro went through her ordeal right in front of me:

Corporal Atwill
Private Haynes
Private Jefferson
Private McDowell
Private Stanard
Sergeant Wheelwright

Sergeant Cabell
Private Crockett
Private Hartsfield
Private Jones

When the girl from Waynesboro finally somewhat completed a second pushup with all of us shouting, "Brother Rat," in support, they let the rest of us go back to our rooms. But one Cadre member kept her out on the stoop straining just outside our room. Within minutes, we could hear the RDC president screaming at her. We all knew his voice well by then.

"Are those tears, Rat? They look like tears to me, and don't forget our Honor Code when you answer, Rat!"

"Yes, sir. Tears, sir."

"Do you miss your daddy, Rat?"

"Yes, sir. He was Class of 1975, sir!"

"Well, good for him cause you're in the Class of Nothin, and that's where we plan for you to stay. You can't even do a couple of push-ups with your Brother Rats. Why don't you go home to Daddy? Would you like to call him right now and tell him to come and pick you up?"

"Yes, sir!"

At this point, I couldn't resist peeking out our door through our just-cleaned window. The RDC president had actually gone from yelling in this girl's ear from behind to getting directly in her face by straddling the railing and standing on the edge of the stoop three stories above the courtyard. He'd lean in to her face and yell at her and then lean back to hang out over the courtyard. I honestly thought there was a chance the girl would crack and try to push him out into thin air.

Instead he released one hand from the rail, held it out to her like he was holding a phone, and said, "Take this and call your daddy. Tell him to come and get you and that you'll never wear the ring. Do it, Rat!"

Her right hand shaking, she pretended to take the phone from the Cadre member and put her still-trembling hand to her ear. "Dad!" she yelled. "Please come and get me!"

The RDC president then pretended to rip the phone from her hand and slam it down on the metal railing, with the banging of his ring seeming to rattle our door's window — and my nerves. I stepped away from the window then, but heard him yell, "Go pack your bags, Rat. Your daddy's coming to get you and take you out of Barracks and my life forever."

And that's exactly what happened. The girl's roommate later told me she came back to their room crying and shaking and actually started frantically packing. She didn't go to DRC formation at lunchtime or her afternoon class. Instead she went down to the pay phones to call her father in Waynesboro.

I can only imagine his thoughts during that drive west on 64 and down 81. I never wanted to put my mother or Nick through that same drive — and I didn't, even when I was sorely tempted in coming months and years. Everyone was tempted to leave at least once and they're fooling themselves if they say otherwise.

For Parents Weekend in October, we played Furman in football. My mother came, of course, but so did two other people I'd basically thought of as surrogate parents since I was very young — and especially after my father died when I was eight.

Nick Adams and Bradley Bell were my father's two room-mates at VMI all four years he was there. Though they went their separate ways after graduation, they stayed connected like the blood brothers I'd always heard they were. When my father died, they both returned to Richmond for the funeral and liter-ally shared blood from their ring fingers with mine to link us forever as well.

I know that may sound like a corny thing now — espe-cially with a grieving eight-year-old girl — but that's just the way they were and are. In an ironic twist of fate that wasn't lost on anyone who experienced it or heard about it, my father spent a year battling lung cancer before it got the best — and worst — of him.

Though tobacco provided his grandparents and parents and ultimately my mother and me with millions of dollars, my father never smoked a single cigarette, cigar, or even a joint, if I'm to believe my mother. Many a night back at my grandparents' house on Monument Avenue or in my hay at VMI I found myself won-dering what kind of God would take my father from us in his twenties while allowing lifetime smokers to escape unscathed far into the old age I'd never get to share with my dad. Of course those smokers made the Shields family wealthy, but that didn't help my father, my mother, or me.

After my father died and I mixed even more Shields blood with his best friends, Nick and Bradley became my surrogate fathers. Especially Nick. He lived just down the street from us — at least when he was in Richmond.

I'd grown up in New York City before my dad got cancer and we moved back to Richmond. We moved in with my grand-parents, who welcomed all three of us like children. I lived there until I came to VMI, and my mother's still there, sleeping in my dad's childhood room.

—◊—

My mom and Nick and Bradley were waiting for me out on the Parade Ground after our Saturday morning parade. I hadn't seen any of them since my mom had dropped me off in August, so I couldn't help tearing up as I made my way past all the other parents and cadets to Nick's VW wagon

My mother was putting out paper plates for our tailgate party but abruptly dropped them on the table when she saw me coming. We shared a long hug — my first truly human touch since I shook hands with Laura in August — and her hands immediately went to my hair, running them through my short black locks after I removed my gray cap.

"Your hair looks great, Ginny," she said, taking a step back to slowly look me up and down. "And so does that bright white uniform."

"Thanks, Mom. I think," I said, returning her smile.

Nick and Bradley had stayed back at the car to let us have our time together first, but I couldn't help pulling away from my mother to go to them. Nick was first, hugging me tightly and then pulling back to look me straight in the eyes and say, "Hello, Rat Shields. Nice haircut. How come they didn't shave it off like the boy Rats?"

"You know they don't do that anymore, Uncle Nick. Hey, Uncle Bradley," I said, hugging him and stepping back for the requisite eye-locking I still found awkward. "Are you going to give me grief about this haircut as well?"

"I'll leave that to Nick. He always tried to wear his hair longer while he was here, and look where that got him," Bradley said as he rubbed Nick's closely shaved and nearly bald head.

"Hey now," Nick said, swiping Bradley's hand away. "I have an old Corps haircut, while Miss Virginia here looks like she could be on the cover of Cosmo. Well, maybe not with that uniform getup."

"What? Y'all don't like me in white?" I asked, while trying to strike a model-like pose. "You should see me in my gray blouse. I turn heads every time I walk through W&L. Well, I actually haven't been allowed to walk downtown yet, but heads will turn when I do."

"You look great," my mom said, again running her hand through my hair.

"You hungry, Rat?" asked Uncle Nick.

"No sir," I replied, without thinking, but then recovered with a joke by saying, "I think I'd rather eat down in the mess hall than have one of your overcooked burgers that I can see — and smell."

"Now stop that sir stuff, Virginia," said Nick, laughing. "You've obviously been calling way too many people sir and ma'am lately." Turning back to the grill, he added, "I know these burgers aren't going to be nearly as good as I remember your grandfather making right here on this Parade Ground during our first Parents Weekend say, oh, twenty years ago. In fact, that's when I met your grandparents, Virginia, God bless em."

"Nick offered to bring them with us from Richmond today," said my mom. "But your grandfather just wasn't up to it, Ginny. You know he'd be here if he could. Nick has promised to cook up this exact same meal for them when we're back in Richmond tomorrow night."

"Well, I'll get to see them at Thanksgiving, and Grandma can make her huge turkey with all the fixings. Uncle Nick, are you and Uncle Bradley going to be in Richmond for Thanksgiving?"

"You know I wouldn't miss it, but Bradley just told me he was heading to Charleston this year. Something about a better invite."

"I was kidding about the better invite back in Charleston, but I am actually heading back there this year as of now. At least for Thanksgiving. We'll see about Christmas. The truth is my father invited me to their house, and it's sorta hard to say no to that even after all we've been through. Or, actually, after all we've not been through."

"That sounds like a story that needs to be told over a beer downtown after the game," said Nick. "Can you go out to dinner with us after the game, Rat?" he asked, turning back around and pointing his dripping metal spatula at me.

"I've heard we can go as long as we're with a parent, so I think so. We might even get to stay out later if we win."

"That's the way it was for us as well, and I think we did win on Parents Weekend back in eighty. But I couldn't go out to dinner because my parents weren't here and they wouldn't let me go with your grandparents, Gin.

"Little did I know that Win and Sarah would become my mother and father in every sense of the word except birthing this big butt of mine," he laughed, patting his rear end. "Back then it just seemed like yet another stab in the back to a nineteen-year-old orphan."

"I see you're still playing the orphan card, poor little Nick," said Bradley. "Gin's grandparents have been better parents to you than my actual ones. I might as well have been an orphan for as little contact as I've had with them — or my brother. Thanksgiving will sure be interesting. My brother's bringing his wife and two teenagers, whom I've met all of once. I don't have the balls to bring William — at least not yet. Oops, pardon my French, Virginia."

"What, you don't think I've heard the word balls once or twice in Barracks, Uncle Bradley?" I laughingly asked. "I'll have to ask my French professor what the translation is for testicles," I added. "Seriously, Uncle Bradley, I think you should take William to meet your family. You're going to have to tell them that you're gay sometime."

"I know, I know," Bradley nodded at all of us. "Y'all have been so welcoming to William, but I just don't think that would be the case with my family after all these years. We'll see how Thanksgiving goes when it's just me. Maybe Christmas."

"When did you tell everyone you were gay, Uncle Bradley?" I asked. "Y'all have never told me."

"That's an easy one," he replied. "I told everyone here, plus your father, on graduation day. I'd tried to get up the nerve our entire First Class year, but could never find the right time. We were having lunch at the Southern Inn and I think it was that second bottle of wine that Win ordered that finally loosened my tongue. That may be what it takes to tell my family as well, after all these years."

"Well you really need to tell them, Uncle Bradley, but OK, all you orphans," I said, changing the subject. "This child is hungry, and I only have a half hour before I have to be back in Barracks to march down to the stadium with the Corps."

"Speaking of Barracks," said Bradley. "Where's your room on fourth stoop?

"We're in Old Barracks, Uncle Bradley. Room 414."

Uncle Nick snapped his head up from the grill and said, "Incredible. You know we were in 441 that first year in New Barracks, right Virginia? What an ironic play on numbers across the years."

"That is pretty wild, Uncle Nick," I said. "I'm learning that this place is full of ironies."

"Well your father sure loved ironies like that, Gin," said Bradley as he unloaded another folding table and some chairs from Uncle Nick's wagon for us to set the table and eat a quick lunch.

As expected the hamburgers were perfectly cooked. Uncle Nick said he'd gotten the juicy burger recipe from a chef in Manhattan who put a tablespoon of butter in the center of each patty to melt and keep the meat moist while the burgers grilled. The sandwiches and conversation sure beat mess hall food and all of the yelling.

—⁕—

We lost the game, but they still announced in Barracks that Rats who had parents visiting could go out to eat with them and that we didn't have to be back on Post until nine. Mom had packed pretzels and other snacks to have out on the Parade Ground after the game, and I brought Laura out with me to meet the three of them.

Everyone was intrigued by my dyke and peppered her with questions about being in the first class of females in Barracks. I can remember standing there in awe of this woman who seemed so much more mature than me, watching her and listening to her answers as she looked each of them in the eye to relate various stories — both good and bad — about her cadetship thus far.

I'd heard many of the tales back in her room those first two months, but I'd never heard her say what she told all of us that day: "It's never been about being in the first group of females for me. It's always been about getting a diploma you can't get anywhere else and using the experience to serve others."

As I watched Laura walk back to Barracks after declining my mother's offer to join us for dinner, I found myself thinking that it was the first time I'd heard someone speak of the word "service" in that way. When I think about it now, she was likely referring to both military service in the traditional sense and service to society as well.

Laura truly saw her experience at VMI as a way of preparing her to serve — whether it was her country, her soldiers, or others. She'd ultimately make a sacrifice that sometimes came with service in the name of freedom, but the world was a different place on that brisk fall day back in 2000 before everything changed less than a year later.

After packing up Nick's post-game tailgating gear, we drove downtown to Spanky's. While we ate our sandwiches, Mom, Nick, and Bradley all regaled me with memories of many meals there, including several about my father's love of good food, beer, and company.

"We chowed down at this very table with your father many times," said Nick. "And we he often ate at that big table over there when your grandparents were in town and took all of us out to dinner. The first time, I hadn't had a beer since the day I came to VMI and felt drunk after just one glass from the pitcher. Your grandfather kept pouring em for the three of us, and we were lucky to weave our way back to fourth stoop without getting stopped in the Ratline."

"Yep," said Bradley. "Your dad could sure drink some beer, Gin. So can your grandfather, now that I think about it. Can you believe that the drinking age was eighteen back then, and that even that minimum wasn't strictly enforced? And that your grandfather probably had a cigarette lit throughout dinner on many of our meals here? That was before he finally gave them up for good. The cigarettes, I mean. Not the beer — or the bourbon or cigars for that matter."

"I can believe it, y'all. Grandma wouldn't let him smoke in the house, so I used to go out in the backyard with him to ask about Daddy and VMI. He was the very first person I told that I wanted to try VMI, and he's still one of the very few graduates who's told me he supports what I'm doing."

"Hey now, Rat," said Bradley, banging his ring on the table. "You know you have the support of Nick and me as well. What you're doing is amazing and so much harder than what we went through — no matter what we may say about the old Corps."

"He's right," said Uncle Nick. "What you — and Laura — are doing at VMI is truly a very special thing. In the short time we spent roaming around Barracks this morning, Bradley and I both feel VMI is much better thanks to the presence of women in Barracks. It was barely controlled chaos in Barracks back in the early eighties, and we could get away with practically anything with the Rats — just as long as it occurred inside Barracks walls. It seems much more organized now without being easier by any stretch."

"I've heard that from others as well," I said. "We think we have it tough, but I can't imagine what it was like for Laura during her Rat year. She still won't talk about some of the stuff that happened."

"Speaking of stuff that happened, have we ever told you about Bradley's Citadel blouse and what your father did for him and our burgeoning little class twenty years ago?"

"No. What the heck was Uncle Bradley doing with a Citadel blouse?"

"Do you want to tell it, Bradley, or should I?"

"You tell it better, Nick," said Uncle Bradley. "I can't believe we've never told Virginia this classic VMI — and Chip Shields — story."

"Well, I'm not sure where to start," Nick said while pouring another round and pointing to my mother's empty wine glass to see if she wanted another.

"Yes, I'll definitely need more wine," my mom said, sighing. "It's a long story when it's told by Nick."

"I'm usually paid by the word, smart aleck," Nick smilingly snapped back at my mom before looking at me. "Well you know Bradley's father and brother went to The Citadel and they were none too happy about him coming to VMI, right?" Nick asked me.

"Yea."

"Well they sent Bradley here to Lexington with his brother's Citadel blouse, saying he'd save the Bell family big bucks by using it instead of buying a new one at VMI.

"Can we get another chardonnay for the lady, please?" Nick asked the passing waitress and taking a gulp of beer before continuing. "On the day all of the Rats were to get fitted for blouses, Bradley told a jerk corporal named Jackson that he had brought his brother's blouse from The Citadel and he only needed to be fitted for one VMI blouse. And then all hell broke loose.

"The corporal he'd told this to grabbed the blouse from him and disappeared for what seemed like an hour while we stood around waiting for whatever very bad thing was obviously about to happen. The next thing we knew, they were kicking in the doors of the entire fourth stoop and yelling at all the Rats available to get outside by the Old Barracks railing.

"Once everybody was out there," Nick continued, smiling at the memory, "the RDC president walked into the courtyard with Bradley's blouse and yelled up at us about how Rat Bell didn't deserve to wear a VMI blouse and that he could just get his sissy butt back to South Carolina. He may have used a few stronger words than that, right, Rat Bell?" Uncle Nick asked Uncle Bradley.

"Uh, heck yea," Uncle Bradley chimed in, continuing the story. "I believe the female anatomy was involved. So, anyway, he then took a lighter and torched my blouse. I guess they'd put lighter fluid on it or something beforehand because it basically disappeared into thin black air.

"But it's what happened next that we wanted to share with you, Virginia," said my mom.

Uncle Nick then said, "Bradley was standing there straining, looking down into the courtyard, and tears were streaming down his face and onto his fatigues. The next sound we heard was your father yelling, 'Brother Rat,' at the top of his lungs. Then all of the Rats took up the chorus and came over to surround Bradley in a sea of puke green fatigues.

"There would have been maybe two or three hundred of us crammed around him ten deep," Nick continued. "It was awesome. Then we all went back to our rooms screaming, 'Brother Rat.' I truly think our class starting coming together that day, and it was all thanks to your dad."

"I'm honestly not sure I could have made it through that day without what your dad did, Virginia," said Uncle Bradley. I think the RDC president and all of the upperclassmen who witnessed it were in awe of your dad's guts out there on the fourth stoop."

"I can't believe I've never heard that story. Why didn't one of you or Dad tell it to me before now?"

"You know your dad would never have shared that story," said Uncle Bradley. "He just wasn't that type of man. And I guess that we never in our wildest dreams thought you'd be a Rat here someday and really understand what happened. I can promise you that your dad or grandfather wouldn't have sent you here with one of their blouses, though I think their uniforms and other VMI stuff are probably still up in that tightly packed attic your grandparents very loosely maintain back on Monument."

"And your family still disagrees about you coming to VMI, Uncle Bradley?" I asked.

"Oh, very much so. As y'all know, I've rarely been back to Charleston, which I dearly miss, but Beaufort has been a blessing. And I love it when men from Charleston — or their wives or boyfriends — drive down to my shop for clothes instead of going to my dad's tired old store on King Street."

"What an amazing story," I said, looking at all three of them in turn. "I think of Dad a lot back in Barracks, and I'll smile every time I put on this blouse now. Is it weird for y'all to see me in a blouse and with such short hair?"

"As a mother who struggled getting you out of torn jeans or running shorts and t-shirts, I'll take any sort of blouse. But yes, it's pretty strange sitting here with you and these two guys that I can still picture in their blouses, with their rings resting on the table just like they are now. Well, at least Bradley's wearing his ring. Aren't you ever going to get your ring resized, Nick?"

"I've got it right here in my pocket, actually," Nick said, pulling it out of his khakis and putting it on his pinkie. "I really should send it off to Jostens, but I never think of it til I get it out again for another trip here."

"Do you still have Dad's ring, Mom?"

"Of course. It's actually in his nightstand, just where he left it when he when he came back home after his last stay at MCV. He was barely strong enough by then to hold his hand up with it on."

After a pause I asked, "Do you think it might be all right if I kept it in my desk here until I get my own?"

"Your dad's already with you in so many ways, Virginia, but I think it's a great idea," said Bradley. "What do you think, Beth?"

"I love it, and so would he. I'll give it to you at Thanksgiving when you're home if we don't see you sooner than that."

"I'm actually speaking to one of my former professors' journalism classes later this month, Beth," said Uncle Nick. "Why don't I bring it to Gin then? I might even be convinced to spend the night at Moody Hall and take this pretty little Keydet out to dinner."

"I don't think I can head off Post for dinner during the week, Uncle Nick, but any visit with you would be great — especially if you come bearing a ring."

"Spoken like a true woman," said Nick. "Don't ever lose that side of you in this place. I lost a bunch of things here, and I'm still looking for one or two of them."

"I won't. Laura is a living example of surviving and thriving here while staying one hundred percent female."

"She really seems to have her act together," my mom said.

"I hope all of you will get to know her this year. I'm so lucky she's my dyke — and friend."

"You should ask her to come to Richmond sometime," said Nick. "I'm sure your grandmother could find a spare bedroom in that huge house."

"That would be great. I'll mention it to her when I stop by her room tonight. She's actually studying for a test Monday because she's hoping to get all A's for the entire year and finish as a distinguished graduate."

"What's she doing after she graduates?" asked Bradley.

"Well, she's on an army scholarship and has a four-year commitment, but she plans to be a lifer like her dad. She's hoping to be a military intelligence officer."

"Back when I was in the army, we thought combining the words 'military' and 'intelligence' was a huge contradiction," said Nick, repeating an old joke. "I guess times have changed."

"Not really. People still use that line with Laura whenever she tells them her plans, but she doesn't care. In this new world where so many insane people on the planet seem to have it out for the United States, any kind of intelligence work is going to be more important than ever. Laura really believes it's the best way she can serve her country."

"We had a BR like that back in our class, didn't we, Bradley?" Nick asked. "He was RDC president and is now a colonel somewhere at the Pentagon. He's on his way to be a general for sure. I think he may have been branched military intelligence right out of VMI as well."

"See what I mean?" I asked. "Laura's no dummy. She's trying for the branch where she thinks a woman can do the most good for our country. And it's not an act like some of the macho guys at VMI right now who run around yelling stuff about killing the enemy. Laura thinks we don't even know who the enemy is half the time and that some of them are living right here in our country."

"This is heady stuff, you three," said my mom. "Why don't you and Bradley finish off that pitcher, Nick, and let's get this girl back to Post. That big king bed back at the Hampton Inn is calling my name."

Though I honestly would have preferred walking back to Post to process the evening with the three of them, they drove me back to Jackson Arch. I hugged each of them tightly before heading back into the Ratline in Jackson Arch.

When I think back on it, all three of those long hugs felt like they were trying to let me know that they completely understood what I was going through once I passed through the stark arch and that they were trying to transmit the strength I needed to make it through the Ratline. Though I felt I already had the mental and physical strength needed, a little more never hurt on some of those long days and nights to come.

They drove away, and I hit the Ratline to Laura's room. She was alone and had only her desk lamp on to illuminate her book and notebook. "Hey, dyke. How was Spanky's?"

"It was great," I said, sitting on her hay in the dark. "My mom, Nick, and Bradley really seem to know what we go through here. We actually talked about you and your plans a bit. They're impressed."

"Well, unless I ace this test on Monday, those plans might be just that. I've heard they really look at grades when it comes to getting the army branch of your choice, and I want to make sure they're as good as possible."

"I'll take that as a sign you don't want company tonight."

"Yep, it's just me and my books tonight and probably all day tomorrow."

"Mom had asked me to see if you wanted to go to Peaks of Otter for brunch tomorrow, but I'm guessing not."

"That sounds fun, but I'm going to stick with my study plans. I'd love a rain check, though, Gin."

"You got it. And they also said they'd really like you to come to Richmond sometime. Maybe you can come for one of the breaks next semester or if I ever get a free weekend or part of one."

"That sounds great. We'll see after you get out of the Ratline and I'm feeling better about grades and getting branched Military Intelligence. I will know by then for sure. Why don't you come by the room tomorrow after you get back from brunch, and maybe we'll go for a run or something to clear my head?"

"That sounds like a plan, Laura. Study — and sleep — well dyke."

—⚏—

My three roommates were already back in our room, and I quickly joined the conversation as we all recounted eating out with our parents and other family members and friends.

None of their parents or friends had any past connection with VMI, so they'd spent the entire day and evening talking about the minutia of what we were going through. It made me glad that I had Mom, Nick, and Bradley who knew my experiences thus far and most of what was to come.

We didn't have breakfast formation on Sunday mornings, so we actually got to sleep in a bit. My roommates were meeting their parents for breakfast, but they were just heading somewhere in town. None of them had ever heard of Peaks of Otter, and I had to admit that I'd never been and only knew of it from my mom and extended family.

The three of them were waiting in the same spot they'd dropped me off the previous night, and I went through another round of hugs and locked eyes with Nick and Bradley after hugging my mom. I got in the back seat beside her, with Nick driving and Bradley sitting sideways in the front passenger seat so he could speak to all three of us at once.

"I talked Nick into taking the Blue Ridge Parkway all the way to Peaks of Otter," my mom said as we headed down the little Letcher Avenue hill through W&L and downtown. "We're going to drive over to Buena Vista and pick up the Parkway outside of town for the pretty drive down to Peaks."

We passed the Hampton Inn, and my mother said she'd slept like a baby. "I wish I had," Uncle Nick said. "Bradley snores even louder now than he did back in Barracks. I almost called your room about two this morning, Beth, to see if you wanted some company in that big king bed of yours."

The car went quiet — unusual for us when we were together — and that got me thinking about my mother and Uncle Nick. At times they did seem uniquely close. But I'd never seen them act like a couple — more like brother and sister.

Though we were blood brethren by definition, I definitely thought of Uncle Nick as a surrogate father in many ways. He'd become even more so when my dad got sick, when he stayed in Richmond for longer periods than ever before and spent lots of time at the house and hospital.

—⟋⟍—

Route 60 heads east out of Lexington and parallels the Maury River for much of the short drive to Buena Vista. My Dad, Nick, and Bradley had all regaled my mom and me about the all-female two-year school on the hill that they once called "Southern See-menary" instead of Southern Seminary. Evidently some of the girls back then had been pretty loose — at least according to the guys. It's now a pretty four-year religious-based school.

About five miles on the other side of BV, we headed up onto the Blue Ridge Parkway, with Nick saying, "I still love this road," as we made the turn to start the drive south.

"You love any road, Nick," replied my mom. "Especially if it leads to a restaurant."

"I used to love any road that led away from VMI, but now that Miss Virginia's there I feel differently. Especially if there's a meal involved that's most definitely not in the mess hall."

"Well, this road right here is leading down memory lane to a pretty darn good brunch, if I recall," said Bradley. "When were we all last here?"

"I knew you'd ask that and I was just thinking about it this morning over my first cup of that good Hampton Inn coffee," my mom said. "You two may not remember, Nick and Bradley, but we last came here in the spring of 1984. Little Virginia was just an infant."

"Are you telling me I've been to Peaks of Otter before today, Mom?"

"Yep, but you wouldn't remember," Mom laughed, looking at me.

"But I do," said Nick. "Your grandparents brought you and your mom from Richmond and stayed in Lexington while the four — I mean five — of us drove down here. I think we even took the Parkway that time as well. I was already into road trips even back then."

"I can't believe y'all took the chance of bringing Mom and me along when it meant Dad might get caught and kicked out of VMI just before graduation."

"We'd all grown a bit more gutsy by then, little girl," said Nick. "We never went out together in town, but we occasionally did trips like this that last semester and only had one close call."

"What was the close call" I asked as Nick veered his wagon into a pull-off with a sign saying it was the highest point of the Parkway in the state.

The four of us got out of the car and went to sit on one of the many stone fences along the Parkway. "So tell me about the close call, y'all," I insisted.

"I can't believe we haven't told you this story before either, Virginia," Nick said, smiling as he thought back to something that happened to all of them almost twenty years ago. "I swear I think your dad may actually have packed his duffel bag that time."

"Lemme tell this one, Nick, OK?" Bradley asked, receiving a nod from Nick to continue. "It's funny how it maybe doesn't sound like a big deal now, but it could have been.

"You see," Bradley continued, "your dad occasionally met you and your mom and your grandparents somewhere between Lexington and Richmond where it was unlikely you'd be seen. Nick and I sometimes joined y'all. We thought there'd be strength in numbers and that most people would assume your mom and you were the sister and niece of one of us."

"OK, my turn slowpoke" said Nick. "No offense, BR, but I get paid to tell stories."

"Only if they involve food," Bradley retorted. "But I guess this one does in the end."

"Yea, I guess it does involve food, doesn't it?" Nick said, laughing while staring down at the Shenandoah Valley below us. "Many of my stories do. Anyway, one April day the three of us had driven up 81 to Edelweiss in Raphine for some really good German food and beer. Your grandparents planned to meet us there with your mom and you. By the way, we need to take you there sometime, Virginia.

"Well, we got there, and y'all were already inside," Uncle Nick continued. "Chip went up to hug your mom and give you an exaggerated kiss on the top of your head before shaking hands with your granddad and hugging your grandmother. We were behind your dad at the time, so we had seen the deputy commandant in civilian clothes sitting at a corner table with his wife. Your dad hadn't noticed him yet."

"Did you freak out, Mom?"

"It didn't really hit me at first that it could be a very big deal," she quietly said, seemingly lost in the memory. "Your granddad, your dad, and your two uncles here went over to the table to say hello, leaving the three of us back at our table. The officer and his wife were just finishing their lunch, and after they left we proceeded to play out all of the mostly bad scenarios that could possibly happen. No one was in a mood to eat or drink much — even Nick here, who always seems hungry and thirsty."

"That's me," said Uncle Nick, still staring down at the Valley and lost in the memory of that long ago day. "I remember it was an unusually quiet meal for this crowd. Your mom and you and your grandparents then headed back to Richmond, and we came back to Barracks in Chip's eerily quiet car.

"We didn't hear anything the rest of that day or Sunday, but then your dad got a message slip Monday morning telling him to report to the deputy commandant's office at thirteen hundred that afternoon."

"We were waiting in our room when he got back just a couple of minutes after one with a completely blank expression."

"We didn't even ask your dad what happened," Bradley said, getting up from the stacked rock fence and walking to the edge of the ledge. "Your dad sat on his cot and told us that the deputy commandant had called him into his office and, after returning your dad's salute, simply asked if it was his wife and child he'd seen at the restaurant Saturday."

Nick picked the thread of the story back up by saying, "I think your dad had thought about how he'd answer a direct question like that many times since he'd married your mom and you'd been born, so he was prepared with a quick answer."

"'Yes, sir. That's correct, sir.' That's exactly what your dad said was his response that afternoon," Bradley continued, looking back at us on the fence and shaking his head at the memory.

"The deputy commandant — I think his name was Snider — then said that was all and dismissed your dad," said Nick. "He couldn't have been gone three minutes. We were just down the stoop from his office."

"The three of us sat around and talked about it for most of the afternoon," Uncle Nick continued. "Sorta like we are now, but not with this great view. We just assumed the deputy commandant was going to tell the higher-ups and your dad would never graduate from VMI after keeping it a secret for so long. But you already know that wasn't the case, Miss Virginia."

"So what happened?" I asked.

"Your father didn't even tell me about any of this until after the three of them had graduated," said my mom. "I was honestly scared to ask until then. I guess it's anticlimactic in retrospect, but the end of this story really is that nothing happened. Your dad kept waiting to get summoned to the supe's office at Smith Hall across the Parade Ground, but it simply just never happened."

"We didn't talk about it much that spring and just assumed the deputy commandant was going through the proper channels to confirm the marriage — and your existence, Gin," said Nick. "But come May and graduation, your dad walked across the stage to get his diploma just like the rest of us — except he had a wife and child sitting in the audience. Little did your dad know you'd walk across that stage one day as well. We'll all be there for you, you know."

"Wow," I exclaimed. "What a great story, y'all. Did anyone ever ask this Snider guy why he never did anything?"

"I think your dad was scared they might still be able to do something even after graduation," said Uncle Bradley. "Nick and I wanted to let sleeping dogs lie, so to speak. I think Snider stayed at VMI for another five years or so, but I have no idea where he is now.

"In a weird way, I think it was an honorable thing that Snider did," Uncle Bradley continued. "Your dad never said this, but I believe he thought that Snider had decided your dad had done the right thing by marrying your mom — and by answering the direct question from him with the only reply he'd decided he could provide."

"This is yet another tale about Dad you three have failed to share with me."

"They'll all come in their time, Ginny," said my mom. "The four of us went through a lot back then. In many ways your first year here is creating a new stage in our lives and a new round of stories you'll likely be sharing with other loved ones someday."

"OK, you three," said Nick. "This talk about Edelweiss has made me hungry. Let's get going before they run out of food at Peaks of Otter."

—m—

When we arrived at the parking lot in front of the main lodge and found that the restaurant wasn't very full yet, we were able to get a table by the window overlooking the lake. "This is sorta surreal," said my mom. "Virginia certainly won't remember, but do you two recall that this is exactly where the five of us sat last time we were here? They put a high chair right here for you, Virginia, and your dad sat next to you, right where you're about to sit down, Gin."

"How do you remember this stuff, Mom?"

"Yea, Beth," Bradley said. "Nick's usually the one who remembers all of his meals, including where he ate, who he ate with, and even every single dish they ordered."

"I do vaguely recall sitting here," said Nick, smiling at me. "I kept feeding you bites of ham from the buffet, and you loved it."

"I still do, Uncle Nick. And I noticed a big pile of ham slices up at the buffet with my name on it."

After ordering iced tea with our various preferences for sweeteners, the four of us went up to the buffet, which we had to ourselves. I pointed to the little "Virginia Cured Ham" placard placed above the pile of slices and said, "See? The ham really did have my name on it."

"And that's going to be my appetizer," said Nick, smiling and filling his plate with ham and a couple of oversized biscuits. I saw him stop to talk to the waitress and figured he was probably asking them to bring out a new batch of fried chicken so it would be hot and crisp. Nick did stuff like that all the time and even made special toppings requests for his burgers at McDonald's so the beef patties would be fresh off the greasy griddle. Yes, even my Uncle Nick goes to a McDonald's outlet occasionally. He says he likes the French fries.

My mom, Uncle Bradley, and I spent a little more time up at the buffet, adding the typical Southern appetizers of mixed salad and still-warm bread to our plates. Back at the table, the waitress I'd seen Nick talking to was uncorking a bottle of white wine — which I then surmised was the reason for their earlier conversation.

"I hope a light German Riesling was OK for everyone. I figured it would work with ham, chicken, or whatever else we had."

"You and Bradley might be on your own today," said my mom. "I'm guessing Virginia here doesn't want to risk heading back into Barracks with wine on her breath, right? And I'd already decided to be the designated driver for all of those Blue

Ridge Parkway curves heading back today so you and Bradley could imbibe freely on your continued ride down memory lane."

"Well, maybe I shouldn't have gotten a bottle, but I'm guessing Bradley and I can handle it. Can we at least toast Chip?" asked Nick, raising his glass.

"Why sure," said my mom, raising her glass of sweet iced tea and nodding at me to do raise mine.

After Nick said, "To a friend, husband, and father," the four of us clinked glasses, with Nick and Bradley going through that whole eye contact thing with me and each other again.

"So I gotta ask. What's the deal with the locked eyes when y'all shake hands, hug, toast, and stuff?"

Nick laughed and said, "I guess we've never really told you that either, Gin. I'm sure Bradley here probably remembers better, but I think your dad actually started it with the two of us way back in the fall of our Rat year. We'd noticed that when he and your grandfather shook hands, they'd hold their grip and eyes for several seconds more than seemed normal.

"When your dad would see us again, even after a short separation, he did the same with both of us. I guess it's a VMI bonding thing in some way, because you're the only other person we do it with besides your grandpa. It stays just us, OK?"

"That's very OK with me. Since Dad died, all of y'all have tried so hard to fill the huge hole he left for all of us. Don't think I haven't noticed and appreciated it. I've missed sharing VMI with him, but all of you have helped with that too."

"We miss him too, honey," said my mom, looking down at her plate. "I'd give anything to have him walking up to the table right now with a big plate of fried chicken."

"He could eat some chicken, couldn't he, Mom?"

Before she could answer, Nick said, "In many ways your dad and grandparents introduced me to good food — especially this Southern stuff — and I guess it eventually led to this crazy and quite fattening career of mine."

"I always thought it was ironic that he never got fat or had high blood pressure or bad cholesterol numbers when they tested him," my mom said. "He ate like Stonewall Jackson's horse. It was one of his life's many ironies that he died of a cancer he didn't cause instead of a heart attack he might have had by eating all of that supposedly unhealthy food."

"Well, if I keep eating all of this sweet Southern cooking and reviewing all of those restaurants for Michelin and others, I'll be the one having the heart attack. But I'll die fat and happy."

"All of you need to stay healthy, Uncle Nick. If Dad couldn't be at my graduation, the three of you better be."

"That's a promise," said Nick. "Who would have thought that you'd be in the audience at Cameron Hall for your dad's graduation and then walk across that same stage some twenty years later?"

"That's a few years from now for sure, but I plan to be there and have you three in the audience. Oh, and Grandma and Granddad too. I wish they could have come this weekend."

"You know they would have been here if they felt up to the trip," said Nick. "They brought us up here a few times during our cadetship."

"I'm still amazed how little I know about my other grandparents, but Grandma and Granddad make up for that."

"They sure do, honey," said my mom, looking at me. "They welcomed me from the day I met them, and we couldn't have asked for more of them after your dad died and they were experiencing their own heartbreaking grief."

"And speaking of your dad," said Nick, getting up and nodding toward the buffet. "I'm going back for some of that fried chicken." The three of us exchanged knowing smiles — and memories — before Bradley also headed back to the buffet.

"Those two are amazing men, aren't they, Mom?" I asked as we watched them walking away from our table.

"Yea. I don't know what we would have done without them — and especially Nick — before and after your dad died. He dropped everything to be in Richmond, and I know he missed several big assignments — and meals — to be with us.

"I wish he'd talk more about your dad," she continued while looking at Uncle Nick up at the buffet. "He just told me recently that he'd held your dad's head over a cracked MCV toilet many times during his chemo and that they'd joke that they had become brothers in bile along with being blood brothers. Like me, he also changed those diapers your dad had to wear near the end many times. He says he gets knots in his stomach every time he thinks about all of us losing him."

"Me too," I said, following her gaze. "It was bad enough back home, but somehow it's even worse sometimes at VMI. I feel like he's watching me in the Ratline, and I guess that's a good thing, but I miss sharing this time with him so much."

"I know, honey. He'd smile at the thought of you in that blouse, but he'd also be glad that your two adopted uncles have been here for you as much as possible."

Nick and Bradley both came back to the table with a plate of chicken, and Nick also had a large plate of desserts to share. Nick and Bradley had more chicken, and Mom and I shared some chocolate cake, but we spent the rest of our time at the table sharing VMI stories separated by two decades and a dead father, husband, and best friend.

After lunch the four of us walked around the little lake, pausing several times in the woods on the opposite bank to glance back at the old hotel and restaurant.

—⚏—

We got back from Peaks of Otter late in the afternoon because Nick insisted that we take the Blue Ridge Parkway again, with Mom driving and me beside her in the wagon's front seat leaning against the side of the door so I could see and talk to everyone. From the backseat Nick and Bradley continued to hold court with stories about my dad and their time at VMI. I'd heard most of them by then, but it still amazed me how the two of them or my mom would share something new almost every time I saw them. I think having me at VMI was bringing back a flood of memories about my dad for all three of them.

They dropped me off at Jackson Arch, and it would be among many times I'd have to say good-bye to one or more of them in front of that iconic statue. I could already feel a sudden and deep loneliness that Uncle Nick had warned me would happen.

He sensed my thoughts and quietly said, "You'll sometimes think that the difficult good-byes don't even make our visits worthwhile, but I promise you that every hello and our times here together will make the tough good-byes OK." I tried to remind myself of that as they drove away to head back to Richmond for Bradley's flight back to South Carolina and, for

Nick, an overnight flight to Paris. I jumped in the Ratline to face all that VMI could throw at me.

I stopped by Laura's room like I had the night before, and she was still at her desk studying. "Did you even sleep?" I asked, only half-joking.

"Of course. I stopped about eleven last night and didn't start up again til just before nine this morning after a couple of cups of strong coffee from the PX."

"Do you want me to run over there to get you another cup?"

"No, I'm good. I skipped lunch, so I'm probably going to head down to the mess hall for a quick bite of supper before hitting the books again."

"I'm stuffed from that huge buffet up at Peaks of Otter, but I don't have any choice on marching down to the mess hall and at least looking like I'm eating. I'll bet they'll be in prime yelling form tonight now that our parents are gone."

"It shouldn't be too bad. Lots of their parents were here as well, and believe me, it doesn't get any easier saying good-bye year after year."

"Why didn't your parents come this weekend, Laura?"

"They flew here from Dad's assignment in Kaiserslautern, Germany, my Rat year, but it's too far and too expensive on an NCO's pay. When they come for graduation, it will be the first time they've been here since Parents Weekend back in '98.

"I'm hoping my dad will be stationed at the Pentagon by then," she continued, while looking out her window. "It should be his last assignment, and we'll likely only overlap in active duty for a year or so. They've even bought the house where they'll retire out in the country near Winchester, where my dad was born and I grew up."

"Wow! I can't imagine my mom not being able to come to VMI a lot more often than your parents could. And my uncles Nick and Bradley too. By the way, I think Uncle Nick's dyke was from Winchester as well."

"Let's ask Nick next time we see him. You're very lucky to have him and others so nearby, but I've done OK. Several professors and the Keydet Club sort of adopted me over time, so I always had somewhere off Post I could head. My soccer teammates and my roommates have also always been great about including me in stuff when their parents visited as well."

"Well, I'd love to include you next time my mom or others are here again. And I really want to go up to Peaks of Otter with you before graduation. I'll bet it's beautiful in the spring."

"Let's make it happen. Graduation will be here before you know it — at least I hope so. But if I don't keep studying until SRC, I'm not going to nail that test, and I'm gonna blame you for getting branched Field Artillery or something instead of MI."

"Sorry. I'm outta here. Do you need me to run by after SRC for anything?"

"No, I'm good. I'm going to work at my study carrel tonight cause you know how my roommates can be in here after a weekend away. I'll see you in the morning. I'll probably fall out of BRC and throw my hay on the floor til your first class, so if you want to come by a little before nine to roll it back up, that would be great."

"Will do, dyke. Oh, and I'm sorry I got back too late for that run you mentioned," I said as I headed out the door.

—∿—

I did return to Peaks of Otter many months later with Laura, and though neither of us ate any fried chicken, we did share the same walk around the little lake after lunch. We talked about her impending graduation, officer's basic camp at Fort Huachuca, Arizona, and where she hoped she might have her first assignment. Neither Laura nor I could have dreamt on that innocent April day up at Peaks of Otter what the following months would bring to our lives.

—⁓—

After I left Laura's room, I raced up to my room in the Ratline without getting stopped a single time, thinking that most upperclassmen were either still out with their parents or snoozing in their rooms. My roommates were already back, and we exchanged more Parents Weekend stories until SRC.

SRC formation and then eating down at the mess hall were both surprisingly uneventful. There wasn't much screaming, though I did get lectured for not eating much. When they brought fried chicken to the table and I couldn't hold back a small smile, it provoked some more half-hearted screaming from one of my corporals.

As everyone had predicted, I did get depressed after Parents Weekend and already looked forward to another football weekend with my mom, as well as with Nick and Bradley if they could make it again. You were kept so occupied as a Rat that you really didn't have time to think about stuff like that very much. The Ratline, classes, and all kinds of military minutia kept me too busy to daydream about my extended family much, though some nights I did lie awake in my hay and remember their VMI stories and how I was now making many of my own.

The football team had two away games before another home game, and only Mom and Nick came to that one. We tailgated and Laura came out for Nick's burgers again. We lost to William & Mary, if I recall correctly, but they still let us go out to dinner if it was with a parent.

—⁓—

Before I knew it, Thanksgiving arrived, and I got to enjoy my first trip back to Richmond. I invited Laura, but she said she was staying in Barracks to get a head start on studying for exams. She did mention that a Physics professor and his wife had invited her to share Thanksgiving uptown with them at their house on Lee Avenue, so I didn't press her on coming with me.

I caught a ride to Richmond with a Second who kept a car uptown, but he only agreed after I said I'd pay for gas. You could always get a ride to Richmond, and at times it seemed like half the Corps of Cadets was from there or nearby.

The Second seemed pretty surprised when he dropped me off at our house, but he didn't say a word. But I had a not too funny feeling I'd hear some rhyming "rich" comments back in Barracks.

That kind of stuff had stopped bothering me by November. Nick said Dad had heard many of the same things when they were there, with "son of a rich" often being added to the epitaph. Those guys who'd yelled at my dad had obviously never met my grandmother, who was standing at the door waiting for me as I walked up the steps. She and my mom were both as far from being that "b" word as was humanly possible.

Grandma engulfed me in a hug, and the smells of my childhood came flooding back along with tears I couldn't stop from flowing onto my grandmother's pale blue blouse. Grandma always smelled like the kitchen, where she'd been when she must have seen me arrive on one of their security system's monitors. I correctly guessed we'd be having fried chicken tonight and suspected my mother and Nick had something to do with the menu.

Grandpa was next. He smelled like whiskey and tobacco, though I'd heard he was limiting himself to a cigar or two a week and good bourbon only on special occasions. His hug was as firm as ever, and then he pulled back, placing a hand on each shoulder and looking me in the eye. "That haircut becomes you, Miss Virginia. But I'm betting you're pretty glad to be out of your gray blouse and in those blue jeans and gray TJ sweatshirt for a few days."

"I am, Grandpa," I said, returning his gaze.

"Well, I still wish I could have seen you in it for Parents Weekend, but your mom shared the pictures, and you were looking quite the Shedet in that blouse."

"I just got demerits the other day for failing to have a good crease in that very blouse, but I'm glad you like the fashion statement, Grandpa."

Mom was next. Though I'd been with her at the final home game just a few weeks earlier, it felt very different seeing her back in our house. We hugged long and hard before she pulled away, wiped a tear from her eye, and said, "Nick's flying in from New York, and he promised he'd make it in time for dinner tonight."

"That's great. I figured he was coming tonight when I smelled fried chicken on Grandma."

"That's my favorite perfume," Grandma said, mischievously smiling at me and pretending to dab some behind her ears. "But it does make me think of your father, who you look like more than ever with that short hair. He loved fried chicken. Especially mine."

"Well, I hope you're frying up lots cause the greasy fried chicken at VMI just doesn't cut it. That fried chicken does make me think of Dad sitting right where I'm sitting in the mess hall, except I'm getting yelled at because I'm smiling while trying to keep grease from trickling down my chin."

"You can drip all you want here, Gin," Grandma said over her shoulder as she slowly made her way back to the kitchen with my grandfather's arm around her waist.

"She and your grandfather here were so excited for tonight and the long weekend," my mom said. "I think they talked about every single meal we'd eat and what I thought you'd like best."

"You'd think they were owners of a restaurant who were planning menus for some visiting food critic," I joked, adding, "Oh yea, there is a food critic visiting, and there he is."

I'd seen Nick through the window over my mom's shoulder, and he came through the front door without knocking, yelling, "I smell fried chicken," before he realized we were right inside the door.

He quickly hugged my mom and then gave me a long hug and eye-lock that was about as close as I would ever come to a fatherly greeting the rest of my life. It felt very good.

We all went to the kitchen and sat around the big island counter while Grandma continued to fry what looked to be about two dozen pieces of chicken and fret over the various side dishes she was taking out of the fridge. During dinner in the kitchen, Nick described the food he'd eaten in New York for Michelin the past week, providing detailed morsels as only a food writer can about meals at Windows on the World, Tavern on the Green, and Elaine's.

While he was talking, I made a mental note to myself to try to be more descriptive in my Rat English essays. I remembered Mom saying that Nick's father had been a literature professor down at VCU and that flowery description seemed to come natural to him. Nick never talked about his dad, who'd died before I was born, and I sometimes felt guilty about talking about mine so much around him. I guess he understood and still does that some people need to talk about their dead fathers and some don't or can't.

It felt great to relax at that big kitchen counter while I ate, with familial conversation replacing all the yelling back in the mess hall. I think everyone there knew what I was feeling and tried to keep the conversation away from VMI as much as possible.

Grandma had fixed apple pie, prompting Nick to ask what she planned for dessert on Thanksgiving Day. "Pecan pie, of course," she said, smiling at the thought. "I was just thinking this morning when I was rolling the dough for this pie that we served pecan pie during your first visit Nick, when Chip brought you here for Thanksgiving back when you were Rats."

"I'd almost forgotten that, Sarah" said Nick, looking at Grandma. "I'm not sure I've missed more than a handful of Thanksgivings — or pieces of pie — with y'all since. The two of you and Chip made me feel like a part of the family that day." Raising his glass of ruby red wine, he said, "You still do."

We finished our pie, and everyone stayed in the kitchen to help Grandma clean up. She made a pot of coffee, and we all sat or stood around the counter talking about tomorrow's Thanksgiving dinner.

"I'm bringing the wine as my contribution, if that's OK," Nick said. "I tasted some incredible pinot noirs from Oregon's Willamette Valley when I was at Windows on the World, and they gave me a few bottles for us to enjoy tomorrow. It was hard to keep from opening one of them on the short flight down here. I think they'll go great with turkey."

"You think anything goes great with turkey, Nick," said my mom. "Last year I think it was French burgundy that had you gushing over the gravy."

"It's the same grape as the Oregon pinot I'm bringing. You'll see. They're doing some amazing stuff in the Northwest."

"Well, Grandma's doing some amazing stuff right here in her Richmond kitchen, so it should be a match made in heaven," said my mom from her barstool at the counter. "Or should I say 'pairing,' wine snob?" she added while looking over at Uncle Nick standing at the sink drying pots.

I couldn't help yawning. It was almost eleven, and I'd been up since five, when they'd kicked in our doors for a run as a reminder that we were still Rats and would be when we got back Sunday night.

We all headed upstairs. Nick slept in the same room he probably had used since the first Thanksgiving he'd been here. Mom slept in Dad's old childhood room, where we'd both slept many nights after he died. Grandma had said my room was the same as I'd left it in August, and it was.

I walked into my old bedroom, and it all felt so foreign. I was a completely different person from the one I had been just three months ago, and so many of the things in my room seemed to be from another life and another person.

I had to smile at the posters of Dylan from 90210 and also Jakob Dylan from the Wallflowers. My mom says my dad loved listening to Jakob's dad, so I guess that's why I had a special fondness for him that goes beyond a schoolgirl crush. Then there were my many colorful lava lamps on my dresser and nightstand. And the now seemingly childish books, like my Nancy Drew collection on my small wooden bookshelf's scarred shelves.

It was nice to fall asleep knowing for certain that my door wouldn't get kicked in the next morning. Earlier that day, Uncle Nick had given me Pat Conroy's *The Prince of Tides* after I told him I'd read *The Lords of Discipline* back in August in preparation for VMI. The last thing I remember was turning off my light after reading just the back cover and dropping the book on the floor.

I probably slept better that night than I had since mid-August and had just barely opened my eyes to a sun-filled room when Uncle Nick half-heartedly kicked my door in and yelled, "Get up, Rat!"

I couldn't help laughing as he ran into the room with a big smile on his face and jumped on top of me. "I'm guessing this isn't the way they're doing it in Barracks. If a guy jumped into your hay like this, he'd be headed off Post before BRC, wouldn't he?"

"Very funny, Uncle Nick. I can't believe I fell asleep last night thinking this was the first time since August that I absolutely knew nobody'd kick in my door, and what do you do?"

"Kick in your door, Rat. I couldn't wait any longer. Your grandma is down there fixing blueberry pancakes, and she said we couldn't eat em til you got your lazy Shedet butt out of bed."

"Oh, I can smell them now. Let me put on a robe, and I'll be down there in a couple of minutes. Thanks for waking me up...I think."

"Sure thing, Miss Virginia. I promise not to do that the rest of the weekend."

"Yea, right. You'll probably want me to run with you or something this afternoon."

"Not a chance, kiddo. This day's all about eating. Well, every day's all about eating for me."

"Get outta here so I can grab my robe. Pour me a cup of coffee, and I'll be right down."

After coffee and more than two dozen fluffy pancakes among the five of us, we spent the rest of the morning in the kitchen talking about past Thanksgivings and how my family always made a big deal of them and most other meals together.

Once Grandma put the turkey in the oven, Uncle Nick and my granddad went into the den to watch the pre-game show in advance of the pro football game. Though I would have been just as happy going in there with them and trading more VMI stories, I decided to stay in the kitchen with Mom and Grandma. I should have known that they'd have VMI stories of their own.

"So we tried avoiding anything having to do with VMI as much as possible last night," said my mom. "But you're fair game today, Ginny. How's it going? Truly."

"It's pretty much the same since I last saw you at that football game. They still yell, and I still take it too personally — just like Uncle Nick predicted — but I'm keeping a pretty low profile. When someone finds out Dad went there, they sometimes give me grief about not being worthy of a ring like his, but I can really tell exactly when they learn he's dead. They don't yell at me as much then. At least not about not being a deserving VMI daughter."

"That's good, honey," said my mom. "Nick and Bradley would have someone's butt if they heard they were using your father as a way to get to you in any way. They'd both be in Barracks tomorrow if you said the word."

"You know the way it works, Mom. Boys will be boys. And you'd be surprised how many of the female upperclassmen yell at me as well. But it's rarely about Dad anymore or how I'm not worthy as a VMI daughter trying to be a cadet. I think my dyke, Laura, put the word out that they couldn't go there. But some of those girls can sure do some serious screaming. You wouldn't believe the mouths they have. A couple of them are worse than the guys."

"Well you're not going to believe this, but I thought the same thing about my roommates and then housemates back at UVA," Mom smiled. "These were supposedly prim and proper Richmond girls and they had trash mouths right out of the gutter. It sounds like that hasn't changed a bit."

"Nope, but somehow the yelling by the girls doesn't have the same effect as the guys. I generally don't take it as personally coming from them for some reason."

"That actually makes sense," said Grandma. "My guess is that most of the guys — even your friends from back in Richmond — resent that you're there. When they yell, you think they mean it. The girls are probably just doing their jobs, and when they yell at you, just remember they're still remembering what it was like to be in the minority when they were Rats."

"You're probably right, but it's still hard. When I'm getting screamed at — especially down at the mess hall — I keep thinking about how Dad must have handled it better. He seemed to handle criticism so much better than me. I used to think that it was due to all the stuff he went through about our family's tobacco money, but Uncle Nick told me he was that way from the day he arrived at VMI."

"He was, honey," agreed my mom. "I never knew anyone who handled criticism better than your dad, but you should remember that he was already carrying that tobacco albatross like a noose long before he was a Rat. Maybe that made a difference."

"Well, I wish it could that way for me too," I said. "I mean I've never broken down and cried at the mess hall, but I've come close. If that happened they'd be all over me. And that's including some of the toughest girls who I don't think have shed a single tear in their lives."

"It's natural to take it personally, but those two in the other room claim the only time it really gets personal is when one or more of those in power decide that they don't want a specific Rat — or even an occasional upperclassman — to get a ring. That's not going to happen to you, so all that yelling isn't personal."

"I know. I know. But it's still hard."

"Well, it should be all over by February," said Mom. "Well at least from what I remember your grandfather and father saying."

"That's true," I said and silently prayed she was right about the Ratline ending soon. "But it's still VMI long after the Ratline ends, you know."

"Every person handles each trial at VMI differently, and you're doing just fine. Your dad would be so proud."

"Thanks, Mom. I think I'm going to head into the den with the men for a bit. They're probably already trading more VMI stories, and maybe I can chime in with a few of my own."

"I'm sure they'll appreciate a woman's perspective," my mother said as I headed out of the kitchen. "Just remember you're still my little girl."

—m—

I spent the next three hours as a little girl, a granddaughter, a daughter, a friend, and a VMI woman. Granddad and Nick traded tales about VMI and Dad, and I chimed in when I could with my own cadet stories and memories of my father. At times I still couldn't believe that I was going to VMI — and that I couldn't share it with my dad. I think Granddad and Uncle Nick sensed that and really tried to include me in the conversation.

—m—

The first NFL game of the day had just ended when Mom came in to tell us that Thanksgiving dinner was almost ready. She and

Grandma had set the table in the dining room while I was with the men, and I apologized for not helping. But Mom said, "We wanted you to have that time with your grandfather and Nick. I want you to realize how all of us know what you're going through and that we will support you in every way possible. Even if that means leaving VMI."

"I'm not leaving VMI Mom," I quickly and firmly replied. "Once I decided to go, there was no way I was going to leave without a ring and a diploma."

"That's great Ginny," said my mom. "But just know we're here for you. Nick has told me so many times that he would be in a car or on a plane in a second if he heard you needed him in Lexington. Have you told her that, Nick?"

"Not in so many words, Beth. But you know I would, Gin. During the second semester of my Rat year after Ratline had actually ended, I really wanted to leave and didn't think I had someone I could call. I was wrong. Your dad got me to call your granddad, and he was in Lexington two hours later in that old Volvo wagon of his."

"Nick couldn't leave Post because he was on confinement for some silly infraction," said Grandpa, who was likely smiling at the memory of his own confinement to Post at some point. "So I swear we must have slowly circled the Parade Ground a half dozen times on foot as I listened to him whining about how he didn't think he could make it," said Grandpa, looking at Nick. "I told him I'd thought the same thing many times when I was there and that it would pass."

"It did," said Nick. "As you can see with this sparkling new ring right here on my finger," said Uncle Nick, banging it down on the dining room table.

"Oh my gosh, Uncle Nick!" I practically shouted. "I can't believe I didn't notice it before now! When did you get it re-sized?"

"It was in my pile of mail yesterday when I got back to the apartment, but I forgot to wear it last night and walked back down there this morning to get it. It's actually a funny story, but I wanted to wait til I was wearing it to tell y'all.

"So I finally called Jostens about a month ago to get all of you off my back about it getting it resized, and they said I just needed to go to a jeweler to check my new and much larger ring size. I went to Schwarzschild's in Carytown, of course, got this fat finger measured, and then sent my original ring to Jostens for resizing.

"About a week after I sent it, they called and left a message that basically said my finger was now too large and they couldn't resize it. So get this. They made me a brand new ring using the original mold from back in '82. And — get this part too — it was completely free!"

"You're kidding!" exclaimed Grandma.

"Nope," laughed Nick. "I called them back and they said it was part of some lifetime guarantee or something they had with VMI — at least back then. They'll replace it if it's stolen, you lose it, or if your finger gets too fat. The woman I talked to said she knew of one guy from the Class of 1960 who had already received a new one five times for various reasons."

"That's my class," said Grandpa. "I'll bet I even know who that is."

"I didn't ask and she probably wouldn't tell me, but I still can't get over the free replacements. Or how it feels on my hand — and actual ring finger instead of my pinkie — after all these years.

"I haven't tried yet," Uncle Nick continued, "but I'll bet I can't wear it while I'm typing up my review of Windows on the World — which I absolutely positively have to do by tomorrow. My new little Toshiba laptop is waiting for me upstairs."

"I'd love to read it," I said. "My Rat English teacher keeps telling me it's all in the details, and I'm betting that's the way you write, Uncle Nick. Lots of details."

"That's especially true when it comes to food. It's really all in the little details most people don't know until you tell them through your words. Like I really take pride in figuring out the ingredients of a dish and then describing them in my reviews and articles. The chefs love it too. Especially when they fool me."

"What do you mean?" asked my mom.

"Well, take this oyster stuffing Sarah made this morning. I intentionally didn't watch her mix it back in the kitchen because I wanted to see if I could guess the ingredients she used. I know I've had it more than a dozen times over the years, but I've never asked for the recipe. Here goes.

"I taste…sourdough bread, celery, onions, oysters, sage, and basil," said Uncle Nick after taking another bite. "How'm I doing, Sarah?"

"You're right on those six, but you're missing a crucial one."

"Hmm," he said, taking another bite.

"Sautéed onion?"

"No, but close. It's chopped and sautéed leeks," said Grandma, smiling.

"See what I mean?" said Uncle Nick, banging his ring on the table. "Sarah here loves that she stumped me, and so do chefs. They like making one thing taste like another. Like leeks tasting like sautéed onion to me."

"Did that happen up at Windows on the World this week?"

"No, but that doesn't mean I didn't have an incredible meal and that I'll put in lots of tasty details before you read it on my laptop tomorrow."

We spent the rest of Thanksgiving dinner talking about food, writing, and — of course — VMI. I couldn't stop thinking about Nick's ring and what it would be like to put mine on almost two years later. I'd brought Dad's ring home from VMI with me and put it on my bedside table, but it would go back in my desk drawer when I returned to Lexington on Sunday.

I helped Grandma and Mom with the dirty dishes while Grandpa and Uncle Nick watched another football game. Though I had contact with females at VMI, it was completely different from the ease of being around these two incredible women. I vowed to keep this sense of peace back in Barracks when possible.

As would be the case whenever I came home from VMI for the next four years, time flew in Richmond. We spent Friday and Saturday eating and talking, with long walks in the Fan. I went for a walk whenever anyone asked, and the company ranged from just Mom and Nick several times to the five of us strolling down to Joe's Inn for breakfast Saturday morning. I knew most of the long-time waitresses, and they all complimented me on my short haircut, but I noticed all of them seemed to have a sweet spot for Nick — and it wasn't just because he'd once written about Joe's for *The New York Times*.

Looking back more than a decade, I know it may seem strange that I didn't have any friends over to the house during my time back home, but during that period in my life I really just wanted to be with my extended family. Nick tells me my dad very rarely had anyone over to the house when he came home from VMI as well.

Even though it was in the forties outside and we could see our breath when we talked, Grandpa and Nick grilled out Saturday night. They'd asked me what I wanted, and I'd told them hamburgers. Neither of them needed to remind me that it was my dad's favorite thing to grill on weekends and that he'd done so very often on the old Weber they were still using.

I stayed outside with the two of them while they cooked and couldn't resist lightly tapping the hot metal top of the grill a couple of times just to feel my father's presence in my warmed fingertips. I could almost hear him telling Grandpa not to let the burgers stay on the grill too long. He liked his burger medium rare at most. So do I.

They gave me the burgers to carry inside, where Mom and Grandma had decided we'd all eat in the kitchen again. The thick granite counter my grandfather had ordered from Luck Stone long ago easily accommodated the five of us, and as always they left the bar stool where Dad always used to sit empty.

The kitchen grew silent, except for the sounds of pleasure as we each bit into our burgers. I'd cut one of them in half for Mom and Grandma to share, but the rest of us began working our way through the thick burgers and the buns Grandma always got at Ukrop's.

"Mine is just how Dad liked em," I said.

"We spent many a Saturday night in this exact spot when he was in high school or home from VMI," Grandma said.

"My memories are mostly of being here as well." I said. "Including many of those Saturday night burgers, Grandpa."

"Your dad would still probably say I overcooked em, wouldn't he, Nick?"

"They never were, but he'd still say they were just to get under your skin, Win."

We sat in the kitchen that night for another two hours, including sharing a batch of brownies my mother had made that afternoon that still gave the kitchen a wonderfully warm smell and feeling.

About ten Grandpa tapped my arm, looked me in the eye, and asked, "Would you like to join Nick and me in the den for a bourbon, Ms. Ginny, or hang out here some more with the ladies?"

I'd tasted bourbon a few times in high school, and Virginia Gentleman was a popular bottle to hide in Barracks back at VMI, but Grandpa or Nick had never asked me to drink anything but beer with them. So I said yes, and looking back I'm so glad I did.

Grandpa had four large leather chairs facing the TV in the den, but he didn't turn it on when Nick and I took two of them and he went over to the bar. I was facing away from him, but I heard the familiar tinkling of ice falling into our three glasses, the opening of a bottle, and seemingly generous amounts of liquid being poured over ice cubes three times.

He brought a glass to me first, leaning down with a grunt before handing it to me with a wink. He then gave a glass to Nick, who'd taken the chair next to mine. Still standing, Grandpa held out his glass and said, "To the Corps. And to a son, father, and friend who would be very proud of his daughter right now."

We clinked glasses, and Grandpa walked slowly over to his well worn chair, sitting down with a sigh and taking a long drink of the now-cool whiskey. I took a small drink as well and, after a stifled choke that made Nick and my grandfather smile, immediately noticed the warming effect it had on me.

"We've spent many an hour in here, pondering the ways of the world. Haven't we, Nick?" asked Grandpa.

"Yes, sir," replied Nick while gazing at Grandpa. "That's a lot of water — or I guess I should say bourbon — under the bridge."

"I remember the night you three graduated and came back here to this very room. I'm pretty sure I opened a second bottle of Virginia Gentleman that night. A. Smith Bowman up in Fredericksburg wasn't making the more interesting smaller batches like this Bowman Brothers here back then, but it didn't seem to get in our way."

"No, sir. If we could have a dollar for every fifth of Virginia Gentleman consumed by VMI cadets and alumni, I guess we'd be millionaires."

"I guess someone there probably is," I joked.

"The president of the company is a VMI grad like you'll soon be, Ginny," my grandfather said. "I just saw him the other day at the Commonwealth Club, and he sent a glass of this stuff straight up over to me. I bought a bottle at the ABC store the next day just for you and Nick. And me, of course," he added, winking at both of us while taking another sip.

"Your dad didn't really like the Commonwealth Club, Ginny," said Nick.

"No, he didn't," said my granddad. "He never liked anything I did that used money made from tobacco sales. I guess that was pretty much anything, huh?"

"Pretty much, Grandpa. Is that why he never worked for your company?"

"Yes, honey. He swore he wouldn't be involved with the sale of tobacco, and he kept his word until cancer took his life anyway."

"But we moved back down here from New York because he got sick, right?"

"Yes. After his stint in the Army and medical school at Columbia, your dad was doing great work at the Cancer Research Institute up there. But he and your mom felt that coming back to Richmond was best.

"The Medical College of Virginia was — and still is — doing some amazing things with cancer treatments," continued Grandpa. "So the three of you came back to Monument Avenue and lived upstairs. But that only lasted six months I guess.

"I'm still not sure that being around all of those cancer patients at MCV — most of whom had smoked and many who still did — didn't kill him as much as the actual cancer. He hated it there."

"I'm glad Dad died at home, though"

"Me too Ginny," said Grandpa. "He stopped the chemotherapy because the doctors said it might only prolong his life for another month at most and he'd be in a lot of pain. He actually lasted a month at home and with much less pain than if he'd stuck with that harsh chemo regimen."

"Why wasn't I there when he died?" I asked.

"We thought it best that you weren't. You were only eight. You were close by with your grandma though. But you should know that he looked your mother straight in the eye and made her promise to say good-bye to you — and she did. Along with me and your mom, Nick and Bradley were at his side when he died out there in the living room where we'd set him up. Can you believe that he had a bite of leftover hamburger that day? It was a Sunday, and I'd grilled some the night before because I knew the end was near. That was his last meal."

"Wow. I didn't know any of this," I said. "I was so young. Thank you for telling me, Grandpa."

"Except for when we were Rats — when we pretty much had to eat anything — your dad wouldn't eat the burgers at VMI," Uncle Nick said. "He always made peanut butter and jelly sandwiches whenever they served those god-awful burgers. Once I ate your dad's burgers back in Richmond when I visited that first Thanksgiving back in '80, I knew why."

"I have to eat the burgers in the mess hall now too. But I don't think I'll have another one after Breakout. I'll eat PB and J too, just like Dad."

"Your dad would smile at that, Ginny," said Grandpa.

The talk that night inevitably revolved around VMI, and we shared stories that only people who have been there can share or understand. They told me things about my dad's time there that I hadn't heard, and I told them about the good and bad times I'd already experienced in my three short — but seemingly long — months there. Before I knew it, Grandpa was opening another fifth of bourbon, but it was just the traditional Virginia Gentleman this time.

—⚬⚬⚬—

I woke up the next morning with my first bourbon hangover and immediately headed to the bathroom for the aspirin. There was classical music playing in the adjacent bedroom where my parents had slept, so I knocked softly.

My mom said, "Come on in, Gin," adding, "You know you don't have to knock," as I opened her door. "I'm surprised you're up this early, you Virginia gentlewoman, you," she joked as I came in with a water glass in my right hand and aspirin in my left. "Did you need some aspirin?"

"Oh yea," I said, gulping both aspirin at once. "How'd you know I'd have a hangover?"

"I was downstairs earlier and caught your granddad carrying an empty bourbon bottle out to the recycling bin."

"That wasn't the only one he opened. We got halfway through a second one before the three of us called it a night around one."

"I figured as much. Grandma and I went to bed about eleven, and we didn't want to interrupt all of that VMI talk."

"It was amazing, Mom. They made me feel like one of them. And so connected to Dad."

"That's great to hear. They have a way of doing that, don't they? They're two very special people, and I'm glad you're getting a chance to see that. They're both so proud of you, and it's not just because of what you're doing at VMI. We all miss your dad, and I think they see you as a physical reminder of everything good about him."

"I felt that exact thing last night. It was almost like they were talking to him instead of me. It was sort of eerie, but it made me feel very special at the same time."

"It makes sense. You are very much your father's daughter, and he was Nick's best friend. And your granddad's only son. At least by blood."

"But I'm also my mother's daughter," I said. "And I'll never let anyone forget it."

"I know. I know," she said, taking my left hand. "Thank you. But the three of you and Bradley have this connection with VMI that only those who have been there can completely and wholly share."

"I just hope I can share a ring and diploma with every one of you someday. It all seems like it's just much too hard and way too long right now."

"I know it's cliché, but you truly have to take it one day at a time at that place. Before you know it, you'll be home for Christmas. Then there's Breakout. And then you're a Third thinking about getting your ring and your diploma."

"I dread going back this afternoon and facing the Ratline and exams."

"I know, honey. But they'll start leaving you alone when exams get closer. Your dad always said it almost felt like a real college when exams approached each December and May."

"I know, but it's just so hard to juggle the academics, the military, and the physical and mental stuff from the Ratline."

"That's what everyone says, but it's what makes VMI so special and bonds you to people like your grandfather and Nick. And your dad."

"You're right. I kept thinking that last night when we were drinking that darned bourbon and sharing stories. It was really special and I'll never forget it."

"That's why your grandma and I didn't say good night. Your grandfather had mentioned that he and Nick planned to do it, and it sounds like he'll be glad he did."

"I can't remember if I thanked him and Nick last night, but I will this morning when I see them."

"Nick's already out for a run, and your grandpa's waiting for you in the den to see if you want to walk off that headache in the Fan."

I threw on some jeans and a Redskins sweatshirt, headed downstairs, and found Grandpa reading a book in the den. "Do you have a headache, Grandpa? I sure do."

"Of course not. I've had years of training. I don't wish that on you, but I suspect that with your genes you'll get used to bourbon as well."

"Well, I consider it well worth it for the conversations we had last night," I said as I leaned down to give him a hug. "Thank you so much for including me."

"It was actually our pleasure Gin. There will hopefully be many more like that here and in Lexington. You're doing a very special thing there, and we all want to share it with you."

"Well, I can't thank you enough. Whatcha reading?"

"Oh, it's another copy of that same Pat Conroy book Uncle Nick gave to you last night," he said, holding it up. "Conroy doesn't write many of em, and it's really good, as expected, thus far. Nick says it's some darned fine writing and I agree. He made you read *The Lords of Discipline*, right?"

"Yea. Last summer. They don't do some of that serious harassment stuff anymore, but it was still good preparation for me. Nick says his father gave it to him the summer before he went to VMI as well."

"It's a bit more complicated than that, little girl, but that's for another talk and another bottle of that Bowman Brothers."

"I'll hold you to that. You wanna walk?"

—⁓—

We walked down to Joe's Inn and drank a couple of cups of coffee while sitting at the bar and talking more about my dad, VMI, Nick, and whatever else I asked my dear grandfather. I wanted to order breakfast to get something in my stomach, but Grandpa said my mom and grandmother were making another one of my favorites back at the house.

I could smell the sausage as soon as we walked in the back door. Mom was at the stove, and I could see Grandma in the dining room setting the table with Nick. He'd already showered and was looking much better than I felt.

"Can I help, y'all?" I asked as I walked into the kitchen.

"We're all set, Gin," said my mom. "Nick knew where everything was."

"How was your run, Uncle Nick? You obviously felt much better than me first thing this morning."

"I just got in a couple of quick miles over at Byrd Park so I wouldn't feel as guilty about these big flaky biscuits and that sausage gravy I'm about to devour. And yes, I'm thinking I probably feel better than you this morning."

"It was worth it. Thanks again for that talk. It meant a lot to me."

"Hey, that was more than a talk. It was a conversation between three VMI family members. And maybe a little bourbon was involved."

"More than a little," said Grandma. "I saw that empty bottle in the recycling bin, as well as that open bottle in the den. That must have been quite the conversation."

"It was, Grandma."

"Well, good. Now let's get some breakfast on the table."

—m—

The rest of the morning and early part of the afternoon went much too quickly. I think everyone was aware of how much I dreaded going back to Lexington because they didn't bring VMI up at all. It was like it was just after my father had died. Nobody wanted to talk about it because they thought it would upset me.

The opposite was actually true then and now. Talking about it, especially with those who had been through something very similar, was actually good for me.

"You know y'all can talk about VMI today as well," I said when everyone was back in the kitchen and helping Grandma and my mother with clean-up. "It's actually OK."

"I know, I know," said Nick. "It's just that many cadets don't want to be reminded of going back there. I remember when I used to come back to Richmond and stay here instead of down the street. I couldn't stay at my apartment yet cause it reminded me of my dad. And staying here with your dad and good ol Sir Winston here kept reminding me that I'd be going back to VMI sooner or later."

"Well, just like last night, I generally like talking about it. I'll bet my dad did too, huh?"

"Yes, he did," said Grandpa. "He liked to talk everything to death back then."

Grandpa's use of "death" in relation to my dad brought a rare silence to the kitchen, as everyone looked down at whatever clean-up task they'd undertaken.

"Oh, I'm sorry," said Grandpa to all of us once he realized his mistake. "It's just that Chip was always such an analyzer. Whether it was about my involvement back then with what he called death sticks or how he was reacting to the pressures of VMI at times, he was always analyzing everything practically to . . ."

"He did the same thing with his cancer," said Mom, cutting my grandfather off before he said death again. "He researched and tried everything with his doctors until they finally told him it was hopeless."

"I sort of remember that even though I was so young then," I said.

"I think that up until that point, he didn't really believe that cancer of all things was going to kill him," said Nick, getting up from his barstool.

We finished the dishes and other clean-up in silence, and I knew everyone was thinking back to when my father finally gave in to his cancer. It was the first time I really realized what it had meant to him and my mom to come back to Richmond and then this house.

We spent the rest of the time before I had to leave in the den, with football playing low in the background on the TV and everyone still trying to avoid talking about me going back to VMI. Every time I mentioned it the conversation became awkward, so I gave up.

Nick had told me the night before that he was speaking to journalism classes at VMI and W&L on Monday and Tuesday and had offered to give me a ride back to VMI. Grandpa had volunteered to go along, and as alumni they were going to share one of those Spartan rooms in Moody Hall. I'd heard the rooms there were almost like our Barracks rooms, but I still looked forward to staying in one of them someday as an alumnus.

We left about three because Rats had to be back for SRC formation. Once in the car, the talk immediately turned to VMI. It was like it was now OK because it was just the three of us. Again they made me feel like part of a very special group of people.

The drive back to Lexington went much too quickly, and before I knew it we were crossing the Maury and staring up at the bleak backside of Barracks, which was looking more and more like a prison to me with each passing day as a Rat.

"You'll probably eventually get rid of that sickening feeling in your gut that I'll bet you're experiencing just about now, Ginny," said Nick, using the rearview mirror to look at me in the backseat. "But you'll also never tire of the elation you'll feel seeing it in the mirror whenever you leave. Those feelings actually reverse over time, but it takes just that — time."

They dropped me off in front of Barracks, and though I planned to see them the next day after Uncle Nick spoke down in Scott Shipp Hall, I still locked eyes and hugged both of them tightly. Most of the upperclassmen hadn't returned from Thanksgiving yet, but I did stop by Laura's room to see if she was there, and of course she was at her desk studying.

—ᴍ—

As Nick and Grandpa had predicted and as would be the case, the period between Thanksgiving and Christmas seemed more focused on the academics side of school rather than the military. Cadre gave us more time to study, and they didn't wake us up for a single sweat party after the first Monday morning following Thanksgiving break. That morning was apparently just a traditional wakeup call to remind us we were still Rats. As if we didn't know.

Winter had really set in by the time the first of December arrived, and I couldn't help but be depressed at waking up before sunrise and marching to supper when it was already dark. To know that I had three and a half more years of this was depressing at times. One day at a time was my mantra then, and it often still is.

I felt well prepared for most of my exams, though college-level chemistry still wasn't my strong suit — just like back at TJ when I got my only C. Grandpa thought it had something to do with the manufacture of tobacco products being chemistry and that my dad had said that cigarettes were truly a mad science. I could just picture and hear my father saying something like that to Grandpa.

My last exam was on December 20, and I got a ride back to Richmond with a female First who, like Laura, was in that first class of female Rats. Unlike my dyke, however, she really didn't like talking about her VMI experience. So most of our ride together was silent. I knew I'd be talking about VMI soon enough back on Monument Avenue, so I didn't mind.

Christmas back home was similar to Thanksgiving, but longer in both length and breadth. It gave me the sense I didn't need to rush to say and do everything in the four short days and nights I'd had at Thanksgiving. Grandpa was sitting on the front porch when we pulled up, and the First didn't get out of her car to meet him after I'd said good-bye through the window.

"I'd like to have met her," Grandpa said after hugging me and putting his arm around my shoulders as we watched the First drive away in her little blue Miata. "Your mom told me you were catching a ride with someone from the first class of females."

"Yep. Unlike my dyke, she didn't seem to want to talk about her experiences. I told her you were a grad and I really think she figured you were like most alumni who hate females being there."

"I think I may be one of the few from way back that has embraced the concept, so I can understand that. I thought maybe since I supported my granddaughter going there that she might feel differently."

"Me too. I even told her that you'd supported me from the day I told you I wanted to go there, but she didn't really seem to believe it," I said as we walked up the steps. "She's very different from Laura."

Grandma and my mom were in the kitchen, and I smelled the meatloaf as soon as I walked through the door.

—◊◊◊—

My Uncle Nick later told me that my first Christmas away from VMI was remarkably similar to the one he had experienced back in 1980. He was there both times, and I just wish my dad could have been with us as well.

We took long walks like we had enjoyed at Thanksgiving, and I went with anyone who asked. We lingered over meals, talking about the past back when my dad was alive, but also about my first semester at VMI. But mostly we just sat around the house, embracing each other in a way I think only my grandparents, my mom, Uncle Nick, and I understood.

We even repeated an evening in my grandfather's den, with Granddad, Nick, and I sharing several glasses of small-batch bourbon late into the night. I didn't even have a hangover the next day, prompting Nick to say during a crisp early-morning run that I was becoming more and more like my dad every day. Looking back, I think that particular Christmas was when I first realized I was becoming a Shields woman. And a VMI woman. I believe my father would have been so very proud.

—⁕—

My three weeks away from the Institute went much too quickly, but I also found myself anxious to return to Lexington. The sooner second semester started, the closer we were to Breakout and becoming a class instead of a mass of Rats.

Once we returned rumors soon surfaced about when we would break out. Of course the sweat parties and other physical and mental pressures intensified, but so did the jokes from Thirds that we wouldn't get out of the Ratline until May.

I'd heard this always happened and didn't take it too seriously, but I still couldn't wait for Breakout to mark my first big accomplishment following in the footsteps of my dad. And it finally happened in late February.

—⁕—

After I told him about it later, Nick said our Breakout was remarkably similar to the Class of 1984's Breakout back in 1981. Laura told me that it was the same for her and the first group of females to become VMI Fourth Classmen in 1998.

After seemingly endless mornings and nights of runs and sweat parties, Breakout for the Class of 2004 began in earnest on a cold Saturday afternoon. We went for a long fourteen-mile march in the afternoon, and that was followed by a sweat party by the First Class that night.

We then had several other sweat parties and they also took us out on a run of several miles with our rifles. My shoulders still ache at the memory, and Uncle Nick recently told me his do as well whenever he remembers a similar run with rifles before their Breakout.

It was by far the most intense few days of workouts our burgeoning class would face. They awoke us a bit before five on Wednesday for another long run. Then, after an adjusted class schedule and changing into fatigues, we were taken into Jackson Memorial Hall for a speech about the fabled VMI family by the First Class president. During the speech I found myself wondering if a female would ever be a class president at VMI.

We were then run into New Barracks for whatever would come next.

What came next was Breakout. It started with a short but hard sweat party in New Barracks. They then sent about a hundred of us us at a time down to the rifle range, where I was in the screaming first group of Rats charging up the hill as Seconds pushed us back down. The Seconds finally allowed us to pass. Then we had to make our way through a muddy pit filled with Thirds who made our trip through the mud as messy and slow as possible.

Once our three groups had passed through these two trials as a mass, we ran back up to the parade field for a final short workout before being sent into Old Barracks. There the Class of 2004 officially came into existence with our first old yell:

Rah Virginia Mil
Rah Rah Rah
Rah, VMI, '04 '04 '04

It bounced off the old walls of Old Barracks like old yells had for decades. We then gave old yells for our dykes in the Class of '01 and even somewhat begrudgingly for the classes of '02 and '03.

That night we shared a steak dinner with our dykes down in the mess hall. Mine was cooked perfectly medium rare, just like Dad liked it.

I had an eight o'clock Calculus 102 class the next morning. I knew I'd get an A when I was working on the problems. My dad was always good at math too.

—∽∿∽—

Everyone in our newly formed class thought there would be a letdown after Breakout, but it certainly didn't happen my first spring at VMI. Though we still had much less freedom than they had over at W&L and any other college, it felt like we were at a very different place after we became the Class of 2004.

It was hard to pinpoint just one thing that made the difference, and to try to explain it to an outsider is futile. But regaining small human pleasures and privileges made all the difference to us

that cool spring. The lack of the many time-consuming requirements from the Ratline made the many things that remained
seem easier to bear.

—⁂—

A wet March, when everything on Post remained gray, including
our uniforms, finally turned to April and our long-awaited spring
break. I'll always remember my first spring week away from VMI
because it involved the first of many trips to Charleston and the
South Carolina Lowcountry.

My mom and Nick drove over from Richmond and picked
me up for the drive down to Bradley's hometown. As he would
do on many future visits, Bradley even made the short drive up
from Beaufort for the first three days of our weeklong stay in the
Holy City. Though we didn't visit his adopted town on this first
Lowcountry visit, the three of us would eventually make our way
to bucolic Beaufort many times.

Though it was more than a decade ago, thoughts of that
week away from VMI and in a city I'd come to know well and
love remain vivid in my mind. It was during that trip that I had
my first taste of shrimp and grits when the three of them took
me to Slightly North of Broad to try Chef Frank Lee's take on a
Southern classic and much more at his groundbreaking farm to
table restaurant. This was well before farm and even sea to table
dining became popular at more recent Charleston additions I've
also grown to love, like Husk, McCrady's, FIG, High Cotton,
Circa 1886, and more.

Nick splurged at Wentworth Mansion for the week, my mom
and I stayed at the pretty-in-pink Mills House, and Bradley had

a carriage house room at the historic John Rutledge House Inn during his three busy days and nights with us. As with more recent visits with and without some or all of them, I ate well, walked many miles along streets dripping with history and Georgia moss, and made several excursions into the South Carolina Lowcountry.

After we checked-in at our three hotels spread across downtown Charleston, we met at the bar at Charleston Place's elegant Charleston Grille so Nick could introduce us to Chef Bob Wagonner. Uncle Nick seemed to know everyone in the restaurant business and it was fun for me to enjoy a slice of his world. Afterwards, we walked down Market Street to SNOB for my first taste of Chef Lee's cooking.

Uncle Nick had — and still has — this strange restaurant rule about nobody being allowed to order the same thing, but I can still remember all four entrées we ordered that night. Uncle Nick ordered the Carolina rabbit roulade for himself, while Uncle Bradley had local Palmetto pigeon, and my mom ordered the crab-stuffed flounder with sautéed shrimp. I only know all of this because I recently asked Uncle Nick about the first time I had shrimp and grits and he reminded me of where it was and what everyone else ordered. When he reminded me of my first shrimp and grits, he also told me that his rule about nobody ordering the same thing at restaurants was originally my dad's idea long ago.

After we shared a dessert — according to Uncle Nick — of *crème brûlée* with four spoons, Uncle Bradley waved the chef over to the table from his open kitchen. Even back then, Chef Lee sported his trademark long and bushy sideburns and a big smile at our compliments on his food. Incredibly, Uncle Nick had never met Chef Lee and grilled him about his shrimp and grits recipe. After describing the dish in detail, he returned to the kitchen and came back with four recipe cards for us, saying they had so many requests for it that he'd had cards printed. I still have mine, though it now has various food stains on it:

Maverick Shrimp and Grits
Frank Lee, Executive Chef, Slightly North of Broad

Creamy Grits
4 cups Water
1/2 tsp. Salt
2 tbs. Butter
1 1/4 cup Stone Ground Grits
1/4 cup Cream

Bring water, salt and 1 tbs. butter to a boil. Stir in grits. Reduce heat to low and cook, stirring occasionally, until grits are thick and creamy (approximately 40 minutes). Remove from heat and finish by stirring in cream and remaining butter. Keep warm.

Shrimp and Sauce
20 Shrimp, peeled and deveined
4 oz. Country ham, julienned
4 oz. Smoked pork sausage, cut in circles
4 tbs. Fresh tomato, seeded and diced
4 tbs. Green onion
1/8 tsp. Fresh garlic, minced
Pinch Cajun spice

1 tbs. Water
3 tsp. Butter

Sauté ham and sausage in 1 tsp. butter. Add shrimp and sauté for 1–2 minutes. Add garlic and Cajun spice. Sauté for 30 seconds. Add green onion and tomato. Add water. Finish with remaining butter.

<u>*To Serve*</u>
Spoon grits onto plates in equal portions. Place 5 shrimp per person on grits and spoon equal parts of topping over each.

Yield: 4 Servings

After dinner, Bradley took us on a walk south of Broad all the way down to the Battery, pointing out many historic houses and gardens along the way. As we made our way back up King Street, he stopped under a gas streetlamp at a two-story house just before reaching Broad. "That's my parents' house," Bradley said quietly while gazing up at the house where only one second story window was lit. "I guess my parents are up there watching the local news like they've probably done almost every night since I was born."

With those words, he started back up King without us. Bradley didn't say another word, except for a quick good night and thanks, until we dropped him off at the John Rutledge House Inn on Broad Street. We then silently made our way over to and up Meeting Street to the Mills House, where my mom and I hugged Nick good night before he strolled east over to the Wentworth Mansion.

Over the next two days with Bradley, he further introduced me to the city he loved without being able to live there. He took the three of us to the Gibbes to stroll through the permanent collection and even arranged a private walking tour with one of the many tour companies located downtown. On the second evening, Bradley met me and my mom back at the City Market for a horse-drawn carriage ride over to Wentworth Mansion, where Uncle Nick was waiting for us at the bar of Circa 1886, which Nick told us had opened in 2000 to rave reviews.

Less than a month after that very special meal, I'd find a clipping of Nick's own review in my tiny VMI mailbox. It was postmarked Paris. Nick's review allowed me to relive that memorable dinner with people I loved in a city I'd grow to love as well.

I wish I still had the menu from that night, but I do have Uncle Nick's review touting the she crab soup, spicy grilled shrimp over green tomatoes, fresh locally-caught snapper, and fried angel food cake for dessert.

When I can afford it, I stay at Wentworth Mansion and eat at least one meal at Circa 1886, where Chef Marc Collins has quietly gained quite a following with locals and visitors in the know like me, my mom, and my uncles.

After dinner, Bradley walked us back to the Mills House, where my mom and I sat up in our two queen beds until after midnight talking about how my dad had never made it to Charleston. I fell asleep with thoughts of him and me walking these streets together under the moonlight.

—◊◊◊—

Late the next morning, the four of us met to stand in line at Jestine's Kitchen for shared breakfasts of scrambled eggs, grits, sausage gravy, biscuits, and lots of coffee. Bradley then offered to take us on a tour of several plantations in the area and this would be the first of many times I'd find myself in another century in the Lowcountry. I can't remember for certain and I'll have to ask my mom or Uncle Nick, but I think that Bradley took us out Ashley River Road to both Magnolia Plantation and Drayton Hall.

I know for certain that we ended up at Middleton Place in the early-evening because we ate at their cozy restaurant after a long walk around the manicured gardens. William, Bradley's partner in business and life, even drove up from Beaufort after he closed their shop. I've since been back to Middleton Place several times to wander the grounds, stay at the contemporary Inn, and even paddle their nearby creek in my bright red and yellow kayak — the team colors of the VMI Keydets.

We headed back to Charleston during a pretty sunset talking about what else we could do in Charleston after Bradley and William left for Beaufort early the following morning. They gave us several good possibilities, including lots of restaurants, a boat ride out to historic Fort Sumter, a trip out to Folly Beach for a long walk in the sand, and shopping on King Street. And, no, we didn't step foot in the menswear shop on King Street still owned by Uncle Bradley's father and now run by his brother.

As with many later trips to Charleston, the days became a blur of talking, walking, and eating. Nick still often reminds me of eating oysters out at Bowen's Island and our lunches and dinners at classic Charleston restaurants like Poogan's Porch, Robert's, with their operatic chef, Magnolias, Hominy Grill, and more. Some of them are now closed, but I've returned to several and others we tried many times with Uncle Nick, Uncle Bradley, my mom, or alone. That routine of talking, walking, and eating, is one I repeat as often as possible since that first spring stay in a truly holy and tasty city.

—⁓—

When we got back from my first Charleston idyll, the Corps of Cadets returned to the whites we'd worn when we first arrived in late summer. Of course, this brought back memories of that first week and the bleak period at the beginning of the Ratline when no end seemed in sight.

The Firsts, including Laura, burned their gray wool pants in the Old Barracks courtyard, and as I watched from the fourth stoop, I couldn't help smiling at the story about the burning of Uncle Bradley's Citadel blouse during his first week at VMI.

Barracks certainly brightened a bit when we switched back to whites. My second semester classes had been going as well as those of first semester, thanks to the studying seeds planted by my granddad, Uncle Nick, Laura, and others. Good grades made almost everything easier at VMI, even after you got out of the Ratline.

The first week of May was probably the best week I'd had at VMI thus far. The First Class had their eyes on graduation morning, and the three classes below them had their sights set on the new privileges they'd enjoy the following year.

Laura had told me our class would get a taste of the new privileges right before graduation. Former Rats got several Third Class privileges, including moving our eyes around while in formations. I know it all seems like small stuff that shouldn't matter, but back during that spring it was a big deal to me and my classmates, as well as upperclassmen gaining even more seemingly trivial privileges.

As with December and as Laura and Uncle Nick had predicted, I also embraced the spring's exams period, when academics mostly trumped military on the priority list. Of course, the May weather also helped.

My exams went well again, and the day before graduation, I learned that I'd be able to wear academic stars my Third Class year thanks to my 3.6 grade point average. My mother had kept a pair of my dad's academic stars and I planned to wear them on my blouse come August.

We awoke to a cloudy drizzle on graduation day, but that didn't seem to affect the mood in Barracks and down in Laura's room, where I headed one final time to wake her up. She joked with me that there was no need to roll up her hay or put her rack up against the wall that morning, and I looked forward to the May morning in 2004 when I could say the same thing to my dyke.

Later that morning, as Laura walked across the Cameron Hall stage and got her diploma, I could picture myself doing it in three long years. I'd look up into the stands where Mom would be sitting, and I'd see her, Uncle Nick, Bradley, and my grandparents — all with that look in their eyes.

—◊—

I did exactly that on a crystal-clear May day more than a thousand days later. About seven hundred and fifty of those days were spent at VMI, and I can tell you that it wasn't without some pain and maybe a little joy. But my dad would have said that's life, and he'd be right.

He also knew about death, and I guess we all do. But I think the decision to go to VMI when you're still a teenager like me puts you closer to death in many ways. No, I don't think this. I know it.

You see, my dyke Laura walked off that stage and toward a new and often terrible world that none of us could have yet imagined. She did know we had enemies, and that's why she wanted to serve our country and help find them. She just didn't know the hatred some of those enemies had for us and what they might do to show that hatred to us and the rest of this troubled world.

Her great grades at VMI had indeed helped her get into the army's Military Intelligence branch, and those same grades likely helped her get a sought-after first posting in Europe. While still at her officer basic course at Fort Huachuca, during which she wrote me several long letters of encouragement, Laura told me that her father had finally been posted to the Pentagon for his last assignment with the U.S. Army and that she hoped to get to Arlington to visit him and her mother in September.

She did just that on Tuesday morning, September 11, 2001. She was truly in the wrong place at the wrong time and was killed by several of those enemies she'd planned to help find in coming years. Laura was buried in Winchester's pretty Mount Hebron Cemetery on Friday, September 14, and her father was buried next to her the following day.

—⟶⟶—

More than a decade removed from it, I finally need to write about 9/11 and Laura's funeral three days after the planes hit and our world changed forever.

I'd been back at VMI three weeks by then so I could get a head start on track with my team as we prepared for what we hoped was going to be a very successful season. I was in my Tuesday physics class when the head of the department came in to tell us that classes had been released and that we were to report back to Barracks.

As word spread Barracks became quieter than I'd ever experienced it. And then I got a status slip note to call my mother. She had taken on the task of telling me about Laura.

Her funeral on Friday was held graveside. I stood behind Laura's mother, who I'd met at Laura's graduation. She would bury her daughter one day and her husband the next. My mother, my grandparents, and Uncle Bradley stood with me. There were dozens of other people who had been part of Laura's life while her dad served in the army, as well those from VMI and during her much-too-short service to her country.

There were also at least ten VMI cadets in coatees, including me, as well as many other men and women in dress uniform from all four branches. I recognized several of them as VMI classmates of Laura.

I'd been asked to be a pallbearer, but I'd said no. I just knew that carrying her casket would bring me to my knees — and it wouldn't be from the weight of lovely Laura. Uncle Nick had volunteered to take my place.

Uncle Nick and the other pallbearers, including Laura's Marine Corps brother and two of her classmates in dress blues, took the casket out of the hearse and placed it on the graveside stand. As we stood there waiting for the service to start, I noticed that Uncle Nick had stayed by the casket beside that sad, gaping hole in the ground.

Looking me straight in the eye where I stood just ten feet away, Nick placed his right hand on the coffin, lifted it high into the air, and brought it down onto the wood with a loud bang. It was like a gunshot in the still September air.

Everyone was jumpy, including me, inevitably thinking bad thoughts about guns and terrorists. But then he did it again and beckoned me over with his left hand.

Never taking his eyes off mine, Uncle Nick took my hand, placed it on top of his, and brought it down hard on the casket for a third time. Many others with VMI rings then joined us as we gave our own impromptu twenty-one-ring salute to my dear dyke as we surrounded her coffin with very loud VMI family love.

Nick felt me go weak in the knees, and he used his free arm to steady me as tears flowed down my face and neck onto my coatee's white collar.

Then Nick, who I'd never heard yell a single word, screamed, "Brother Rat!" as his ring and my hand hit the coffin once again. The others joined in, and I looked over to see my mom and grandma yelling those words as well. Another arm came around my shoulder, and my grandfather stood beside me, banging his ring in unison with Nick's, joining in the chorus, and letting his tears flow onto his shirt collar and his red, white, and yellow tie.

Nick let go of my hand and backed away, as did the others. Before I followed his lead, however, I placed both hands on the mahogany and said my own silent good-byes to my dyke and the life we knew before 9/11.

I honestly can't tell you about the short service for Laura, which I numbly watched through tear-filled eyes in the embrace of my mother and grandfather. I have no further memories of that sad September morning. I don't remember any details of the reception that followed — which I still think is a stupid name for a gathering after a funeral.

Uncle Bradley drove me back to Lexington without a word, while Nick took my mom and grandparents home to Richmond. I also have no memory of walking back to my third stoop room and into the arms of my waiting roommates.

I just remember the sound of the bugle that night at taps and then again in the morning for reveille. It signaled the start of another day on that fabled little hill in Lexington.

Epilogue: Nick

When I left for VMI more than 30 years ago, I never could have imagined the life I'd lead and the people I would meet and love — and sometimes lose. I also couldn't have imagined the daughter of my best friend attending VMI, graduating, and honorably serving her country in a way her dyke, Laura, would have very much understood and appreciated.

I don't get to see Virginia as much as I'd like because she's served in many far-flung places around the world. I can't even pronounce the names of several of the cities and countries where she's been posted.

Like Laura, Virginia commissioned as a Military Intelligence officer and has spent her entire U.S. Army career finding terrorists who seek to do harm to our country and the Americans she so bravely serves. Virginia would never say this, but I believe she chose her life's work the Friday after 9/11, when Laura was buried in Winchester's Mount Hebron Cemetery.

I've returned to Winchester and that peaceful hillside cemetery with Virginia several times over the years. We always kneel together, look each other in the eye, and bring our rings crashing down on that cold granite tombstone.

As it says on Virginia's state flag and on many VMI rings, "*Sic semper tyrannis,*" Laura and Virginia. Thus, always, to tyrants.

THE END

CPSIA information can be obtained at www.ICGtesting.com
Printed in the USA
LVOW04s1516200814

400098LV00023B/1283/P